Peri Minneopa Is Back

"Readers will be drawn to Peri's spunky personality and independence; she refuses to hide behind her affectionate, protective fiancé, police detective Skip Carlton, even when flashbacks double the stress of car chases and shoot-outs. Readers will appreciate Carline's effective cliff-hangers and her ability to build truly creepy scenes, especially when Peri unearths sinister secrets in a prime suspect's home. Carline also puts considerable effort into her depictions of PTSD, OCD, and autism. This is a satisfying mystery that will leave readers eager for Peri's next investigation." – *Booklife Reviews*

"MURDER BYTES gives readers new insight into Peri—her trademark wit, tenacity, and self-awareness are coupled with a surprising vulnerability and heartfelt emotion, and you just can't help but root for her. In a sea of fictional PIs, Peri Minneopa is a standout. Grab your copy of Gayle Carline's latest. You'll be hooked from page one!" – *Janis Thomas, bestselling author of WHAT REMAINS TRUE*

"Readers who enjoyed Peri's prior escapades will relish the new challenges she faces in Murder Bytes, while newcomers will appreciate that the story and background are complete in one book, holding the rare ability to both compliment prior productions and create a satisfying stand-alone, high-octane mystery." – *D. Donovan, Senior Reviewer, Midwest Book Review*

MURDER BYTES

A Novel

by
Gayle Carline

This is a work of fiction. All characters, organizations, places, and events portrayed in this novel are either products of the author's imagination or are used fictitiously.

Cover art by Joe Felipe of Market Me (www.marketme.us).

ISBN-13: 978-1-943654-14-7

 Published in the USA by Dancing Corgi Press

This book is dedicated to family ties.

CHAPTER ONE

DEV NEEDED TO be somewhere else. Not stuck behind a dumpster, negotiating with an unwashed, unkempt, unpleasant man, over a stupid jacket.

"Fifty bucks, man." The man squinted, dilated eyes staring at the sun. "This is Italian leather."

Dev wanted to throw Homeless Man a ten and point out the windbreaker was neither Italian nor leather. But the morning sunlight was invading his pounding head, and the smells coming from the dumpster reached into his stomach and tossed it like a salad. A very old salad.

More importantly, he was losing precious time.

He withdrew two twenties from his pocket. "Here. Does this work?"

The altered-statesman stretched his hand out and grinned showing three teeth, all rotted. "Sweet."

Deal done, Dev slipped into the jacket and zipped it up. It smelled tangy, but he couldn't afford to mind. There were stains on his shirt, stains he needed to hide.

The whine of police sirens made him flinch.

Homeless Man chuckled. "That's my swan song, man." He ambled away from the dumpster, headed toward the freeway.

Dev watched a parade of flashing lights whip into the hotel parking lot next door. He backed a few steps, his racing heart urging him to turn and run.

Instead, he forced himself to walk toward the university. His legs twitched, ready to take off, and his pulse throbbed violently. Around the corner from the fast food joints and gas stations, California State University, Fullerton, stretched across 236 acres of prime real estate. The glass-and-steel buildings, punctuated with jacaranda trees, closed in around him. The scent of star jasmine floating on the warm June air sickened him.

Relax, he kept telling himself. *Only a guilty man runs.*

While he strolled, last night's events galloped across his mind. He knew he'd been in the hotel lobby, waiting for...someone—a sales rep? From there, images flashed, brief, chaotic, in no clear order. Blonde hair and floral perfume...white sheets and blood...the tang of copper...a shiny, sharp edge, and a scream.

A second scream, from the maid, had awakened him to the horror in the room. He bolted, half-dazed, half-mad, fully terrified.

God, my head hurts.

The university campus was too deserted to hide him. At the corner of State College, he recalled a bakery down the street. Panera, or one of those chains, it didn't matter.

He needed to clear his head, figure out his next move. Coffee sounded like a good start. He opened the door, flinching at his reflection as he did. But the server barely glanced at him as she gave him coffee, and took his money.

He shouldn't have run away, but the deed was done. With a sigh of reluctance, Dev Minneopa pulled out his cell phone and called the only person who could help him.

CHAPTER TWO

PERI MINNEOPA DRAPED her tall frame across a lounge chair, surveying her surroundings.

Soft tones of green, from pale to dusky, painted the yard. Breezes whispered through the swath of shocking pink bougainvillea, carrying hints of scent from nearby plumeria.

The garden was an oasis, yet all she could hear was the hammering and yammering of the construction team in her house. She took another swig of coffee and closed her eyes, reminding herself that she made this choice.

God, why did I make this choice?

The French doors from the kitchen opened, letting more decibels into the yard for a moment. Peri glanced back to see her fiancé, Skip, shuffling toward her. He'd acclimated well to using a cane. His limp was almost unnoticeable.

"Morning, Doll." Leaning in, he gave her an affectionate peck on her lips, his mustache brushing her face.

"Is it too early for a martini?" She nodded toward the house. "They insist on getting started at seven-damned-o'clock every morning."

Skip smiled as he settled into the second lounge chair, placing his mug next to hers. "Jared and Willem promised eight weeks, right?"

"Eight of the longest weeks of my life."

"Well, don't stick around. Go for a run. Visit Blanche. Clean out your office."

Peri watched her fingers trace the arm of the chair. "Not in the mood to run, Blanche is out on a call, and...I don't know, Skip, I can't seem to find the energy to dig through all those files. All that paper."

"Maybe call the therapist?"

"Already got an appointment, later today." A small alligator lizard caught her eye, parked on a paving stone, soaking in the morning heat. "I don't think she's helping me that much. It's not like I have PTSD. I'm not anxious, or afraid. I'm just...not me."

"That's part of it, Doll. That's why we keep doing the homework, until we feel like ourselves again."

She tried to smile, but it felt like a grimace. "I really hate going through this while you're going through your physical therapy. It feels like I'm not being very supportive."

He rose and slid into her lounge chair, wrapping her in his arms. "Hey, we're doing great. If anything, we understand each other even better."

"I wish I was back in my old house. I'll love this place when it's finished, but in the meantime, all the noise and the mess—ugh."

"Who knew your house would sell so quickly? And I did offer to let you move in with me. You still can, anytime."

"Yes, but I want to do this right. Buying this house together means it'll be ours, not just mine or yours." She didn't need to remind him of their previous, disastrous attempt to live together. Snuggling into his chest, she took a deep breath. "Two weeks down, six more to go."

A song softly hummed amid the background cacophony of drills and hammers. Peri stretched across her fiancé to wrestle her phone from the table. She didn't recognize the number, but answered anyway.

"Hey, Sis, it's Dev. I'm in trouble."

She sat up, pushing against Skip. "Dev? What's wrong?"

"I can't explain it over the phone." His voice sounded raspy. "I'm at Panera on State College."

She ran her fingers through her blond hair. "And?"

"And what?" His voice got a little louder. "I need you to meet me here."

"Oh, so you snap your fingers and I'm expected to jump?"

She could almost hear the wall of stubbornness building. It was a family curse.

"Forget it. Sorry I bothered you."

"Dev, don't. I'm sorry. I'll be right there." Peri ended the call and turned to Skip. "My brother's in trouble. Want to go for a ride?"

CHAPTER THREE

SKIP WORE HIS usual flinty expression as he drove. "Did he say what kind of trouble?"

"He didn't say." Peri stared ahead at the road, trying to will him to drive faster. "I'm not sure which is weirder—that he called, or that he's here in town."

"When did you ever hear from him without prompting?"

She tapped the console. "Hmm, never. And I haven't seen him since Erik's funeral."

"I still can't believe you grew up calling your parents by their first names."

"I still can't believe I'm grown up." She pointed to the right. "That's it."

Skip pulled into a spot and Peri unbuckled her seatbelt before the car stopped rolling. He reached across her.

"Easy. It's all gonna be okay."

She leaned back and took a deep breath. "I guess. Everything feels so—I don't know."

"Like you're running to catch up with it?"

"Yes." She pursed her lips. "One more side effect of the shooting?"

"Possibly, but then again, patience has never been one of your strengths."

She punched his arm and got out.

Inside, she saw a semi-familiar face tucked into the corner booth.

"Last time I saw you, you were a little tanner," she said, sitting.

He gave her a shrug, saw Skip, and froze.

"Dev, this is my boyfr—my fiancé, Skip Carlton." Peri slid over, to allow Skip to sit next to her. "Now, what's the problem?"

Dev glanced from Peri to Skip and back a few times, silent. She reached under the table, gave Skip's thigh a little squeeze, and he rose.

"I'll be up front, having coffee."

Peri studied her brother. The same blue eyes as their father, same crooked smile as their mom. He gripped his coffee cup in both hands, his knuckles swollen and knotted. Another familial trait.

She glanced down at her own hands. *Were my knuckles always this big?*

Dev leaned over the table and spoke in a whisper. "I had a meeting last night—with a sales rep, I think. I woke up this morning in a hotel room with a dead woman. I have no memory of what happened in between."

She hadn't been sure what to expect, but this wasn't it. Her eyes widened. "What did the police say?"

"No idea. I ran outta there before they got to the room."

"Are you *kidding* me?" Peri's voice climbed an octave.

"Keep it down, will you?" He grabbed her arm. "I realize I have to go to the police. I just—needed someone to talk to first. I needed my little sister."

Peri sat back and stared at her brother, crossing her arms over her chest. "After not contacting me in over a year, after making me chase you down to even figure out where you were for the past, I dunno, seven years? Now you need me to get you out of a jam."

His eyes narrowed as he rose from the booth. "No, I guess I don't. I'll take my chances with the cops."

Peri held up her hand. "Whoa, there, Bugsy. Sit down. I didn't say I wouldn't help. I'm just not loving the way you only want to see me because you're in trouble. I'll get over it."

He slumped against the vinyl and leaned his arms on the table, staring at his mug.

She broke the silence. "Okay. My fiancé happens to be a detective with the Placentia Police Department. He can go with us to the station so you can give your statement—and that shirt of yours for processing. I'm guessing that's not your blood on the collar."

He pulled the jacket further up on his neck, and gave her a quick nod. Peri looked around and found Skip, on the other side of the bakery. At a small gesture from her, he began to make his way toward them.

"I gotta hit the head," Dev said, sliding out of the booth.

"Can't it wait?"

"Sure, if I want to piss myself."

"Okay, but don't wash. You might have evidence on you."

9

"Whatever." He slipped around the corner as Skip reached the table with a curious look.

"He went to the bathroom."

Skip sat and finished his coffee as she explained Dev's predicament.

"Let me see what I can find out." He pulled out his cell phone and placed a call.

Peri strained to hear his half of the conversation, but it was no use. Skip had that remarkable ability to speak quietly and be understood by the person on the other end. Years of police training had also honed his poker face, so she couldn't even read his expression. He ended the call and returned to his coffee.

The little patience she had evaporated. "Well?"

"Well." He took one more sip. "There is a dead woman in the Holidaze Hotel and Spa on Nutwood. Initial guess is exsanguination—there's a lot of blood. Fingerprints aplenty, along with a man's jacket, size 38, with a visitor's ID in the pocket from Howard Aerospace Company. Dev...Chaplain?"

"Chaplain. What an ass."

"Because...?"

"Because he's using our 'real' last name." She wiggled her fingers in quotation marks. "When Helen and Erik married and moved to California from Minnesota, they decided to take a brand new last name. Erik proposed in Minneopa State Park."

"And using Chaplain makes you mad." Skip was stone-faced, but Peri could detect amused disapproval in the slight cock of his head.

"Yes, Minneopa is our legal family name. How dare he deny it?"

"Right now, he's denying his place in an interrogation room. Stay here. I'll go get him."

Peri picked up Dev's coffee cup, smelled the contents, and set it down. Smelled like coffee. *What was I was expecting, alcohol? I'm not a P.I. anymore.*

Skip returned to stand by the table. "Your brother's in the wind."

CHAPTER FOUR

WILLEM REESE-CHEN WAS standing on the flagstone walkway when Peri and Skip pulled into the drive. The popular interior designer was in high demand by many homeowners, as well as major real estate developers, but he had carved his schedule out for the woman who had saved him and his partner, not to mention their dog.

Moonie the pit bull sat at his feet, legs spread awkwardly and tongue lolling.

"I brought a visitor with me today." Willem greeted Peri with an enormous hug and a small kiss on the cheek. "Moonpie just had to see her Miss Peri."

Peri laughed and bent down to rub the wriggling dog's ears and jowls. It felt oddly comforting to give the massive head a massage. "I may have a treat or two in the house."

Skip shook Willem's hand, and gestured toward his nearly-bald head. "That's a new look for you."

Willem ran a hand across the stubble on his scalp. "It's actually grown a little. Seems the dye I used last time for that blue ombre turned my hair into kindling."

"Oh, no, I think you look good," Peri told him.

"Jared likes it, and that's all I care about." He turned toward the front door. "Shall we take a look at the progress? I want to make certain you're both happy."

"If Peri likes it, that's all I care about." Skip stepped forward and kissed Peri's forehead. "I'm going over to the station and check up on that little problem."

Peri turned to him. "The police? Do you have to?"

He cradled her hands in his. "We need to be above-board with this. Nothing hidden."

She released him, nodding. "You're right. And thank you."

Willem followed Peri through the gated atrium leading into the house, surveying the newly planted gardenias and oriental bamboo trees. "What little problem?"

Peri shrugged. "Family drama, if you get what I mean."

"Oh, honey, I totally get that." Willem opened the door. The sounds of construction spilled out. Moonie took a step into the house, pricked her ears at the noise, and found a cool corner of the atrium to flop down and close her eyes.

After an hour of staring at bare studs, paint samples, and window-covering options, Peri lost her ability to pretend she cared about any of it.

"I'm sorry, Willem. I realize I have to make some decisions. Can you leave the samples for me? I promise I'll make up my mind by tomorrow."

He smiled. "Ah, Peri. Sure, I'll wait."

She hugged him again. "Really, I don't want to take advantage of you. I'm just…"

"Not quite yourself?"

"You've noticed?"

"A little. It's hard to push through trauma, especially when you don't want to change the view on the other side."

"You're right. I want the normal I used to have. Not this one." She smiled. "Thanks."

Willem touched her arm. "Is everything all right with your family?"

His tenderness made her want to cry. She shook her head. "My brother's in trouble. I honestly don't know much, except that it's bad, and the police are looking for him."

"Oh, honey." He put his arm around her shoulder. "Will he come looking for you?"

"Already did. He wanted me to help him, or so I thought. And then he ran."

"The police won't—hurt him, will they? I mean, might he be violent?"

A fragment of a memory flashed through her mind. She and Dev were playing hide-and-seek in the fields behind their house—or at least she thought they were playing. When she finally found him, he was so angry, he slapped her face, telling her, "When I grow up, I *never* want to see you again."

He was 14. She was only 10.

Peri shook the image from her head. "I honestly don't have a clue."

"If you need anything, you call me and Jared." He gestured toward the atrium. "And come over and pet Moonie whenever you want. She can make anybody feel better."

Two air kisses toward her cheeks, and he was out the front door. Grabbing her laptop, Peri returned to the backyard and began to search online for her brother. She thought the internet might hold some clues to Endeavor Minneopa, aka Dev Chaplain.

A general search turned up nothing interesting. A few social media hits, mostly on business-related sites. No website of his own, no blog, nothing personal. *That's the story of your life, big brother—nothing personal.*

She did find public records. Dev graduated from the University of Arizona with a degree in business. Bought a house in Vegas in the '90s. Sold it ten years later. No marriages, no births. Nothing special.

Digging a little deeper, she discovered a news article on an engineering-related website. Dev was marketing director of an engineering startup. The new firm was selling a product that promised what no one else's could—a universal translator for machine language. The article used a lot of technical jargon, but from her limited understanding, the device could talk Android or iOS, Mac or PC, Xbox or Nintendo.

The implications were enormous. This product broke through all current encryption codes. If that's what Dev was selling, who were his buyers? Peri needed to talk to an expert. But first, she needed to find Dev.

She read another article on the startup, looking for the location of the company. A flash of anger and pain hit as she read the words "Fullerton office." Dev had taken up residence in the city next door without telling her.

The police, no doubt, had already located her brother's home, as well as his workplace. If he was half as bright as he used to be, he'd steer clear of those areas. Where else would he go?

As a child, Dev liked to play by the railroad tracks, mostly to watch the trains shooting by. He'd stand the direction the train was traveling, his eyes closed and arms out, as if wishing himself into one of the cars.

Fullerton's train station was near the middle of downtown. Travelers could catch Amtrak and the Metrolink, going north to Los Angeles, or south to San Diego. In LA, there were other trains and buses to transfer to and keep moving. In San Diego, the border was only a few steps away.

Both were good options if you were trying to disappear. It was a long shot, but she grabbed her keys. As she picked up her phone, it vibrated. It was her therapist on the line.

Crap, I forgot. "Hi, Dr. Andrews, sorry I missed my appointment—family emergency. I'll have to call back and reschedule, okay? Thanks, bye."

She ran to her car, tossing her phone into her tote as she went.

Chapter Five

Peri passed the mini-mart and the small café, pausing at the ticket office to find a schedule. The first train left in 30 minutes, going north. The next one was 15 minutes later, going south.

Her search of the northbound platform came up empty. The southbound platform was across the tracks, accessible by a pedestrian overpass. Trotting up the stairs sent a tingle down her spine. The enclosed grating around the walkway made it look like another overpass she'd once had to crawl along, to get away from a crazy woman out to kill her.

Her fingers could still feel the metal cutting into them, and her body weight trying to pull her down. The approaching train had roared below her, rattling her hands loose. As she fell, Benny caught her arm, Benny who had never been a hero.

Why didn't I get PTSD from that? I'm fine walking over this bridge. Why did it have to be gunplay that got to me?

A figure sat alone on the last bench. His back was turned, but Peri recognized the blond hair and filthy jacket. She strode down the platform, eyes focused on her target.

"Miss Peri." A familiar voice distracted her. Benny Needles stepped in her path, waving his hand in front of her face. "Miss Peri, it's me, Benny."

The short, rotund man in the gray suit before her, had been her part-time client, part-time assistant, and full-time pain in the ass for a few years. With the closing of her detective agency, he was now her—friend, she supposed. He hopped gently, from foot to foot, in his excited way.

"Benny, so nice to see you," Peri said, still inching forward, looking at the figure ahead.

"Miss Peri, look." He held out his blue silk tie. "Look what Sam got me."

"Give me one min—I just need to—could you—" she stammered as she shifted right and left, attempting to get past him. At last she stopped, defeated, and looked at his tie. "Yes, Benny, it's a nice tie."

"No, the tie pin. It was Dino's." He beamed. "I'm wearing Dean Martin's tie pin."

"Yeah, it's great." She looked back up at her prey. The bench was empty. "Dammit."

"What's wrong?"

"I was following someone and he got away."

Benny frowned. "I thought you quit being a detective."

"I did. This was…a friend of mine." She craned her neck, hoping to spot Dev laying low, further down the sunny platform. "He, uh, he forgot to give me his address."

"Guess what I'm doing today." Benny was relentless, tagging along as she walked.

She worked her way back toward the stairs. "What?"

"I'm going to Los Angeles. Well, not Los Angeles, really. I'm going to Hollywood."

"Uh-huh."

"Sam is going with me. We're going to find Dean Martin's stars on the Hollywood Walk of Fame and eat at a fancy restaurant."

"Uh-huh."

"Miss Peri." Benny barked her name, causing her to stop and look at him. "You are being very impolite. You are not listening to me."

"Look, Ben, it's important that I find this guy. But I was listening. You're going to see some stars or something, right? At the observatory or something?"

Benny glared at the ground, his face flushed. "No. I am going to see Dean Martin's stars on the Hollywood Walk of Fame. If you want to find that guy so bad, why don't you just call him?"

"I don't have his num—oh, wait." She pulled out her phone and looked at the incoming call record. Dev's phone number was her first call of the day. She looked up to thank her friend, and saw him huffing away, down the platform. "Aww, Ben, I'm sorry."

Guilt was immediate and severe. Peri usually made allowances for his Asperger's, but she had blown him off. *I'll apologize when I see him again.*

She pressed the Dial icon on Dev's number. By the fourth ring, she was pretty sure he'd ditched the phone.

"What do you want?"

"You know what I want, Brother. You've got to come in if you want my help."

"Why should the police look any further than me? I'm the perfect suspect."

19

"True, but you have Skip and me to help you clear things up. Plus, the further you try to run, the guiltier you look to the cops." As she talked, Peri moved around the platform, attempting to hear Dev's actual voice. "Looking cooperative will help your case a lot more than running."

"Or maybe I'll look like a guilty man who cooperates to look good."

Peri spotted him, under the staircase. She maneuvered past the last clump of people and stood there, staring at him. "You want to try this again?"

"Not really. I've been pretty good at hiding, even from Miss Smarty Pants Private Eye."

"And yet, here we are. There's no statute of limitations on murder, Dev. You'd have to hide forever."

"Miss Peri, is this your friend?" Benny had returned, despite his apparent bruised feelings.

"Benny, this isn't a good time—" She turned back to see her brother dash around the staircase and run up the steps. Running after him, she called out. "Dev, stop running, you idiot!"

He stopped in the middle of the stairs.

CHAPTER SIX

"THAT USUALLY DOESN'T work," she said, as Dev lifted his hands over his head. Coming down, out of the shadows, was a uniformed police officer. His face was clean-shaven, pink and cherubic, his blue eyes wide enough to see white outlines. His gun was drawn and pointed at her brother.

"Holy Hell." Peri took a step back, her hands held away from her body. "Officer, don't shoot. Dev, do everything he says."

The officer shouted orders over her voice. "Hands on your head! Turn around!"

Peri tried to shout above his commands. "Don't shoot him! Dev, listen to him!"

The three stood, suspended in the moment, Dev with his hands waving upward, Peri and the officer screaming commands.

A low, booming voice cut through the chaos. "Everyone calm down now."

A second officer stepped out, past the younger one. Short, muscular, and tanned, Peri was certain he juggled tractor tires for fun. He said something to his partner, looked at Dev, and demonstrated with his own arms what he wanted Dev to do.

21

Dev placed his hands on top of his head, and turned around. The second officer nodded, and proceeded down the steps, handcuffs already out.

The first policeman began shouting again. "I said hands on your head!"

"His hands are—oh." Peri saw that the officer was coming for her. "Hey, no, I was bringing him in."

"Who are you?" He motioned with the gun for her to obey.

Peri clasped her hands on top of her head and turned. "I'm a private investigator. You can check the wallet in my bag for my ID."

"Miss Peri, are you still working?" Benny had followed, yet again. "You said you were just looking for a friend."

"I was, Benny. I'm not working. It's complicated." Still nervous about the shouting and the guns, she knew it could easily get worse again with Benny on the scene. *Where was that freakin' train to LA, and why wasn't Benny on it?*

"That's my friend." Benny pointed at her with a half-eaten Danish. "You let her go."

The officer's hands shook as he brought Peri's arms down behind her back. She felt the sweat on his palms, heard his ragged breathing. He twisted her wrists behind her to accommodate the handcuffs, and she was happy for her recent yoga classes, to keep her shoulders from cramping. *He's young and tense. Won't take much to set him off.*

"It's okay, Benny." She managed a smile. "I'm just going to answer some questions, then I'll be home."

He did not look convinced. "It doesn't look okay. I'm going to call Mr. Skip."

"Down the stairs," the officer ordered.

"Yes, sir, let me take it slow. We don't want to fall." She gritted her teeth as the officer gripped her arm. "Yes, call Skip, Benny. I'm being taken to the Fullerton Police Department."

Benny's eyes were wide and he nodded like a bobble-head doll. "I'll get help, Miss Peri. You can count on me."

At the bottom of the stairs, the officer gave her a quick, mechanical pat-down. "No gun?"

"No."

"I thought you were a P.I."

She stared at his still-pink cheeks. He couldn't have been more than 25. A mere puppy. "Like I said, check my wallet. You'll find my license."

"But no permit for concealed carry?"

"I don't like guns." She flinched. Two years of saying that, but now she meant it. "Me and Sam Spade."

"Who?"

She blinked at his cluelessness. "Bartender at Craftsman."

"What's he got to do with it?"

Peri shook her head, and noticed Benny, still hovering with the small crowd that had gathered. She nodded at him, as the officer dragged her into the waiting patrol car.

"Call Mr. Skip, Ben."

Benny stepped up to the officer, his expression as stern and earnest as a trial attorney. "You are making a big mistake. Miss Peri is a private investigator. She never breaks the law. Except for the time she broke into that man's office, but she didn't take anything. He was already dead. And when she picked the lock—"

"Benny." Peri wished her hands were free so she could slap them over his mouth. "Stop helping, and call Skip."

"You don't have to yell at me."

"Sorry." She did not have time for this. "Please call. I'm counting on you."

CHAPTER SEVEN

THE POLICE CAR smelled like old socks and sour milk, overlaid with cherry-scented disinfectant. They'd put Dev in a separate car, so Peri sat alone in the backseat, hands uncomfortably clasped behind her back, seatbelt rubbing across her collarbone. She looked at the back of the young officer's head. His hair was cut short, leaving his pale neck dotted with angry red bumps.

The older officer drove, wearing the same unreadable expression that Skip often did. How did he keep his cool around his fly-off-the-handle associate? Did the department pair them so the more experienced man could desensitize the rookie?

Doogie Howser, Fullerton PD, she thought, then, *that's not nice. He's a perfectly fine policeman, doing his job. It's your fault for letting your brother slip away the first time.*

She wiggled her fingers to keep them from growing numb, and sat as far back as she could manage. The police station was less than a mile away. She could make it.

In the meantime, how would she explain her presence at the train station? It was simple enough in her head. She wanted to find her brother and bring him to the police. The location was a lucky guess, based on their

25

history. Still, she didn't exactly have proof that she and Dev weren't planning his getaway together.

It would depend upon him vouching for her, their stories remaining consistent, and Skip verifying it all.

I hope we can convince the cops. Orange is not my color.

Officer Doogie cranked his neck around and addressed her. "So—breaking and entering? When was this?"

She glared at him. "Pretty day, isn't it?"

"That's not what I asked."

"That's all I'm answering."

Officer Doogie turned back around. She could see the angry flush blossoming on his ears.

At the station, Peri searched in vain for a friendly face while being led toward the interview rooms. "Is Detective Berkwits around?"

"How do you know the detective?" Officer Doogie held a door open for her, and she walked to the table in the middle of the small space. "Been arrested before, eh?"

"Did you not run my license?" Bowing slightly, she held her hands away, hoping to be uncuffed. "I'm a P.I. I worked with the detective on a case."

He freed her and motioned to the chair. "We'll see about that."

"By the way, I didn't get your name."

"Officer Darden."

"And your partner?"

He frowned. "What does that matter?"

"It doesn't. Just wanted to think of you as a team. Starsky and Hutch and all that."

"Starzy and what?"

Peri sat, head in her hands. "Never mind, Officer Darden. Thanks for the lift to the station. Tell your partner I said he's a good driver. Real careful."

Darden slammed the door on his way out.

Wow, he needs a sense of humor. She looked around the room. Nothing but a table, two chairs, and a two-way mirror. Everything was beige. It made her feel beige— bland, lifeless. Her shoulders slumped forward, elbows shoving against the wooden table top.

The therapist had suggested meditation for stress— always wanting her to find her "happy place." Peri still wasn't convinced, but she closed her eyes, trying not to smirk, and let her mind wander.

Paris. She visualized that afternoon in the Jardin des Tuileries, with a glass of wine and a plate of crepes. It was a beautiful day, and the sun warmed her face. It was all B.S.—before shooting.

Now, she couldn't find the happiness, or sadness, in anything. Just irritation, which ran through her bloodstream. She wanted to punch the beige wall, but settled for deep breathing.

"Peri, it's good to see you." Detective Berkwits put a cup of coffee in front of her and sat down, holding a Manila folder. "Although these aren't the best circumstances. What's going on?"

"Mistaken identity," she said, attempting the *Reader's Digest* condensed version. "Well, maybe more like wrong place, wrong time."

"Tell me what happened." He put the folder on the table.

Her tale expanded to the unabridged edition, as she recounted everything that had happened since Dev's morning call. When she got to the part where Officer Darden's gun was pointed at her, tears fought to escape from her eyes. She rubbed her forehead with her knuckles, with enough pressure to distract herself.

"Has your brother ever had violent tendencies?"

"Not when we were kids—most of the time." She shrugged. "Look, the truth is, I have no idea who my brother is now."

The detective nodded, and looked through the folder. "Fair enough. Since the murder happened in Placentia, we've turned him over to Detective Logan and the PPD. As far as your role in this, your brother swears you're not involved." He held up a paper. "So does a Mister Benny Needles, and Detective Skip Carlton. I'd say you're in the clear."

"Thank you, Detective. Can I go now?"

"I assume you plan on helping your brother get out of trouble."

"Yes—well, as I told Dev, Skip and I will look into the evidence and make sure he's not just the most likely suspect. You know me, Detective. I won't try to get him out of trouble if he really did it."

The detective smiled and handed her the folder. "That makes me feel better about giving you this. Seems that we have a little background on the murdered woman. Tressa Velasco. She was under investigation. We've sent this on to Logan, but I thought you'd appreciate a copy."

"Investigation for what?"

"We're not sure. The FBI asked us to put some intel together. They were coming in next week to brief us on what they're investigating, and what other assistance we might lend." He nodded toward the folder. "We've got a call in, to let them know of Velasco's death. I can't promise to keep you in the loop but I'll probably be giving the PPD more info. I'm sure you've still got your sources."

"Detective, you are a prince." Peri took the folder and stood. "Now, how do I get a ride back to my car?"

"Ah, I have a driver waiting for you." He walked her out of the room and down the hall to the desk captain, where a tall, handsome man leaned on a cane. "Detective Carlton, perhaps you can give this woman a lift."

Peri put her arms around Skip, and looked over at Berkwits. She held up the folder. "Thank you, detective. I do appreciate this."

CHAPTER EIGHT

"WHAT WERE YOU doing at the train station?" Skip asked as they walked to his car.

"I had a hunch. Dev used to love trains as a kid. It wasn't an obvious place for the police to look."

"Peri—"

"Don't take that tone with me. I'm not a little kid to be scolded."

"And yet, you got tangled up in your brother's arrest."

"Because Officer Doogie jumped to a bad conclusion."

He frowned. "Officer *Doogie*?"

"Sorry." Peri opened the door to the SUV, then turned to face him. "No, I'm not sorry. That kid can't be more than 25, with his little peach-fuzz face. He was shaking, he was sweaty, ready to come unstuck any minute. I was afraid someone was going to take a bullet."

She scrambled into the seat and faced forward, brushing a quick tear from her eye. A few seconds later, Skip slid in behind the wheel. She felt his body move forward to find the ignition, back to find the seatbelt, but she refused to look at him. As she reached for her own belt, warm lips touched her cheek. She turned and kissed him back.

"Must have been scary for you," he whispered.

"I can't control it." A willful tear slid down her cheek. She wiped her face dry in protest, sniffling back the waterworks that threatened to break the dam.

"You will." He put the car into gear and pulled out into the street.

While he drove, Peri reviewed the folder on Tressa Velasco, giving Skip the highlights as she read. "Tressa, 35, works at Howard Aerospace Company—oh, they're in Fullerton…got her bachelor's at University of Arizona, her masters at Cal State Fullerton…electrical engineering. Why would she be in the hotel room with Dev? Did he know her? Maybe she was trying to buy his company's device."

"What device?"

She turned to look at him. "Read an article about it. I don't get the whole thing, but it sounds like it can translate computer language, so that your Apple can talk your Samsung, or your Xbox can talk to your Playstation."

"Wow, that's kind of a big deal. Wonder why we haven't seen it in the news."

"I found the article online. Obscure engineering news site." She fanned the papers against her chin. "Article said they were a startup company. Perhaps they're not well-known enough to make the big news cycle. Or maybe…"

The silence grew, until Skip said, "Maybe what?"

"Maybe it's still in that, what do they call it? Beta phase? Like, they're testing it out with a few customers before they unleash it on the market."

"So our murder vic was looking to buy the device as a guinea pig, right?"

"Maybe. Would a big company like Howard Aerospace buy unproven pieces of equipment? And would they send an engineer to buy it? Is that why Tressa was in the FBI's sights?"

"Wait—FBI?"

"Yeah, that's why Fullerton had this folder. The FBI asked them to find out about Tressa. The Feds were supposed to come in and brief the PD on it next week. Guess that won't happen."

"So, why did Berkwits give you the folder?"

"Professional courtesy. He already gave a copy to Logan, but thought I could also use it, my brother being involved and all. I think you should start at Howard Aerospace, and I'll go to Dev's office. See what we can find."

"Whoa, there." Skip stomped the brakes hard at the light. "We are not working a case. I'm still on disability and you're, well, not you."

"Yes, but I told my brother I'd help him. Actually, I kind of said we'd help him." Peri saw the muscle in his jaw tighten. "I realize how it sounds. It exhausts me to think about it. But Dev's my brother and I have to help him, even though he hates me, and by the way, I'm not that happy with him at the moment."

"At the moment?"

She sat back, combing her fingernails across her scalp. "Yeah, at the moment. Fifty-one years, and I'm still little sister, looking up to her big brother. I don't trust him. But all he'd have to do is show me some tiny measure of brotherly affection, and all would be forgotten. How sappy am I?"

Skip reached for her hand and squeezed it. "Just enough, and the right kind. The kind of sappy I like."

Peri looked back down at the papers. "Hmm, Tressa's credit card shows a couple of recent purchases, Jeweler's Touch for a little over $600, and David's Bridal for a couple thou."

"Who's the lucky guy?"

She shuffled through everything the detective gave her. "Doesn't say. But I bet we could find out."

"Peri, we are not investigating."

"But there's so much information here. I've never had this much dumped into my lap without asking. It's begging me to do something, drive somewhere, talk to someone."

"We're letting the Placentia PD handle this. Logan's good, you know that. He won't just hand your brother to the DA's office and wash his hands."

She closed the folder. "You're right. Logan is a good detective, so is Spencer, even if he is an ass. I can trust them to dig into this case."

"You haven't heard the news, have you? Spencer retired."

"Oh, wow." Peri smiled. "Who's Logan's new partner?"

"Reed Powell. He got a promotion."

"He's pretty nice, for a cop."

Skip smirked. "That's the right attitude."

CHAPTER NINE

SKIP PULLED INTO the parking lot at the Placentia Civic Center. It sounded grander than it looked, a cool swath of green grass surrounding three buildings—City Hall, the police department, and the library. A tall tiled fountain sat in the center of a ring of pergola. Most of the time, recycled water tumbled down the blue tiles, although today it was dry.

They were buzzed in by the desk clerk, Evelyn, who told them Detective Logan was in the Crime Scene Lab with Jason Bonham, the forensics specialist. Peri saw Jason in the window and waved. Logan was facing away when Jason waved back. The detective stretched around to see the visitors, nodding in acknowledgment.

Jason leaped from his chair to hug Peri and shake Skip's hand at the same time.

"I'm here to give you whatever info I can," Peri said, holding up the folder. "I'm assuming you got this packet from Detective Berkwits. They'd been working with the FBI, although they weren't supposed to be fully briefed until next week."

"Yep." Logan held up a similar folder. "So…she's an engineer for a big company. He's a marketing guy for a small company. They end up in the same hotel room. This doesn't look like a coincidence."

Peri straightened up, her eyes wide. "Detective, what if it had nothing to do with business? Tressa's credit card statement says she bought a wedding dress recently. Who was she marrying, and is he the jealous kind?"

"It's an angle we need to look at," Logan said, continuing to skim through the folder's contents. "Sorry this involves you, Peri. It's hard when a family member gets themselves in this kind of trouble."

"Thanks. It's not..." She struggled for the words. "Ideal. Especially when my brother and I haven't been close for a long time."

"Estranged?" Jason asked.

"Not really. I mean, we didn't have a fight or anything. Dev decided not to be part of our family. I never knew why."

The lab door opened and Logan's new partner, Detective Powell stepped in. "Logan, can I see you?"

Nodding, the detective left the room. Peri sat down next to Jason. "So, learn anything so far on the murder?"

"I just got started. Blanche has the body, the clothes are all here for processing." He gestured to the table. "Photos, fingerprints, DNA swabs, I'm getting organized. Gotta make certain I'm processing the right things in the right order."

Logan entered, wearing an expression that was stony, even for him, and holding a blue cloth grocery bag. "Looks like we don't need to process anything. Dev Chaplain just confessed to the murder. Even handed us the weapon."

Peri jumped from her seat. "That can't be—it's insane."

Skip put his hand on her arm. "Peri, you said yourself, you haven't been around Dev for a lot of years."

"Yes, but…" She pointed to the bag. "How did Dev get the weapon to you?"

"What do you mean, how?" Logan asked. "He just gave it to us in the interview room."

She planted her hands on her hips. "After he was frisked by the Fullerton police?"

Logan stared at her. "So, the officer didn't do his job right."

"And what pocket did Dev pull it out of?"

"It was stuck down the back of his pants, covered by his jacket."

"Oh, really?" Peri pointed again. "How long has it been in that bag? You should check my brother's backside for cuts."

Logan looked down. There was a silver tip protruding from the bottom of the bag, and the material was being sliced, slowly, with the weight of the knife. He put it on the table.

"Okay, so what?" he asked at last.

"So I'm changing my mind," she told him. "Based on this evidence and his confession, I don't think he did it."

"It doesn't matter what you think," Logan said. "He confessed."

"Let me talk to him." Peri grabbed his arm. "I'm begging you. At least, follow through with the evidence, the autopsy. Make certain it agrees with what he says happened. What will it hurt you to cross your I's and dot your T's?"

"Don't you mean—" Jason started.

She waved at him. "Shh, I'm trying to save my brother, if that's possible."

Logan looked from her to the knife and back again. "Because it's you, we'll dig a little deeper. Come on, I'll take you to him. He's still in interrogation."

CHAPTER TEN

SHE FOLLOWED THE detective to a room with a table and two chairs. It was a carbon-copy of the interview room in the Fullerton station. Same-sized room with same-beige walls, same cheap-but-indestructible table.

Dev hunched over a legal pad, writing. He kept his head down as she sat.

"Want to tell me what this is about?" she asked. "You ran away from the cops, begged for my help, ran away from me, then suddenly you confess? Plus, literally pull the murder weapon out of your ass—what's up with that?"

He stopped writing and looked up at her. His eyes were red, as though he'd been crying. "I wrote it all down, Sis. Leave it alone."

"I will not leave it alone. Not when it doesn't make any sense." She stood and paced the small room. "What happened to you, between your arrest and being brought here?"

"Nothing."

"Why should I believe you now? You didn't even tell me that you knew her."

"How do you know?"

"Geez, Dev, she's an engineer, you're the marketing guy for an engineering firm, you're both in the same hotel room. You both went to University of Arizona—did you meet there?"

"Oh, screw you." He scooted his chair to face the wall.

"How well did you know her?"

Silence.

Her voice raised a decibel. "How. Well. Did. You. Know. Her?"

More silence.

She walked to him, and glared at the side of his head, waiting for him to face her. He refused. She put her mouth up to his ear and snapped, "I'm going to talk to you whether you look at me or not."

Dev cringed and ducked away, turning to scowl at her. "You don't have to shout."

She stood and crossed her arms. "I can help you. Even if you're telling the truth, even if you're guilty, I can still help you. But I need to have the real story."

"I don't want your help." He stared at her, his face mottled. "I'm begging you, now, don't fight this."

She went back to her chair and sat down. "Who got to you, and how?"

He opened his mouth, lips trembling, before looking around the room, and lowering his eyes. His hands were on the table. He lifted his right in a semi-fist and pounded his left palm, then brought them both to his chest. "Forget about me. Seriously."

The door opened, and Detective Powell walked in. "Afraid it's time for processing."

Peri nodded and rose, tears in her eyes. "Can I at least hug him first?"

"Sure."

She put her arms around her brother. His body remained upright, but he patted her on the back a couple of times. "Goodbye, Periwinkle."

The detective escorted him from the room. Peri followed them out but returned to the lab. Jason was placing items on a table, writing on labels.

"Hey, Peri, Skip said to tell you he's in his office."

Peri reached for a tissue on his desk. Seeing her dab at her eyes, Jason put his arm around her shoulders. "I'm so sorry."

"Just promise me you'll process the evidence. If they stop you, call me. I don't have any clout, but I'll try to do something."

"Sure, Peri. I can tell you already, there were no prints found on the knife."

She sniffled. "I guess he could have wiped them off, but why, if he was turning it in? I mean, how did he even hand it over to the detective without actually touching it?"

"According to Logan, it was already in the blue bag, so he didn't have to touch the knife to turn it in. But there were no prints at all, which is weird. You can check with Blanche, but I could swear I saw defensive wounds on the vic's hands. I'd expect some kind of smeared prints on the blade, or bloodied prints on the handle."

"Was there blood on the knife?"

"Yes, but…" He scratched at the side of his face, combing down through his goatee. "I need to test more, but the stain doesn't look like a knife that's been stuck into a body and pulled away. More like, swiped through a blood pool. But don't quote me. I'm still working on it."

"Thanks, Jason. I'm going to find Skip."

As she walked down the hall, a patrol officer opened the other interrogation room door. A man stood beside him, slender and paste-white, with wire-rimmed eyeglasses. His wrists protruded from his long-sleeved tee-shirt, and his hands were enormous. Peri shuddered when her gaze reached his long yellow fingernails. The officer stepped aside and let the pale man enter first.

She found Skip behind his desk, tossing envelopes in the wastebasket. He glanced up. "Ready to go?"

"Did you see the skinny white guy?"

He nodded. "Vic's fiancé. Art Gibbons."

"Now we know why she was shopping for a wedding dress."

"Yep. By the way, will you be shopping for a big white dress?" He grinned and winked at her.

"I didn't even want that with the first marriage. Not sure I want to be shopping at all."

"How about the ring?"

"A plain band is fine. Why are we working out the wedding plans now?"

"To distract you from your brother's predicament. Plus, you keep putting everything off. I'm okay with low-key. I just need to know where to be and when to be there."

She put her arms around him. "When your house sells and our house is complete, I thought we'd figure it out."

"And I'm okay with that." He rose. "Now can we go?"

"Well…couldn't we listen to the fiancé's statement?"

Skip's shoulders sank. "Yes, if no one objects."

Chapter Eleven

As no one was in the observation room, no one minded if Skip and Peri let themselves in. Art Gibbons sat at the table, ramrod straight in the chair, arms by his side. Detective Powell sat with his back to the two-way mirror.

"So did your fiancée tell you where she was going?" Powell asked.

"She said she had a meeting at the office." Gibbons' voice was flat, robotic.

Peri felt a chill down her back. For just losing his fiancée, he did not appear to be a heartbroken man.

"She never said she'd be at the hotel?"

"No."

"Skip." She touched his arm. "What do your Spidey senses tell you?"

As usual, his poker face remained. "Without any evidence, he's a man who is still processing his fiancée's death. Not just her death, her murder."

"But…?"

He shrugged. "But I wouldn't discount him, if the evidence hinted in his direction. I've seen too many guys like him. Controlled, measured responses to cops, white-knuckle rage as soon as we turn our heads."

"Is that what you see in Dev?"

"No, but perhaps it's worse. I don't get any reading from him at all. Unlike his sister, he's kind of a blank slate."

"Am I that easy to read?" She smiled.

"Are, and was." His hand reached out, settled on her waist. "Even when you were the cleaning lady at the station, I knew you planned your work schedule around mine."

"Why, Skipper, I'm shocked—that you figured it out."

"Did she ever share what she was working on?" Powell's voice interrupted them, turning their attention back to the interview.

"A little. We don't work on the same projects. She's working on the commercial side of the house, some kind of tracking and display system for aircraft. I'm working DoD."

"Department of Defense? Is it classified?"

"Only the encryption parts."

The rest of the interview devolved into the logistics of death. Autopsy, releasing the body, what paperwork to file. When Peri's mother was in hospice, the workers told her and Erik where to go and what to do. When Erik died, Peri assumed the process would be the same, but it was different because his death was different.

For every death, there are things no one knows until it's too late and you need them.

In the meantime, her brother had confessed to something he probably did not do, and she had the uphill battle of finding who did it and fighting to get her brother to recant. "We need my brother's phone."

Skip's eyes narrowed as he stared at her. "Why?"

"Because something isn't right." She shook her head. "He was doing everything to avoid capture. Suddenly, he's writing out a confession. Something happened between the time he got in that squad car in Fullerton, and when he reached the interview room in Placentia."

"I understand, you want to believe he's innocent, but—"

"You didn't see him in that interview room. He was begging me to leave it alone. Guilty or not, who does that? And the knife." She told him what Jason said about the lack of prints. "Plus, it's sharp enough to cut through a bag, but he somehow pulls it out of the back of his pants?"

"Okay, Smarty." He leaned against the wall. "Give me another explanation."

"I don't know." She paced to the door and back. "Who drove Dev to this station? I need to talk to him. How would I get his phone number?"

"Let me find out from the desk who brought Dev in." Skip pulled out his phone and pressed a number. Two questions later, he hung up. "Officer Darden and his partner Officer Gomez delivered Dev."

"And a phone number?"

"Peri, we're not the Police White Pages."

She glared at him. "Fine—I'll call Detective Berkwits. His number's in my phone."

The detective answered quickly. She explained what she needed, and was rewarded with two phone numbers, one for each officer.

Which one to call? She decided to start with the more experienced one. The one she trusted. The one she liked.

"Officer Gomez, this is Peri—"

45

"WHO?" His voice was booming, and she could hear what sounded like a jackhammer in the background.

"PERI MINNEOPA." Skip grimaced, so she left the observation room and walked down the hall, looking for a more private location.

Officer Gomez kept shouting. "YOU'LL HAVE TO CALL BACK. I CAN'T HEAR YOU."

As she opened the door to the next interview room, the phone went dead.

"Well, damn." She sat and looked at her phone. "Guess I'm out of options."

She entered Officer Darden's number and pressed "Call." He was obviously not with his partner—she didn't hear the same cacophony in the background.

"Officer Darden, this is Peri Minneopa. You brought me in today for questioning. I have some questions for you."

"Miss Minnypopa, this isn't appropriate. Who gave you my number?"

"Detective Berkwits, and please call me Peri." This was not going to be easy. "Officer, I just need to ask some questions about my brother's trip to the Placentia Police Station."

"I don't know, Miss Minn—Miss. Let me talk to the sergeant first." The call ended.

Peri held the silent phone in her hand, wondering how to squeeze blood from this particular turnip. She returned to the hall where Skip waited for her.

"Officer Doogie won't talk to me." Hands on her hips, she looked at him. "Skipper?"

"I'm not making phone calls for you."

"But he'll talk to you. You're a detective."

"A detective on disability leave."

"A detective, nonetheless." She draped her arms around him. "Can I ply you with drinks? Sex? Sexy drinks?"

"What are you trying to find out?"

She stood on her tiptoes to kiss his cheek. "One, did he have his phone? Could he have received any calls, or texts? And two, is there any place along the route he could have picked up that knife?"

"Peri, that's ridiculous."

"Maybe so, but I saw Officer Doo—Darden frisk my brother. Which would you rather believe—that he didn't feel a razor-sharp knife sticking out of the back of his pants, or that Dev somehow acquired that knife later?"

Skip nodded. "All right. I'm not convinced, but I am curious."

Detective Logan walked toward them. "Peri, I need you to look at something for me."

The trio returned to the lab. "Jason spotted it. It might not mean anything, but I'm trying to stay open-minded on this case."

"Thank you, Steve." Peri sat next to Jason in front of a monitor.

"I was logging everything we've got," Jason said, "including all the videos from the interviews. I noticed something...unusual when Dev was talking to you."

He held up a remote control and pressed a button. The video was angled over her shoulder, pointing toward Dev. She saw her body tense, her hands in fists, and heard her voice, pleading with him. He stared, mouth parted, eyes red. Looking up at the camera, he brought his right fist smashing against his left palm, and dragged them toward his chest.

"Play that end part back," Peri said, leaning forward. "And turn the sound off."

"What is it, Doll?" Skip asked.

"When Dev and I were little, we learned ASL. Used it like a secret code." Pointing to the video, she sat up. "That motion Dev made—it wasn't an angry gesture. It was sign language."

"What'd he say?" Logan asked.

"He said, 'Help me.'"

CHAPTER TWELVE

BENNY NEEDLES WANDERED down Hollywood Boulevard, reading each star's name as the crowds jostled their way around him. His gray sharkskin suit, crisp white shirt, and silver-blue tie made him stand out among the shorts-and-tees tourists. For Benny, a visit to Dean Martin's stars on the Walk of Fame required at least business attire.

His friend Samantha Hollis walked with him, trying to keep the masses from running him over while he inspected each tile. She had also picked her best outfit for the day, a retro shirtwaist of blue and white polka dots, with a sailor collar. In keeping with her 40s theme, she wore little white gloves and a veiled fascinator that accentuated her short, lavender bob.

"I think Dino's star is just up here, past Wilcox," Sam said.

Benny nodded. "Look, Will Rogers."

"The map says Carol Burnett is here, too."

Benny stopped and looked ahead. "We've been walking a long time. Can we sit down after we find Dino?"

"Yes, I think that would be nice. There's a pizza place not far from here."

"Oh, no." Benny shook his head. "We will go to the Musso & Frank Grill."

Sam smiled. "Alright. We'll go there."

As they continued down the boulevard, Benny stared at the pavement. "Miss Peri was not polite to me today."

"Yes, you mentioned that on the train."

"She wasn't even interested in my tie pin."

"It sounded like she had a lot on her mind. I'm sure she didn't mean to be rude."

"She told me—look, it's Dino's star." He scurried to the tile and gazed at it, hand over his heart.

"It's lovely," Sam said.

"This was his star for movies." His voice softened to a whisper. "February 8, 1960."

They lingered while he cleaned the star, and she took photos.

After ten minutes, Sam asked, "Should we go to the restaurant now?"

He nodded. "We'll pass by his second star, for television, on the way."

"Perfect."

"Thank you, Sam, for coming to Hollywood with me. I always wanted to come and see Dino's stars, but I was afraid to come by myself."

"I'm honored that you asked me."

"Good." He frowned. "Miss Peri told me she was quitting the private eye business. Told me she didn't need me for an assistant anymore."

"Do you think she lied to you?"

"No." He stared at the pavement again. "No, she doesn't lie. But sometimes she doesn't tell me everything. I think she doesn't want to get me into trouble."

"I'd say that makes her a pretty good friend."

"Sam…" Benny kept walking, rubbing his tie pin, his collar moist with perspiration. "We're friends, right?"

She smiled again. "Yes, Benny."

"Good friends?"

"The best."

"Are we…special good friends?"

Sam didn't answer immediately, but let a few seconds pass. "As in, girlfriend-boyfriend special?"

Benny's face flushed scarlet as he nodded.

"I don't know." She patted his arm. "I like you. I like hanging out with you and being quiet with you. I'm not quite ready to feel anything else, but there's no one else I'd rather be with. Can we just be extra special friends before we get to girlfriend-boyfriend?"

"Yes," he sighed in relief. "I like that."

They found Dean's second star, and spent time cleaning, photographing, and admiring it, before strolling on toward Musso & Frank's.

"Miss Peri getting arrested was scary," Benny said.

"Yes, it was."

"I used to be her assistant." He pushed his chest forward. "We solved crimes together."

"Yes. You were a good team."

"She said today that she was just looking for a friend, but I think she was trying to keep me safe again."

They had arrived at the famous restaurant. The room was sparsely populated, but Benny stepped up to the maitre'd and informed him of their reservations. The older man glanced at his book, nodded, and led them to a booth.

"Oh, good, they have spaghetti and meatballs," he said, looking at the menu.

The décor in the restaurant hearkened to the days of old Hollywood glamour. Dark wood, blood-red leather, and low lighting made the place look like a movie from the '40s. Benny studied the room, from wall to wall to floor to ceiling, pointing everything out to Sam.

Some time after they had placed their orders, Sam said, "I'll bet Peri would love this place. They're famous for their martinis."

"Miss Peri loves dirty martinis. Do you think she's okay?"

"She should be," Sam said. "Skip was there to help her."

He nodded. "Yes. But I'm usually her best assistant."

"I'm sure you are."

"Sam…" Benny reached forward for her hand on the table, but couldn't quite take it. He placed his hand beside hers, his pinky finger touching her thumb. "I'm pretty sure Miss Peri needs my help. I can't let her down."

Sam smiled. "If you think so. Do you want to leave now?"

"Oh, no. After we've seen Dino's prints near Grauman's." He looked up to see the waiter bringing his meal. "Miss Peri understands. You always have to finish what you start."

CHAPTER THIRTEEN

PERI WALKED INTO her kitchen, where the construction sounds were at their peak. The not-quite-steady bang of the gun, combined with the relentless whirr of the drill invaded her temples, pounded into her brain.

She found the refrigerator, poured a glass of ice water, and headed down the hall of the spacious ranch-style house, into the master bedroom. After shutting the door, she built a pillow fort on the bed and tucked herself inside, with her laptop.

Armed with more information, she dug through the internet again, looking for her brother. Perhaps he was being blackmailed into confessing. It had the makings of a bad movie script. Take the fall, get a reward. Cash for the family, and a secret gets buried.

What was Dev afraid of losing? Was there a wife or child hidden somewhere? Had he done something in his youth, something without a statute of limitations? That could only be murder. Was he a criminal?

Peri followed any breadcrumb she found. Newspaper articles, social media, all using his "other" name. *Such an ass. How dare he turn his back on everything our parents built? On me.*

There it was. It wasn't family pride. Her big brother had abandoned her. Her hero walked out of her life, ditching her, on purpose. She had spent most of her adulthood chasing him down, pretending to want to "check in," but really wanting his attention. *What is so wrong with me?*

She closed the search sites on her computer, and started up her music app. The Steely Dan channel played *Any Major Dude*. She alternated rubbing the cold glass against her forehead, and drinking the contents. By the time it was empty, Donald Fagen was singing about reeling in the years. The lyrics resonated with her.

The things you think are useless, Dev...

Leaving the music on, she re-launched her search engine and visited sites. Dev didn't seem to do any of the normal social media, apart from LinkedIn, which only gave his work experience and a brief resume. Nothing special, but she made a note to visit the company.

An idea hit her, and she logged into a genealogy website. Sometimes, these sites had more records in one location than if she tried to search for each one individually. She entered her parents' names and found both her and her brother.

Clicking on "Endeavor Minneopa" yielded a few results. A recorded petition to change his name to Chaplain was filed a year ago. Why did he wait so long— was the last time she hunted him down the last straw? There was a document discharging him from the Army— who knew he was in the military?

"I need to talk to Dev's boss," she said as she closed her laptop. Pushing it away, she felt the pillows lean in, embracing her. A nap sounded better than detective work.

She could justify it. Her head was still aching from the muffled construction noises, and probably from her feelings of anger and worry over Dev. Just a short nap.

Who am I kidding? If I lie down, I won't wake up for at least two hours.

A cup of coffee was needed to slap her awake, get her to Dev's office.

She rose from her comfortable pillow haven and got the aspirin out of the bathroom cabinet. After taking two, she smoothed her knit top and leggings and launched her weary body toward her kitchen, aka Cacophony Central.

While her travel mug filled with a dark roast, she looked around at the progress. Cabinets had been installed on the kitchen walls, the fridge had been moved to its final location, and a new dishwasher sat in the middle of the room, awaiting installation. Peri picked up her full mug and tightened the spill-proof lid.

Hank Thomas the construction foreman entered, nodding at her. "Hey, Peri-almost-missus-Carlton. Howzit look?"

She startled at the use of Skip's last name. Was that the way she was going to do things?

"Looks nice, but…" She gestured at the upper cabinets. "Weren't they supposed to go all the way to the ceiling?"

"Well, normally, cabinets don't go that high. Most people can't reach."

"True, but I thought we wanted them to extend to the top, since Skip and I are tall." She pointed underneath. "Now we don't have enough space below the cabinets, on the counter."

Hank took out his tape measure and stretched it, copying numbers into his little book. Peri tried not to laugh. Contractors and their tools—it's all about the inches. He measured four places, then called to one of his workmen.

"These are custom-length cabinets," he barked. "They need to go up to the ceiling."

There was a little grumbling and a few heavy sighs, while the worker glanced at Peri.

"Go ahead and swear about it," she told him. "I would."

A colorful barrage of cursing trailed after him as he left the room. Hank scowled, but Peri laughed. She held her mug up in a salute.

It was a 15-minute trip to Dev's office in Fullerton, according to her car's GPS. She mumbled a few choice words of her own as she drove off. After Dev's case got solved, she'd yell at him for being an ass.

Get Dev out of this jam...then we'll have a come-to-Jesus talk.

CHAPTER FOURTEEN

RO-BET ENGINEERING WAS nestled into the Y where Harbor Boulevard splits in half before continuing north, leaving its tender shoot, Brea Boulevard, to head northeast. Peri got out of her car, glancing up at the tall office building's long white stripes of stucco, alternating with the dark shine of windows.

She entered the building, found the elevators, and stopped at an unassuming door on the 8th floor, with a tiny name plaque. *Suite 810, Ro-Bet Engineering, LLC.*

The small waiting room appeared to have been furnished by liquidation sales. Two unmatched chairs were pushed against the wall, separated by a wrought iron table that belonged in a garden. The receptionist's desk was an olive drab metal, covered in stacks of paper, with a computer monitor from the Jurassic Age perched on one corner.

A young woman sat behind the desk, pale with ink-black hair parted in the middle and drooping into two thin braids. Her dress was similarly dark, drab, and the shape of a burlap sack. Peri couldn't help but think of Wednesday Addams.

"My name is Peri Minneopa." She held out her business card. "I'd like to speak with Mr. Betancourt."

The girl extended her hand with the speed of a sloth reaching for a branch. She took the card without looking away from Peri. "I will see if *Mister Betancourt* is available."

Peri tipped her head and smiled. "Thank you."

The receptionist disappeared through a door. While she was gone, Peri took the opportunity to have a look at the stacks of paper on *Miz Addams'* desk. They were all invoices, organized by company, and arranged by how many reminders had been sent for payment due.

For having such a miracle device, they sure need money.

Ye olde monitor on the desk was attached to a tower on the floor, a small rectangle that might have been beige beneath the layers of dust and fingerprints. A keyboard shelf was tucked away under the desk, so she pulled it out. The monitor brightened with a screenshot of the receptionist, dressed in black with black accessories, and a large python draped across her shoulders. Her mouth was attempting a smile. It didn't look good on her.

Peri heard footsteps approaching and quickly moved to the other side of the desk, pulling her phone out to look busy.

"Mr. Betancourt will see you now." The receptionist's words were loud and over-enunciated, like the bark of a territorial dog.

Peri smiled. "Thank you. I didn't catch your name."

"Miss Keening." The girl stepped away from the door, allowing a tall figure to take her place, as if inviting the bouncer to escort a drunken bully outside.

Peri walked forward, hand extended. He was a handsome man with dark hair and eyes, a chiseled facial structure, and a blinding white smile.

"Miss Minn—ouppa?" He studied her business card, before looking up. "My name is Rodolfo Betancourt. I hope I got your name right."

"Minn-ee-o-pa. You can call me Peri."

"Shall we go to my office?" He turned to the receptionist. "Emily, make sure those invoices go out today."

Emily Keening. The girl looked at the screen saver on her monitor, and gave Peri a sour glance.

Rodolfo stepped aside and allowed Peri to walk through the doorway into his office. It was a dark cavern, twice as large as the reception area. Floor to ceiling windows would have let the sun in, except they were hidden by heavy shades. Rodolfo flipped a switch, hitting the room with a swath of florescent light, before taking his place behind a substantial oak desk. He gestured for Peri to sit across from him in a plush leather chair.

"What can I help you with, Miz—Peri?"

"I'm working with the Placentia Police Department on a case." She paused. Her sleuthing skills felt rusty. "I'm here to discuss one of your employees, Dev Chaplain."

"Dev is our director of marketing. What do you want to know?"

One step at a time, Peri. "What exactly does he market for you, and who would be his customer base?"

"Dev markets all our devices. Mostly, we make routers. They enable computers to communicate via a network. We make and install routers for any kind of business needs, large or small."

"Do you sell any of these routers to large companies, like Howard Aerospace?"

"I wish." He smiled, showing his perfectly white, perfectly straight teeth. "HAC prefers to deal with larger houses that give deep discounts and have certified their software to at least level B."

"I'm sorry, certified software?"

"Our routers consist of three parts, in a way. There's the hardware, or the physical pieces that you plug into equipment, like a computer. Then there's software, which is a set of commands telling the hardware what to do. There's also firmware, which is kind of a hybrid—it's a bunch of physical circuits that have commands programmed into them.

"All the commands, or software, must be run through rigorous testing and documented in order to qualify for different levels. A is the highest, and most stringent, but achieving level B is not that much easier."

Peri looked up from her notes. "And what is your software level?"

"We are currently trying to achieve level B. We haven't gotten there yet. It's expensive, all those hours of testing, and recording everything."

Something in his delivery made her think he wasn't a fan of certification. "So, who are your current customers?"

Rodolfo tapped his fingertips together. "We have a few small businesses in Brea and Fullerton. I can get you their names, if it's absolutely necessary."

"Is there some kind of confidentiality agreement in your sales?"

"No, of course not." He squirmed in his chair. "I just meant, if it was important to you. I mean, you wanted references for Dev, right?"

"Yes, sorry, I got distracted. Back to Dev, how long has he worked for you?"

"Only a year, but he's done great stuff. Doubled our business, and got us connections with software certification professionals. We're not marketing types. Dev's a real salesman."

"Do you know anything about his personal life?"

"Not really. He's a private guy. Never brings anyone to the office parties, doesn't join in any office small talk about family." He leaned forward. "To be honest, I often wonder what he's hiding. I mean, who doesn't at least mention going to the movies?"

"Good point. Well, could there be anyone else in the company he speaks to?"

Rodolfo shrugged. "There might be, but I work the most closely with him."

Peri nodded. "Do you know an engineer named Tressa Velasco?"

"Tressa...Velasco?" He looked up, away from her. "I don't think so."

"She worked at Howard Aerospace—HAC." She watched his face, certain he was lying. There was a wideness in his eyes, an almost theatrical level of denial.

He shook his head. "What did you say she does?"

Not much at the moment. "Electrical engineering. Would it be possible to see Dev's office?"

"Certainly, although it's not much of an office." He stood. "More of a cubicle. Dev's not here that often. He's out, selling."

She nodded, and followed him out. *I get it. Dev's your salesman.*

CHAPTER FIFTEEN

HE STEERED HER out of his office and through a door to the left of the reception desk, into a long hallway. The walls were a dull eggshell color, and showed scuffmarks and dents. They stopped at the door marked, "Offices."

This space was larger, divided into two areas by a half-glass, half-solid wall. There were tables of equipment on the far side, robotic arms, and someone wandering around in a white, hooded suit, with a tray in his or her gloved hand. This side held two rows of four cubicles, with walls covered in a beige, carpet-like material, no more than 5 feet high.

Rodolfo tapped Peri's shoulder and pointed to a cubicle at the end of the first row. "That's Dev's. Feel free to look around."

She walked down the aisle to her brother's cubicle, glancing in the other cubbies as she went. They were all occupied. Her escort stopped at the cubicle next to Dev's and began talking to someone, leaning over the door frame.

As with most pre-fab units, Dev's space had a built-in desk with overhead cabinets and an under-desk safe. Peri slipped on a pair of thin gloves, and sat in his chair, surveying his work environment, trying to get a feel for her brother's style, and maybe his secrets.

He was neat, at least. His desktop was clear of any photos, any mementos, anything that told the world who he was. No papers waiting to be filed, nothing in disarray or disorganization. A blotter with the month and days was centered alongside a plain brown coffee mug.

The drawers were all locked. Fortunately, the locks were simple ones, and no one was watching. She slipped a metal file in each slot and easily popped them. His overhead cabinet held a few books on routers and networking. The drawers yielded files full of marketing brochures. Everything about this office revolved around his job.

Dev almost didn't exist.

Peri shuffled through the brochures, to see if anything fell out. There was one piece of paper that didn't belong—a receipt from the local drugstore. It looked ordinary, but ordinary things aren't hidden unless there's a reason. She snapped a photo of the receipt and continued to sift through the drawers.

As a last act, she picked up his blotter, checking for anything hidden. There were two sticky notes attached to the cardboard backing. One had an obvious phone number, and the initials "T.V." If they didn't mean Tressa Velasco, it was a helluva coincidence. The other sticky was a series of four two-digit numbers, separated by hyphens.

More photos, of both notes, were quickly snapped before she turned the blotter back. The meaning of the four numbers eluded her, but perhaps someone around here knew. She pulled off her gloves and shoved them into her tote. *Maybe Dev will at least give me a hint from his jail cell.*

Walking out of Dev's cubicle, she saw Rodolfo talking to a young, dark-haired woman wearing leggings and an oversized sweatshirt. He glanced up and moved away from her cubicle. Peri stopped him.

"Mr. Betancourt, perhaps you could introduce me. I'd like to find as many people as possible who have had interactions with Dev."

"Certainly. I'm sure our crew is happy to help. Right, Alicia?"

"Of course." The young woman turned to Peri, hand out. "Alicia Duarte, software engineer."

"Peri Minneopa, and no, you don't have to remember my last name. How well do you know Dev?"

Alicia's hands went out, palms up. "Not uber-well. He's hardly ever in here, and he's so quiet. I mean, he's not grumpy or anything. Just…keeps his head down, stays under the radar, that kind of thing. If I say hi, he says hi back, though."

"So, you guys never had lunch together, or chatted about anything?"

"No. I gotta be honest, I got the impression he thought we were all just kids. No offense, and we would have totes included him in our after-hours stuff. We like to go to happy hour, Sunday brunch, movies. He acted like he was too old for that stuff." While she spoke, her hands kept up a myriad of motions, as if they needed to work along with her mouth in order for her to produce words.

"And here in your cubicle, next to his, you never accidentally overheard phone conversations?"

"Um, okay, well, I try not to eavesdrop." If hands could look apologetic, hers were contrite. "But I did hear him, just yesterday. He was talking to someone named Tee. I mean, his voice wasn't, like, upset, but he just kept saying, 'Now, Tee, it's not like that. Just meet me for drinks and I'll explain.' Over and over. Finally, he goes, 'Great, I'll see you there,' and next thing, I see him hurrying past my cubby."

Peri's stomach rolled over. Tee could be Tressa, and meeting her for drinks could have led to a hotel room and stabbing and that would lead to Dev in prison. "I don't suppose you heard where they might have been going for drinks."

"Nah, sorry."

A low male voice interrupted them. "Hey, what's going on?"

CHAPTER SIXTEEN

"JAMES, MEET PERI Minne…" Alicia began.

"Minneopa, and just call me Peri." She extended her hand to the young man at the doorway. "And you are?"

"James Peoples." He was short and square, with brown hair and brown eyes, framed by Buddy Holly glasses. Underneath his baggy tee-shirt and slacks, Peri wasn't certain if he was chunky or ripped. Figuring engineers, she guessed chunky. His voice was soft. "What's up?"

"I'm getting information on Dev Chaplain. Mr. Betancourt was kind enough to let me look through his office, talk to people he knows."

"Dev? Yeah, he's kind of weird." The young man shook his head. "Not very sociable. Kind of acts like he doesn't want to be here."

"That's not true," Alicia said. "Sure, he keeps to himself, but he isn't cranky about it."

James smiled at Alicia, the way an older person does when a young person talks about having experience. Peri filed his condescension under *Things I Don't Like About People*.

"Well, thank you, both—" Peri was interrupted by Ms. Keening, who had entered the room to give a note to

Rodolfo and whisper in his ear. She stood really close, and held her face so near to his, their cheeks touched. Peri regarded the two of them. Could suave, handsome Rodolfo, and goth-yet-drab Emily be a thing?

Stranger couplings have happened. Look at Benny and Sam.

Rodolfo turned to her, "If you'll excuse me, Peri, we'll have to cut this meeting short. It seems a Detective Logan is here to see me. Alicia, could you take over as Peri's escort?"

Peri held her hand out. "Thank you, Rodolfo. It's been a pleasure."

The businessman shook her hand with a smile and left. As Peri turned to speak to Alicia, she bumped against someone else's arm, and in an instant, felt them draw back and heard a surprised, "Hey!"

A tall, pale young man dressed to engineering perfection in Dockers and a short-sleeved dress shirt held a mug away from him, looking at the splatter on the floor.

"Are you okay?" she asked.

"I'm fine, but now I need more hot water. My tea ratio is off."

Alicia stepped between them. "Peri, this is Tim Neal. Tim, Peri is doing some kind of a…background check, is it? On Dev. She wants to talk to people who work with him, or hang out with him."

Tim's light blue eyes flitted nervously between the two women. "I don't work with Dev."

Peri smiled, attempting to put him at ease. "Thanks, Tim. I'm assuming you don't socialize with him either?"

He looked at his tea, squinting. "No. I need to fix this."

"Sure, go ahead." Peri watched the young man leave. "He reminds me of a friend of mine."

"He's a funny guy," Alicia said. "Very particular about everything."

"Nothing wrong with that. If you don't mind, I think I owe him a better apology."

She followed Tim out the door, Alicia on her heels. They caught up with him in a small kitchenette, where he removed the teabag from his mug and placed it in a bowl, before measuring the mug's water level.

"Excuse me, Tim," Peri said, watching his fastidious actions to correct his disrupted drink. "I wanted to apologize again. I had no idea you were behind me. I'll be more careful next time."

"It was annoying." He placed the mug into the microwave. "But easily remedied."

Peri glanced at Alicia, who had moved into the hallway to talk on the phone. "You're probably pretty observant. Was there anyone who did spend time with Dev?"

He bent his upper body away from her, as if the question hurt. "He talks too much. Always asking how everyone is doing. That's a stupid question. We're doing our jobs, like he should be."

Peri nodded. "Just checking. Thanks."

"He laughs with Alicia." Tim was talking to his mug as he sank the teabag and set his timer. "Laughs too much. James hates it, but he hates it more when Dev meets the blonde lady in the park."

"A blonde lady? Was it Tressa?"

He shook his head. "I don't know her name. If I never met you, why would I know who you are?"

"Exactly. Thanks for the information." Peri left, slipping through the receptionist's area, avoiding being spotted by Detective Logan. She'd worked hard to develop a good relationship with him. No need to spoil it by being accused of snooping.

Once in her car, she called Chief Fletcher to see where Dev was being held. They needed to talk.

According to the Chief, Dev was spending the night in the OC Central Men's Jail. By the time Peri found that out, visiting times were over. Having to wait until morning made her peevish, but there was nothing else to be done. She grabbed takeout from her favorite pizza place and headed home.

As she pulled into her drive, her phone played a jaunty tune. It was her best gal pal, Blanche. Her husky voice didn't even wait for Peri's hello.

"I heard you're going crazy in your new digs. Want to come over?"

"That's the best offer I've had all day." Peri backed her car out and headed to the spacious greens of Yorba Linda.

CHAPTER SEVENTEEN

BLANCHE AND HER family lived on the outskirts of the city, in a large house on an even larger piece of land. Peri liked to tease her friend about being in the lap of luxury, but knew it was well-deserved. Blanche had worked hard to become a surgeon, but was forced to adjust her career choices when an automobile accident decimated her fine motor skills. As Assistant Medical Examiner in the Sheriff's office, her talents were put to good use.

Blanche's husband, Paul, was an engineer who had risen to upper management at one of the local aerospace companies. Their two children, Nick and Dani, were thriving young adults in college. The four of them were the warmest and most generous family Peri had ever known.

Peri strolled to the door, knocked once, and let herself in. She heard Blanche's familiar voice as she walked across the threshold.

"Did you bring pizza?"

"Good thing I got a large." Peri walked through the foyer, and found Blanche in the kitchen, slicing limes. "Margaritas tonight?"

"Does that meet with your approval?"

"Olé." She put down the pizza box and picked up a glass to roll the rim in juice and salt. "So, how much have you heard?"

"Only about the construction crew driving you to madness…and that your brother is in town and arrested for murder."

Peri rubbed her temples. "You know the worst part? I'd rather just not get involved. That sounds awful, but I feel tired of it all, tired of investigating things and having to think and be curious. But he's my big brother and I can't not help him."

"Cut yourself a little slack." Blanche rinsed her hands and held her arms out as she moved around the counter and embraced her friend. "You're still fighting your way back from trauma. It's only been four months since the shooting."

"You're just hugging me to dry your hands on my shirt."

"Maybe." She let go and returned to her bartending. "Grab the chips and salsa, and let's go outside. I'll bring the pizza and the booze."

They took their spread to the backyard, where a sleek black dining set glinted in the partial shade of the patio cover, and two large Adirondack chairs overlooked the azure swimming pool. Placing the food and drink on the table, the two friends found plates and cutlery in the outdoor supply cabinet, and settled in for a nosh.

Peri brought her up to speed on her chance meeting with Dev, her arrest, and her subsequent visit to Dev's place of business. "I'm so mad at him right now I could throat-punch him. Who could have gotten him to confess like that?"

"Sounds like someone with enough power to hurt him. Maybe they threatened to kill him, or someone he loves."

"I've never seen him that frightened. Not that I've seen a lot of him as an adult." Peri took a sip of her margarita and marveled at its delicious combination of tart and smooth and salty. "I won't lie, it hurts, to have your own brother shun you."

"He's an ass, if you'll pardon my saying so." Blanche lifted her own glass. "You are a good friend, and a brave and fabulous woman. The world should be knocking your door down, trying to get close to you."

Peri smiled. "So, what do I need to do to get you to talk about the murder vic?"

"For my bestie, that closely-held info comes free." She held up a slice of veggie pizza. "Although this is not a bad bribe."

"So spill."

"I've barely had one day with her and we just sent the blood to the lab for tox screening. I can tell you she had twenty-five stab wounds, none particularly deep, but a few deadly. Carotid got hit, femoral artery, too. Found skin cells under her nails, so we sent that out to be typed."

"So COD was stabbing?"

"Probably. No bruising anywhere, except on the left bicep. Even if she'd been poisoned, the blood at the scene suggests she was alive when she was stabbed."

Peri sat back, sighing. "And Jason's checking the knife that supposedly my brother handed over as the murder weapon."

"Oh, Peri, I'm so sorry. How can I help?"

"Only thing you can do is what you always do. Process her carefully and completely. If there's a contradiction in Dev's confession, it's gotta be in the evidence." Peri took out her phone and ran through her photos. "Right now, I've got a few slips of paper to chase, and that's it. This one has me stumped. Four numbers, separated by hyphens, what do they mean?"

"Let me see." Blanche reached for her phone, studied it. "Paul? C'mere!"

A tall, dark-haired man strolled out to the patio and helped himself to a chip, digging a scoop of salsa with it, and popping it into his mouth. "Where's my margarita?" he mumbled between crunches.

"Glasses are on the counter. Pitcher is on the table." His wife pointed with Peri's phone, holding it up for him to view. "You're an engineer. What do these numbers mean?"

He pulled a pair of glasses from his forehead and sat them on his nose before taking the phone. "They look like the combo to a lock."

"I thought combinations had three numbers," Peri said.

"Almost all do, unless they're specialty locks. We use this kind at my office all the time. One more number means another layer of difficulty to break the code."

Peri sat up. "So, an aerospace company would use these? Like, say, Howard Aerospace? Or, maybe Dev's company—he had a safe in his office."

"Definitely." He kissed Blanche on top of her head. "Did I earn my drink?"

"Hell, yes," Peri told him. "Give that man a margarita. Extra salt."

"Thanks, Peri." He grinned and tickled his wife's neck on his way back into the house. "I never get a good score from the East German judge."

"Your husband's a hoot," Peri said.

"Yeah." Blanche licked at the remaining salt on her glass. "I'm gonna renew his contract. Speaking of husbands, are you and Skip setting the date soon? I don't care how big the wedding is, as long as I'm there."

"We don't want to set a date until Skip sells his house. I really thought his would sell first."

Blanche shook her head. "Nope. Yours was a small house with a smallish price tag, in pristine condition. It was perfect for a young couple. Skip's problem is that his house is the best of the neighborhood, at the top of the food chain. Everyone's looking for a bargain, but they want perfection. They think they'll find a turnkey that they can improve on, and make it worth even more than they paid for it."

"You're right, it's hard to do that with his place. Upscale kitchen and bath, smart home with security system and cameras." Peri downed the rest of her drink. "We're never getting married, cuz he's never gonna sell."

"Don't think that way, Girlfriend." Blanche reached across to rub her shoulder. "It'll find its owner, somehow."

"Right now, all I'd like is for the hammering to stop at my—our—new house. Six more weeks."

"It's like the groundhog saw his shadow, huh?"

"Yeah, the groundhog who was packing a jackhammer."

Blanche laughed. "Seriously, it's all gonna be all right. Keep taking those baby steps, one day at a time, pretty soon you and Skip will look back and see it was worth it."

Peri stood up and stretched. "Beebs, I love you. But if you toss one more cliché at me, I'm going to hork up a hairball, right here."

Her friend laughed again, and joined her, walking into the house and to the front door. Peri hugged her tightly. "Thanks for keeping me sane."

"It's my job."

CHAPTER EIGHTEEN

PERI POINTED HER little blue Honda down Fairmont Boulevard, on the gently curving, lightly hilly road, past all the streets named "Paseo de" something or other, making her way west. The sky had almost completed its transition from the lightbulb bright of the June day, to a dusky darkness. Night skies were never quite ink-black, due to the thousands of lights in thousands of homes across the county.

Her headlights automatically blazed on as she turned onto Esperanza Road, where the real estate catered to lower incomes. Houses were smaller here, and packed more tightly. Train tracks ran beside the road, which had to make life interesting for the residents.

Wonder which side is the wrong side of the tracks?

At the corner where Esperanza morphed into Orangethorpe Avenue, she became aware of a car behind her, without its lights on. *Idiot,* she thought. *I can't tell you to turn on your headlights if I'm in front of you. Someone else will just have to do it.*

The car hung close to her bumper, aggravating her even more. *There's plenty of room for you to pass.*

She kept a close watch in her rearview mirror. "What is wrong with you, you jackass? Go around me."

The speed limit was 50, so Peri pushed her Honda up to 55. The dark car stayed with her.

As a test, she moved from the right lane into the left. The car moved with her. In the near-darkness, it appeared to be a sedan about the same size as her Civic. The front end was square, which would make it older. She couldn't tell what color it was. Gray. Maybe blue.

At Orangethorpe and Kraemer, she was supposed to turn right. Instead, she stayed straight. As expected, the car remained on her tail. Her body began to tremble, making her foot jiggle on the accelerator.

Taking a long, deep breath, she reached out for the phone mounted on her dashboard. She wasn't certain she could dial Skip, but 9-1-1 was always available.

"What's your emergency?"

"Hello, my name is Peri Minneopa." Her voice quivered. "I am being pursued by an unknown person in a car with no lights on."

"Peri, ma'am, are you on foot?"

No, you idiot, she wanted to scream. "No, I'm in my car. Late model blue Honda Civic, license plate 4WKN411. I'm on Orangethorpe heading west. I'm going to turn right on Placentia Avenue and try to get to the police station."

"Understood, Peri. I'll relay to our patrols, see if anyone can intercept. In the meantime, I'll stay on the line until you get to the station."

"Thank you. Who am I talking to?"

"Karen. I used to work the day shift."

"Yes, I remember you. Nice to have you on the line with me."

The dark car maintained its closeness, trailing her like toilet paper on her shoe. Her jittery nerves calmed into a deliberate, furious desire to stop the car, get the bat from behind her seat, and go to work on this driver. She shared the plan with Karen, who laughed before warning her not to try it.

As she approached the stoplight at Chapman and Kraemer, she could see the police station, and nearly leapt from her seat with joy. The light was green, so she decided to go straight and enter the station from Chapman. It would be a left-hand turn with no oncoming traffic.

"I'm almost there, Karen. I'm on Chapman, turning onto All-America W—"

A jarring bang launched her car forward, and tossed her body toward the steering wheel, until the seatbelt jerked her back. She managed to look up and see the dark car pushing her bumper. Her foot hit the brake and she slid to a stop, sideways, her back end in the turn lane and the front end across oncoming traffic.

The other car stopped, too. Peri undid her seatbelt, reached for the door handle to get out and confront her stalker. As she opened her door, the dark car backed away from her bumper, putting the driver within her line of sight. His window was rolled down, but she didn't see a face. Instead, she saw a blur holding a shape she recognized.

A gun barrel.

She heard a familiar pop, and buried herself in the seats, holding her arms over her head. Her back passenger window shattered in a thousand tiny pebbles. She could hear Karen on the phone asking what happened.

"Shots fired!" was all she could spit out.

The sedan sped away, tires squealing and engine roaring. She heard sirens, one whipping past her, and another stopping. The reflection of red and blue lights on the street let her know help had arrived. It had taken perhaps a minute, which felt like a month.

"Miss Peri." A pair of hands were on her shoulders, attempting to ease her from her vehicle. "They're gone. We chased them off."

She looked into a face she recognized, Officer Driver. The policewoman had helped Peri deal with Detective Logan when Skip was in the hospital.

"Gwen, I'm so glad it's you." Peri pushed her body back into a sitting position. "That was nuts."

"Are you okay?"

"Sure." Peri could hear her voice echo, sounding very far away. She took a step out of her car and felt the ground open up and inhale her leg. The other leg followed, so she decided to go, too. *It's warm and dark down here.*

CHAPTER NINETEEN

THE WORLD WAS upside down. A strange young man held her hand, good-looking and broad-shouldered. He wore a blue shirt.

"Hello, there," he said.

Where was she? Who was she? Peri flailed, pushing herself up, off the cot, trying to swing her body upright.

The EMT pressed her shoulders down. "You're okay, ma'am. Please lie back. You were in a car accident."

She fought against him for a moment, before his words penetrated her brain. *Car accident. Yes, from behind. And the gun…*

Calmer now that her memory was filling in the blanks, Peri surveyed the scene. She was on her back, it was night, and there were flashing lights all around her.

The young man smiled down at her.

"Maybe you could bring me up to speed," she said.

"I'd be happy to, if you could give me some information. Can we start with your name?"

A huffing noise startled her, followed by a squeeze on her arm. *Ah, a blood pressure monitor.*

"I'm Peri. Periwinkle Minneopa."

"Good. Where do you live?"

"Hmm, well, I used to live on Bradford Avenue, but I recently moved. Let me think of the address. It's still in Placentia. Sounds Spanish. It's not far from here. It has a 2 in it. Maybe a 1."

The EMT looked over his shoulder at someone. A deep, melodic voice said, "That's probably the wrong test question. She really did just move to a new address."

"Skip." She reached out to him, felt his hand wrap around hers.

"Hey, Doll, heard you got into a pickle." He leaned down and kissed her. "The paramedics are going to check you out."

"My car—"

"Yes, your car got messed up. I called a service, they're towing it to Allen's shop. We'll worry about it tomorrow."

When she tried to sit up again, the EMT put his hand on her shoulder. "Let's finish taking your vitals first, okay?"

"Okay." She turned to Skip. "This was not my fault. I was at Blanche's, for God's sake."

"I believe you. I think your brother's in a lot more trouble than we originally thought." He brushed her hair back from her face. "I'm going to let the EMT finish his job, and then I'll take you home, make sure you're safe."

He strolled away, toward her car and the officers gathering evidence.

"Okay, ma'am, let's try to get you sitting up." The young man steadied her back and adjusted the gurney as she lifted herself into a sitting position. "How's that feel?"

"I'm okay. I think I just passed out."

"I agree. But no one wanted to send you home with a concussion, or possibly a gunshot wound." He leaned down and grabbed an open leather bag, parking it on the edge of his truck's door. As he packed his equipment, he said, "Tell me when you feel like standing. I'll call Detective Carlton over to help you to his car."

"Now." Peri wanted away from this scene. "I want to stand up, and go home."

Skip returned, and helped her into his SUV. She leaned back into the seat, fighting the waves of trembling in her body but allowing a few tears to leak from her eyes, to keep herself from a full-blown weep.

It took another ten minutes for Skip to stop answering questions and get into the car, which allowed her time to calm down. She was silent as they cruised down Chapman toward Orangethorpe Avenue. Skip had the radio turned to the Angels game. The sports channel had a particularly AM-radio vibe to it, which usually she enjoyed. Tonight, it grated. Everything grated on her— the traffic lights, the sound of the engine, the streetlights.

She closed her eyes to shut them all out, but all she saw in her mind was a dark sedan with no lights running up behind her. Her body tensed, braced for impact. She opened her eyes again. The bright lights would be easier to deal with.

"I hate this." She kicked at the floor.

"I do, too." Skip kept his eyes on the road, his expression unchanged.

"I don't like feeling fragile. It's not…"

"Not you?"

"Not at all." Peri crossed her arms and looked out the window. "Can you stay with me tonight? Just because."

"I'll always stay with you, whenever you want." He rubbed his hand along his eyebrow. "With any luck, I'll sell that house and stay with you forever."

She smiled. Rubbing his eyebrow was Skip's tell. No matter how calm his voice remained, she knew how upset he was when he pulled on those brow hairs. "I can't wait."

CHAPTER TWENTY

IT WAS AFTER they had ordered takeout, eaten on the patio, and finally retreated to the master bedroom that Peri had to decide what to do about sleeping. She held up an amber bottle and looked at the label.

"The doctor said you would help me sleep," she told it. "But will you give me better dreams?"

Skip stroked her hair, moving his hand down to slip it around her waist. He rested his chin on her shoulder. "Have you tried them yet?"

She shook her head.

"Well, tonight would be a good night to test them." He kissed her cheek. "I'll be here in case."

"True, but I don't want them to make me feel groggy tomorrow. How long do they last?"

"I don't know." Skip let go of her and took his polo shirt off, tossing it on a chair. "What's wrong with sleeping in? Especially after tonight."

"I have to visit Dev tomorrow. He's locked up at OC, right?" She looked at his broad, muscled back and smiled as she slipped out of her v-neck shirt.

"Yeah, listen...about that."

Her smile faded. "What?"

"I was there when they processed him. Tried to help him through it all." He moved to her, and ran his hands down her arms. "He was really clear, Doll. He doesn't want to see you. Says he'll refuse to go if you visit."

"What right does he have to refuse me? I'm trying to help him, for Pete's sake. Ungrateful brat." She threw the pill bottle across the room, strode into the dressing area, and took off her bra. "I can't understand it. He calls, out of the blue. Swears he didn't do it. Begs for my help. Runs away from us. Confesses to the crime. Asks for my help in sign language—Aarrgghh!"

Shimmying out of her leggings, she kicked them across the bedroom.

"He's not making it easy on you."

"I'm so—ooh, so—frustrated." She stomped toward the bathroom, only to be caught in Skip's arms. It took barely five seconds for her to collapse against his chest. "I've never understood why he didn't love me the way I loved him."

Skip kissed the top of her head, held her close. "I don't understand it either. But if you still want to help him, I'll do whatever you ask."

"I love you, Skipper." She looked down at the floor. "Where did I throw those pills?"

He held the bottle out to her. "I saved them from your rampage."

"Thanks. Regardless of what I do tomorrow, tonight I need to get some sleep, and I don't want to relive that crash, those—" She pushed the word from her throat, "gunshots."

"It's a raw deal. You shouldn't have to go through this, especially when you're still processing the last time."

She embraced him again, enjoying a long kiss that made her insides melt like butter, and erased every worry from her mind. They paused, and she rattled the bottle in her hands before tossing it aside. "I'll take those later."

He chuckled and carried her to the bed, where they indulged each other, tenderly and completely, before she swallowed the little white pill and knew nothing except sweet sleep until the morning light.

Beams of sunlight shooting across the bed woke her. It had to be late morning. She rolled over and checked the clock. *Eleven, damn. I gotta get stuff done.*

As she pushed her body to sitting, her muscles reminded her of last night's incident. She hobbled to the bathroom, clutching the ibuprofen bottle on her way out. Wandering into the living room, she noticed she was hearing a sound she hadn't heard in days. Silence. Blissful, yes, but why wasn't anyone here working?

Her cell phone was on its charger. There were six missed messages, most from Jared and Willem. The first asked if she'd chosen countertops. In the second message, they wondered why she hadn't responded to the first message.

By the third message, they'd heard about her attack. Willem in particular sounded near tears. The fourth message was from this morning, wondering how she was. Jared said the crew would be in at noon.

They both surrendered in their last message, telling her that they would get in touch with Skip.

The sixth message was from her therapist, reminding her to reschedule her appointment. *Yeah, I need to do that. Later.*

Peri pulled the coffee pot from the soon-to-be discarded wet bar in the family room, hooked it up and got it brewing. She found a note with it, from Skip.

Thought I'd let you sleep a bit. I've gone in to talk to the Chief about my extended sick leave, then I'll probably have lunch with the guys.

Please just rest. Love you.

The last two sentences were underlined. She understood. He clearly did not want her to keep digging into Dev's life. After last night, she almost agreed. She took a quick, temperature-testing sip of her coffee, and strolled back into her room. If the workmen were due in less than an hour, she wanted to be dressed and semi-coherent.

As she got ready, she searched for a motive for last night's attack. She'd visited Dev's work. She'd asked about Dev, mostly. Nobody knew Tressa. At least, nobody admitted they knew her, even though Tim Neal said they did.

"Well, somebody there didn't like me," she told the mirror as she applied lipstick. "And I'm going to find out who."

The doorbell rang, followed by a knock, and the sound of a key turning. It had to be Jared or Willem. A tall, bronzed demi-god entered, with a shaggy head of brown hair and a dark stubble of beard that only served to heighten his sexy looks.

"Jared." She greeted him with a hug. Jared Reese-Chen was the spouse of Willem, and the contractor-half of the construction-design team of Chen & Reese. What Willem designed in theory, Jared made reality.

"Willem says not to worry about the paint and countertops for now. He can come up with some combinations to narrow it down for you. He doesn't want you to stress."

"Thank you—and him."

"Can we work in the back today? We have to install some windows, and the pass-through to the patio."

"Sure, I'm going out for a bit." She caught the look of dread on his face, so she added, "Just research, nothing dangerous."

"Okay, but what are you going out in?"

"My car—oh, yeah." She needed to call her insurance agent, get a loaner, do all the adult things she hated. Instead, she wanted to find the car that hit her, but she couldn't do both at the same time. Or could she?

CHAPTER TWENTY-ONE

AS JARED WALKED to the backyard, Peri picked up her phone and searched for a name.

"Benny, how busy are you?"

"Who is this? You need to introduce yourself." His voice sounded even more nasal when he whined.

"Sorry. This is Peri. How busy are you?"

"No, Miss Peri." He sighed. "First you say, how are you and I say I am fine, and then you ask if I'm busy and I say—"

"Benny, I have no time." It took one sentence for him to irritate her. "I need an assistant for a job, like, right now. Can you help me or not?"

"Yes. Yes, I can help you."

"Great. Get a pencil to write down my new address."

An hour later, Peri sat in Benny's classic black Caddy and called upon all her patience not to yell at the little man behind the big steering wheel. They inched their way down Chapman Avenue, to Harbor Boulevard. Traffic was minimal, apart from some sticky stop-and-go at Fullerton College. Peri would have maneuvered her way around the constant stream of cars turning into parking lots.

Benny did not maneuver. He also did not venture above 30 miles per hour. She tried not to fidget in the seat.

"Is it possible to go any faster?"

"No talking." His answer was immediate and clipped. "I have to concentrate."

"Fine." Peri looked out the window and rubbed her temples. She'd forgotten how challenging it was to work with her OCD-Asperger's assistant. Yet, each time he drove her to the point of losing her temper, she would remind herself that this was the way he was.

Someone had corrected her recently, that Asperger's wasn't a "thing" anymore—he was just "on the spectrum." It didn't matter what the label said. Benny would not change, at least not in a major way, and not quickly.

Following her instructions, Benny drove into the parking lot at the intersection of Harbor and Brea, and pulled into a space.

"What are we doing here, Miss Peri?"

"I'm looking for a car." She turned to him. "The trick will be how to find it without looking suspicious."

"What's it look like?" Benny pointed the rearview mirror toward himself and fiddled with his tie.

"It's—just a car, Benny. Stay here and I'll be back." She opened the door to leave.

"I want to help you, Miss Peri." He opened his door, too. "I'm your assistant."

"No, you're not." She picked up her tote. "I mean, I'm not working a case. I just needed a ride here. My car is in the shop."

"Why is it in the shop? And why are you being mean to me?"

Peri stopped and sat back. She didn't have time for this. *Sometimes you have to make time for people.* "I'm sorry if I am being mean. I didn't intend to."

Benny slammed his door. "You are being very mean lately. Ever since you caught that man who was stalking Jared, you have been mean to me. You don't let me help you, you don't ask me about my day when you see me, you didn't even like my tie pin."

His face was flushed, his eyebrows furrowed, his foot wiggling. She'd never seen him so angry.

Leaning back into the car, she sighed. "I am sorry. I don't feel like myself anymore, and I'm impatient with everyone. Here's the whole story. My brother is in trouble. The police think he killed a woman. I don't really want to be in the detective business anymore, but I want to help my brother. Someone hit my car last night, and since I only ever interviewed people from Dev's work in this building, I thought, maybe the person was from this office."

"Oh." His shoulders relaxed. "Then I will help you be a detective one more time to help your brother." His face returned to its normal hue. "What kind of car are we looking for?"

"It's a sedan, no bigger than my car, an older model, dark colored, and should have some damage on the..." She stopped and pantomimed the crash, using her hands as both cars. "on the left front."

He nodded the whole time. "I will look at the cars on this side of the parking lot. You can look at the cars on the other side."

"Sounds like a good plan." She smiled. "Thank you."

They exited the Caddy and walked away in opposite directions. Peri tried to look casual as she strolled up and down the aisles of the parking lot. There were a lot of cars, mostly SUVs. The larger vehicles tended to obscure the ones parked in front of them, so she had to slow down and study each dark sedan, of which there were many.

"It's probably not even here," she mumbled.

The low sound of an engine, complete with tires creeping on pavement, snuck up behind her. She peeked over her shoulder to see a patrol car following her.

Damn. The one thing I didn't need.

Turning, she waved at the officer behind the wheel and his partner. To add to her displeasure, she recognized them both. Officers Gomez and Darden.

Double damn.

CHAPTER TWENTY-TWO

"GOOD AFTERNOON, OFFICERS." Peri gave them her friendliest smile.

Officer Darden came right to the point. "Someone called, ma'am. They reported suspicious activity."

"Is it against the law to wander through a parking lot?"

"It is private property." Darden placed his hands on his belt, close to his holster. "Maybe you're planning to break into cars."

Peri's pulse quickened at the sight of his hand so near his gun. "Seriously? You think I'm a petty thief?"

"I don't know what you are, ma'am," Darden said. "But you have to leave this lot."

"Look, I was attacked last night—" she started.

"We don't care." Darden pointed. "That's the exit. Get back in your car and go."

She turned to Officer Gomez. "What do you have to say about it?"

Gomez cleared his throat. "I understand your desire to find the person who attacked you last night—"

"Okay, then—"

He finished his thought. "But, this parking lot still belongs to someone, and that someone doesn't want you here."

"So you agree with Officer Darden."

Gomez smiled. "Let us say, I understand why he said what he did."

Darden glared at his partner.

Peri raised her hands in surrender. "Okay, I'm gone. They probably weren't here, anyway. My car is in the lot on the other side. I promise I'll walk right over to it and drive away."

The officers stood, eyeing her skeptically.

"God." Holding out one hand, she said, "Pinkie swear?"

Gomez nudged Darden. "C'mon. Let's give her the benefit of the doubt."

"But—"

"But nothing. She hasn't lied to us yet." Gomez turned and walked back to the patrol car. He opened the driver's side door and stood, tapping his hand on the roof.

Officer Darden gave Peri a pointed scowl, and joined his partner. She smiled at him, and strode down the aisle, toward the smaller parking lot.

Bite me, Doogie.

Benny's car was still in its space. She noticed his little, round body in the driver's seat, so she opened the passenger door and let herself in.

"The police say we have to go now," she told him.

He nodded and started the engine. As they drove back toward Placentia, she fumed.

"What's the big deal? I was just walking through a parking lot." She glanced at Benny. "Sorry. You don't want me to talk."

"I don't." He rolled the Cadillac to a gentle stop at a light. "But when we get to your house, I'll show you the pictures I took."

"Pictures of what?"

He looked perplexed. "Of the car you told me to look for."

"What? You found it?" She hopped about in her seat. "Oh, Benny, I could hug you."

"Well, don't. And stop moving around. And stop talking. I have to concentrate."

The ride back to her house was a horrid half-hour of trying to sit quietly and not drag her assistant's phone away from him. By the time they pulled into her drive, she was ready to explode.

"Okay, we're here. Show me the photos." She unbuckled her seatbelt and turned, hands out.

"Shouldn't you invite a guest into the house?"

She checked her annoyance. "Yes, ordinarily I would, and you are welcome to come in. It's just that my house is still being worked on, and I didn't think you'd appreciate all the loud noises and the mess."

"Oh. No, I would not." He took his phone from his pocket, poked at the screen, and handed it to Peri. "Is this the car?"

She swiped through the photos. They showed a small, blue-gray sedan, with a significant dent on the front left corner. The headlight hung askew, and scrape marks down the left side had light blue paint on them, much like the color of her Honda. She kept swiping, until she saw what she was looking for—the license plate number.

"This is it, Benny. This is the car that hit my car, and—" She almost mentioned the shots fired. *No reason to upset him—or myself.* "And, these are perfect. Can you text them to my phone?"

"Of course. I can do lots of things on my phone. Sam showed me." He began poking again. Soon, Peri's phone was beeping at regular intervals, as he sent each picture. "What do we do next?"

"We?" She hadn't thought of her next step as a team effort, or even her next ten steps. But Benny wanted to help. "Well, first, I have to see who owns this car, and turn these pictures in to the police."

"Then what?"

She paused, searching for a task for him. "You know what I'm going to need? A ride to some of the places I want to investigate."

"When do we leave?"

Peri glanced at her watch. "Give me a couple of hours to ID this car, and deal with the insurance company. Pick me up around two?"

"When you say around two, do you mean before two or after?"

"After."

"How much after?"

She shook her head. "Pick me up at 2:15, okay?"

"Geez, Miss Peri, I wish you had said that to begin with."

"I wish I had, too." She pushed her still-aching body from his car, and hurried to the house with as much speed as her tired legs could manage.

As usual, she opened the door to a wall of sound, most of it construction tools, accented by what sounded like rap music in Spanish. She peeked into the kitchen. Everything was looking more complete, except for the cabinets, and countertops, which were still waiting for her color choice. She grabbed water from the fridge, and fled to the bedroom.

Calling the insurance company was first on her list. The faster she had wheels, the less she'd need Benny to tote her around.

If we're ever in a high speed chase, we're screwed.

Her agent was a nice, older man who refused to retire. She gave him the particulars of where her car had been towed, wrote down the information about what to do next, and got off the phone before she accidentally mentioned the bullet holes.

I'll save that for later.

CHAPTER TWENTY-THREE

PUTTING HER "WRECKED car notes" aside, she pulled up the plate for the blue-gray Nissan with body damage. It was registered to Mr. Tim Neal, 27, who lived in Long Beach. Tim Neal, the young, exacting man who worked with Dev.

"Okay, Timmy, what's your story?" Peri typed the name into her search engine, hoping without expecting. What she found was disheartening. "Great. You share a name with a musician. I can dig through pages forever, or…"

She attempted, "Tim Neal Long Beach." As usual these days, it was social media where she hit pay dirt. A graduate of Cal State Fullerton, he was active on Twitter and LinkedIn. Both Emily Keening and Alicia Duarte were friends of his.

"What, Tim, not Rodolfo?" She looked through his posts. Most were short rants about the modern world, mixed with longer raves about the latest video game. "Yeah, you might not want the boss to see the inside of your head."

By 2:14, she stood outside her front door, waiting. One minute later, Benny pulled his Cadillac into the drive.

"Thanks, Ben. We should go to the police station first."

He hesitated. "Do I have to go in?"

"Not unless you want to."

"Because I will go in, Miss Peri, if you need me to, but I'd rather not."

A sheen of moisture glistened around his hairline. Just the thought of the police made him sweat. "Not going to be necessary this time, but I appreciate the offer."

The June sun was high and hot when they arrived at the Placentia Civic Center. Benny pulled to the curb. "You can get out here and I will go park. You have to be finished by 4 p.m."

"Hot date?"

"No." He ignored her joke. "I'm picking Sam up at 6 p.m., and I have to get ready."

"I'll be as brief as I can." Peri rolled her passenger window down, and turned to her driver. "Stay cool. If you feel yourself getting too hot, go sit in the library."

"I'm not a baby, Miss Peri." He scowled. "And roll the window back up. I don't want dirt coming in."

Obeying his command and trying not to roll her eyes as hard as she did the window, she gave the handle a final crank, and got out of the car. The air conditioning was blessed relief as she hit the station door. Evelyn, the front desk clerk, looked at her.

"I'm here to see Detective Logan," Peri said.

"He's not here." The clerk looked back down at her papers. She had a bad habit of acting like Peri didn't exist if Skip wasn't with her. Peri had hoped her attitude would have softened. It hadn't.

"How about Chief Fletcher?"

"He's busy."

Evelyn, cut me some slack. "Can you at least call him and ask if he'll see me?"

"He said not to interrupt him." The clerk wasn't biting. She also wasn't buzzing Peri in.

Peri grimaced, and took out her phone. Fletcher answered on the first ring.

"Chief, I have some new information on my attack last night. Can you ask Evelyn to buzz me in?" She nodded, ended the call and smiled at her nemesis.

Evelyn's phone rang and she picked it up. "Yes, Chief."

The gate buzzed, and Peri entered. The clerk stared at her, phone in hand, scowling.

Peri smiled. "Thanks, Evelyn."

Chief Fletcher sat behind his desk, tapping his pen on a paper. Peri took her seat across from him. "How's the city doing? Staying safe?"

"We were, until your family came to town."

"He didn't do it. I don't understand why he confessed, but he's either being paid or blackmailed or threatened somehow."

"Well, because it's you, we're spending more time on investigation than we ever do on a suspect who confesses."

"Yeah, it's so much better to take confessions from just anyone. Saves money, manpower, looks great on the monthly status report."

The Chief glared at her. "I hope you're not accusing my department of coercing your brother, because I can show you the tapes of his interview if you are."

"No, I'm not," she snapped, before putting her hands up. "I'm sorry. I don't know why I said that. This department is always on the up and up. I actually came here with some info on the person who chased me last night."

Pulling up the photos Benny had texted her, she handed her phone to the Chief. He swiped through them. "You sure this is the car?"

"Reasonably so. I looked up the license plate. Car belongs to a Tim Neal, who works at the same company as Dev."

"Yes, but, his car was in their parking lot. Maybe he's just another employee, who had an unrelated accident."

"An accident that left blue paint, the same color as my Honda, on the front left. My car's damage is on the back right. How many coincidences do we need for a warrant?" Peri did her best to tame her crankiness.

"Well, we can definitely investigate this," Fletcher said. "And by we, I mean my detectives, while you stay out of it."

"You really think that's gonna happen?"

"No, but I am hoping you're spending an equal amount of time with the PTSD therapist."

"Crap, I need to reschedule with her." She sat back. "I wish the whole process moved faster. I've got things to do."

"Like get married?" He smiled.

"And get my brother out of trouble." She saw him open his mouth, and she placed her hand up to stop him. "If he really is innocent."

CHAPTER TWENTY-FOUR

SHE FOUND BENNY sitting on a bench on the plaza, fanning himself with a library brochure. The June afternoon wasn't cooling down fast enough for him, and as always, he was dressed in his Dino-finest, a sleek gray suit with a cream shirt and blue-patterned tie.

"Benny, you could have sat in the library, where it's cool."

He popped off the bench as if ejected. "I didn't want you to have to look for me. A good assistant is always available."

She smiled. "True, but next time, you can just call me, or text, to tell me where you are."

"Okay. Where to now?"

She glanced at her watch. "I think we've got time to see Dev's place. The police have probably picked it over, but I'd like to see if there are any clues they left behind." She pulled up his address on her phone. "It's in Fullerton, near the university."

They got back in the car and headed west, Peri giving enough directions for him to navigate correctly, but not so many that she got yelled at for being too chatty. Twenty minutes later, they were in a parking garage under an apartment building. Benny pulled into a space, and Peri put her hand on the door.

"Not yet, Miss Peri." He put the car in reverse. "I'm not straight in the space yet."

She took her hand off the door handle and waited while he pulled back, then forward, then back again, and once more forward, until her patience broke into small shards.

"Benny." She struggled to keep her voice even. "Why don't you let me out, and then you can get straight in the space while I'm up at Dev's?"

He gave her an incredulous look. "But don't you need me to assist?"

Oh, dear. "Yes, I just meant that you could join me once you're parked. Apartment 315."

Emotional crisis averted, Peri got out of the car, and he continued his pursuit of parking perfection, while she walked to the elevator. A frat-boy odor—beer, sweat, and probably urine—hit her as she stepped inside. She stood in the middle, hoping they had aimed for the corners, and breathed through her mouth for three floors.

Apartment 315 was at the end of a long hallway. Peri grabbed the doorknob to test it, then stopped. *What if he didn't live alone?* She stepped back and knocked. No answer, but she tried once more, just in case.

Impatience won—she tested the door. Locked. Pulling a slender tool from her pocket, she knelt and slid it into the keyhole. Dev's front door proved to be stubborn. The pins refused to lift when she pushed up with her metal pick.

Good thing I have a handy assistant.

One bright spot from Benny's brief incarceration a few years ago, was that many of the other felons befriended him and taught him a few tricks. Peri's favorite was his ability to pick locks.

After five minutes of waiting, she wondered if Benny had decided to drive around the block and come at the parking space from a different angle. She dug in her purse to find something she could use to pry open Dev's door, when the fire exit next to her burst open and Benny stumbled out, wheezing like a bulldog.

"Why didn't you take the elevator?" Peri asked.

He wrinkled his nose. "It smelled bad."

"I agree. We'll take the stairs down."

"The stairs smelled bad, too."

"We'll fly down. In the meantime, want to pick this lock?"

Benny smiled and reached into his breast pocket.

Click-click. "Easy peasy."

They snuck in, slow and quiet. Dev might not live alone, although it was doubtful he had a roommate. Her brother was a solo act. Sharing his living space would only be done in dire necessity.

The small apartment was dark, the blackout curtains allowing only slim strands of light to seep in. Shadows gave shape to a sofa on one side of the room, and a table on the other. Peri found a light switch, which lit a single bulb in a corner lamp. If the room had seemed gloomy before, it was positively suicidal now.

They were in one room that served as a living area, dining area, and kitchenette. The sofa was old and showed the permanent dent of a body. On the far wall, a large TV sat precariously on an empty bookcase. The dining set was a white plastic patio table and chairs.

"Geez, this place is sad," Benny said.

Harsh critique from you, Peri thought. "Yes, it is sad."

"What are we looking for?"

"Right now, I'm looking for two things. One, anything that indicates how or how well he knew Tressa Velasco, and two, any reason he'd take the fall for a murder he didn't commit. Make that three things—I'd also like to figure out why Tressa was murdered."

"You bet, Miss Peri." Benny disappeared into the bedroom, while Peri opened drawers and closets in the living room/kitchenette combo. Nothing leapt out and screamed "evidence" at her, but she dug onward.

The cabinet next to the sink was filled with pills, mostly vitamins and supplements, although there were a few prescription bottles as well. Peri took photos of these, to research later.

"Dex-uh-meth-uh-zone," she read on one of the labels. "Sounds serious."

At some point, she stopped pretending and admitted to herself that she was searching for any significant information at all about her brother.

Who is he?

CHAPTER TWENTY-FIVE

"MISS PERI, I found pictures." Benny emerged from the bedroom, holding a box.

"What of?" She opened it to find two stacks of photos, about a dozen each, and a flash drive.

One stack of photos was scenery. Photos of the Grand Canyon, Zion National Park, Yosemite, and more. They all had the faded yellow patina of time. No one was in these photos, but the back of each said, "Our trip to (wherever)," and the date, all from 2001.

"Nice." Peri read the back of each photo, wondering who the hell "our" included. Family? Fraternity bros?

The next stack were photos of people. Dev was in these, along with a smiling blond cheerleader type woman, a tall, slender nerdy guy, and a spike-haired punk dude. Again, no names, just dates on the back. The backgrounds looked like the scenic photos from the first stack. Peri lined up the dates—yes, Dev and his friends were in Zion together.

She put one photo under a light and studied the people in it. The woman was petite, with her hair in a ponytail. She stood close to the nerd, his arm around her waist. The punker was small and lithe, with white-tipped shards of hair, and he appeared to have a nose stud and a

107

lip ring. He was looking at the girl, snarling, in a Billy Idol pose.

There was no label on the flash drive—not even a post-it note. She picked it up, and turned it around in her fingers. Normally, she took photos of evidence, so she wouldn't remove anything. But this...she looked around for a computer to plug it into. Nothing.

Espionage and blackmail both flitted across her mind. She was willing to believe Dev didn't murder that woman, but was he involved in something else?

Plan B was not optimal, but it would have to do. She shoved the drive into her pocket, along with the two stacks of photos.

In for a penny, in for a pound.

"Here, Benny, put this box back where you found it." As she opened her mouth to add something about being careful, she heard heavy footsteps that stopped at the front door, followed by the sound of a lock being picked. Tapping the light off, she shoved Benny into the bedroom.

"Hey—" He tried to protest, but she placed her hand at his mouth and shook her head.

"Someone's coming," she whispered, and looked around the dark bedroom. The room was as sparsely furnished as the rest of the apartment, but the wide-open closet was bursting with trash bags. She hoped they were filled with clothes and not bodies. A sliding glass door to a balcony caught her attention, partially hidden behind curtains. In a swift, nearly-silent movement, she slid the door open, dragged Benny out with her, and closed the curtains, along with the door.

The balcony was minuscule and empty, except for the one thing she needed. An emergency rope ladder lay puddled in a corner.

"Thanks, Dev, safety first." Peri draped it over the ledge and hooked it on. It wasn't long enough to reach the ground, but it would get them close enough to jump. She motioned for Benny to swing his leg across and climb down.

Benny shook his head, his eyes wide as dinner plates. "I can't."

"You can. You have to." She kept her voice low. "If you get caught with me, it means two strikes on your record."

He continued to resist, so she added, "You've been brave before, Ben. You can be brave again. Dino would be."

At the mention of his hero, he stopped shaking his head. His eyes were still enormous, and his body trembled, but he told her, "Yes. I can be brave. Me and Dino."

Peri thought she'd have trouble getting the little man's soft body over the railing and onto the ladder. But just as he leaned over the edge, she heard noises from the bedroom, like things being thrown. Adrenalin, along with fear for her friend, kicked in, and she lifted Benny like a tote bag and placed him on the ladder.

"Go." She crouched below the railing, waiting for him to get down before she started her descent. As she did, she glimpsed the bedroom through a sliver of space between the curtains. A stocky figure was dragging things from the closet, pawing through them, then tossing them aside.

She was kicking herself for not snooping through the closet, when she saw the tension on the rope ladder slacken. Benny was down. She threw her leg over the side and put her tennis shoe in a rung. As she lowered herself down the ladder, she heard the sliding glass door open. She descended faster, burning her palms as she slid them down the rope.

She was ten feet from the ground when she felt the ladder shake, loosen, and give way. Looking up as she fell was pure instinct. Above her, two large hands threw the ropes outward. She had enough time to curl into a sideways ball before she hit the dirt. There was a bit of landscape on this side of the building, so her face and shoulders hit soil and ground cover, while her hips and legs hit pavement.

Benny ran to her. "Miss Peri, you fell! Are you okay?"

She pushed her body to standing, gasping aloud from the pain in her ankle. "Mostly. Not really. Help me to your car, and get me to the doctor."

"You're kind of dirty."

Peri had been through this before with her friend. Dirty clothes were not allowed in the Caddy. She shoved him toward the parking garage. "I can brush myself off."

He frowned. "Oh, all right. But I'm getting the towels out of the trunk for you."

They made their way to his car, and Peri leaned on the Caddy's fins while he fished for the keys. At the sound of tires, Peri hobbled around to the front of the car, dragging Benny with her. They crouched, out of sight, until it had passed.

"That was a police car," Benny said.

"That was a close call," Peri told him. "Now, I need to get to the hospital."

"Not until I get the towels out of the trunk."

She sighed. Maybe she should let the police handle this.

CHAPTER TWENTY-SIX

"YOU WERE SMART to land on your side," the ER doctor told her. "I think you're just going to have a lot of bruising and general soreness."

"Yeah, lucky me." Peri crawled off the table.

"We can give you some Tylenol with codeine to help you rest." He made notes on her chart.

"That's okay, I'll pass." She limped toward the door. "Are we done?"

"Did you settle with our finance officer?"

"Oh, yes. They don't release my x-rays until I put coins in the slot."

The doctor laughed, which made her grumpier.

"I only wish that was a joke."

She hobbled to the waiting room and looked around for Benny. He had vanished, but Skip was in one of the chairs, watching a baseball game on his phone.

"Hey, Doll." Skip rose from his chair and offered his arm for support. "We have to talk about this. The whole car chase, shooting thing was accidental, but this sounds like it could have been avoided, at least from what Benny told me."

"I'm sure he exaggerated." She leaned into him as they walked out to his car.

"Did he pick the lock to let you into Dev's apartment?"

"Yes."

"Did you have permission to be there?" He assisted her into his SUV.

"Define permission." Peri groaned as she fastened her seatbelt. "He's my brother. Don't siblings have some kind of automatic permission to get into each other's stuff?"

"Maybe when you were ten."

"Well, it's absolutely not my fault that some big lug was also rummaging through his stuff." Peri rubbed her head. "What was he searching for? Maybe the flash drive I took."

"You took evidence?" Skip pounded the steering wheel. "Dammit, why are you even doing this? You should be talking to that shrink of yours eight hours a day."

"I'm not proud of taking it." She slapped the dash in response, then sucked in her breath at the pain. "I didn't see any other choice. And I have been seeing my therapist, mostly. I'm working out my trauma and finding my happy place. I don't want to investigate Dev's problem, but what else am I supposed to do? You tell me, Skip. What if it was your brother?"

"I don't know!"

They both went silent. Peri listened to the whoosh of car tires as they drove. The radio announcer was broadcasting the game. Leaning back in the seat, she closed her eyes. She wanted to cry, but the tears didn't want to cooperate. Skip braked gently, stopping at the light at Kraemer and Chapman. She listened to the blinker, ticka-ticka-ticka.

"Look, you're in a tough position," Skip said, his voice low and soft. "I'd probably be doing what you're doing. I'd tell myself I'm not getting involved, then I'd get involved. But I'm worried about you, and I mean more than I usually worry. I'm afraid that you're not going to be as logical, as smart, or as good at your job, because your trauma and your personal feelings are going to cloud your judgment."

She nodded. "I'm worried, too."

Two stoplights later, Skip sighed. "Okay, I have an idea. I'm still on leave, officially, but what if I helped you? We could team up."

"I thought you were going to help me anyway."

"Well, yes, but I was planning to just wait until you asked for something. I'm talking about seriously working together, as partners."

"Ooh, I've never had a partner before." Peri smiled at him, as he raised his eyebrows. "And no, Benny doesn't count. He's an assistant."

Skip chuckled. "So, what do you say?"

"I say yes. I'd love to have someone to share the load with." She adjusted her seat, causing a twinge of pain in her hip. "Maybe you can keep me from getting so banged up."

"That was definitely on my mind."

"Love you, Skipper." She leaned to kiss him as they pulled into the driveway. "How should we divvy up the work?"

He gave her a sly glance. "I'll take the dangerous stuff and you do the research."

"Very funny. How was I to guess that snooping around at Dev's place would end up like this?"

"Well, here's a general rule to follow—anytime you enter a place without permission, you should plan for the possibility that someone doesn't want you there and might try to harm you."

"Got it." She turned her body toward the open car door and placed her right foot on the running board, preparing to ease the rest of her body out of the seat.

Skip hustled around and caught her, arms wrapped around her ribs, lowering her to the ground. "Rule Number 2—it's not a sign of weakness if you ask for help."

Peri kissed him again. "I guess this partnering thing will take some getting used to."

They went inside and checked out the remodeling progress. Most of the cabinets were hung, but unfinished. One cabinet had five little swatches of paint, in different colors, and a sticky note above them.

Not to rush you, but the guys really need to know what color. Does this help? Hugs—Willem

"I feel horrible," Peri said. "It's not that I can't decide, it's just, I don't really care what color."

"Then pick any of them." Skip opened the fridge. "If you really do care, you'll have a reaction about it."

She stood back and looked at each color, blocking the others from view with her hands. "The middle one."

Skip was laying containers of cold chicken, broccoli, and rice on the plywood that currently served as a counter. "That medium gray?"

"You don't like it?" She started the process over.

He gently pushed her hands down, cradling her face. "I might care even less than you do what color the cabinets are. Medium gray is an excellent choice, if it's one you can live with."

"That's my problem." Her eyes glassed over. "I have no idea what I can live with. I'm not sure of anything. Except you."

They held each other, swaying as if a lullaby played. His arms around her, and the strength of his body, fortified her.

"I'm so hungry," she whispered. "I could eat a car."

"Will cold chicken do?"

They pulled away, and completed their dinner preparation, which they carried to the patio table.

"So, let's make a list of what we know," she said, as she scooped a forkful of chicken and rice. "We'll split up tasks from there."

"Can we just eat first?"

"I guess, but it's already late, and if I want to start tomorrow morning, I should call Benny and fill him in."

"Call him and say you're doing some research and won't need him to drive you anywhere tomorrow."

"No." She allowed a whine in her voice. "Maybe while you're off chasing one lead, I might have to chase another one."

"Doll, I'm pretty sure that's my point about being a team. Let me do the legwork."

"But I thought—"

He put his hand up, pointing toward her hip. "At least not until you've healed a little. Do you really want to be struggling to get in and out of the Caddy all day? And what if you get in another jam? How much punishment can your body take?"

"I hate it when you're right." She sighed. "Now, let me get a notepad. We'll make a plan."

She pushed herself up from the chair and limped to her purse, retrieving a notebook and a pen. *I'll call Benny a little later and explain. He'll probably be happy to get the day off, after today.*

CHAPTER TWENTY-SEVEN

BENNY DID NOT appreciate Peri's call. "Aren't I a good assistant?"

"You're a great assistant, Benny, and I still need you. But this morning, I have to do some research at home. Besides, I'm still pretty sore from that fall yesterday. I'll call you this afternoon with a plan for where we go next."

"Okay." Benny moved from anxious to understanding in two syllables. "When you aren't hurting, I will help you."

She knew Skip's plan was to manipulate her into staying out of trouble. Her sore muscles agreed it was a good plan—for now. After some coffee and ibuprofen, however, they might want to get out and stretch. Maybe go for a walk, or break into an office.

After all, it was Saturday. Who would be working, especially at Ro-Bet?

The drilling and sawing sounds in her kitchen reminded her that some people work on the weekends. She'd agreed to the extra intrusion as part of the accelerated timeline, although as she slipped into the backyard with her coffee, she wondered why they required six days a week for eight weeks. She tried to calculate how long five days a week would take, then four.

How about one day a week? What's the rush?

She opened her laptop and inserted Dev's flash drive into the USB port. Praying there were no viruses, she clicked on the icon. A folder of photos popped up.

They showed Dev's office, the lab and its surroundings. A few of his coworkers were in the photos, going about their business. None of them faced the camera, so possibly they didn't know they were being photographed. At the bottom of each picture was a series of numbers.

Peri got out the physical photos she had appropriated, and lined them up on her scanner. It took several scans to get all the photos, but soon she had the front and back of each one loaded onto her computer.

As a last step, she copied everything onto her cloud, so she could access them from her phone.

I'll flash these around, see what people know about them.

Since this was supposed to be a research day, it was time to fill in all the other players. She knew about as much as she could about Dev, and had a file on Tressa, so the next person on her list was Rodolfo Betancourt.

Rodolfo had a neat, tidy life on the internet. He was a member of LinkedIn, and had an Instagram account filled with pictures of his wife and their dog. His biography on both sites was exactly the same, and purely professional. Much like her brother's stark internet presence, she could not glean anything about him personally, except that he had a cute dog.

His wife looked like she worked out, a lot. Peri found her on Facebook, and discovered she was a nurse and a bicyclist. All her photos were of long, winding roads, and handlebars.

Emily Keening was easier to find. Instagram, Snapchat, she loved all the social media and they all loved her. Each photo had hundreds of views, and likes, and comments like "You're so cute!" and "Love the hair!" The girl was cute, if you liked dour expressions on pasty-white faces. At least her shiny black hair looked healthy.

She was a graduate of Cal State Fullerton, majoring in math. Peri leafed through her notes, until she found Tim Neal. He'd also gone to Cal State Fullerton, as an engineering major.

Wonder if they knew each other then?

One photo was a close-up of her face, kohl-rimmed eyes and cherried lips shining against her pale skin. She looked up at the camera, puckering her lips against her hand. A band of dark metal twisted around her ring finger, culminating in briars that wrapped around a deep red stone.

The caption read, "Don't get excited—it's just a promise ring. But I promise I'll invite you all to the wedding, LOL."

The girl's friends posted the typical comments and replies about how lucky and how wonderful and many blessings. *Mazel tov*, Peri thought, *but could we have the name of the boyfriend, please?* No such luck, as she skimmed across Emily's many social accounts.

Peri moved on, to the next person on her list, Alicia Duarte. Young, perky, and just as social as Emily, Alicia was a recent graduate of Cal Poly Pomona. Ro-Bet

Engineering was her first job, and she was so excited about it, her status updates contained almost nothing else. Her photos were of a small apartment full of moving boxes, but even they were tagged as, "Now that I have a great job, I can afford a great place!"

Peri made notes, and planned to visit her next.

As she got up to brew another cup of coffee, she heard pounding at the front door. It was probably a salesman. Between solar, roofing, and pest control companies, there was always someone trying to get her attention.

She opened the door to a surprise—Alicia Duarte cowered in her doorway, looking over her shoulder.

"Can I come in?"

CHAPTER TWENTY-EIGHT

PERI PULLED ALICIA into the house, slamming the door. The girl broke into tears.

"I'm sorry to intrude I wasn't expected but I didn't know where else to go and you seem like someone who would believe me," she strung together in a single breath, before looking up at Peri with reddened eyes, mascara running down her cheeks.

"Come in and calm down." Peri led her toward the guest powder room. "Wash your face, blow your nose. Want some coffee? Tea?"

"Mmm, just water. Maybe tea?"

Peri smiled. "Clean yourself up, and I'll fix you something."

Moments later, the girl emerged, and accepted a mug of chamomile tea, as Peri steered her out into the garden. Alicia looked around, uneasy.

"Are you sure we're safe here?"

"Safe from what?" Peri sat on one chaise and motioned to the one next to her.

Alicia kept looking, swiveling her head about, taking in every plant, every wall, up to the sky and beyond. Peri eased back in the chair, and watched her guest, as wind whooshed through the bamboo. The girl's tension didn't melt as much as it chipped, piece by piece, from her frame, until at last she sat back and took a sip of her tea.

"By the way, how did you find out where I live?"

Alicia blushed. "I was worried. The way you were snooping around Dev's office, and then I heard about Tressa…I spent a little time Googling you."

"Fair enough." Peri nodded. "So, what's going on?"

The slender brunette closed her eyes for a moment, before focusing on her tea. "First of all, I lied. To you, to the police. I got scared when Dev got arrested. I didn't want to get involved."

"What was the lie?"

"That Dev and I weren't close, that he wasn't part of our group."

"And the truth is?"

"The truth is, he's super friendly, always going to happy hour with us, or the movies. Super helpful at work, too. To be honest, I think he kind of likes me, but he never said anything or tried anything. I mean, our age difference is pretty big."

"Why did you lie to me?"

"I wanted you to think he was a loner, so you wouldn't think we were involved in anything illegal."

"Because…Dev was into something illegal?"

"Oh, no." Alicia placed her mug on the accent table with both hands as if setting down a bomb. Sitting forward, at the edge of the chaise, she gestured about, her hands choreographed to her words. "Dev was never into anything illegal. He just wanted us to get to Level B certification, and he was willing to do anything to get it. I mean, not anything as in illegal. Just…anything else."

"Like what exactly?"

Her hands fluttered into her lap, like trained doves. "Tressa."

"He did Tressa?"

"God, no." Her hands flew again as if startled. "I mean, so, he knew Tressa from college, and he heard she was working on a DoD project that required software certification."

"DoD—Department of Defense, yes?"

"Uh-huh. Anyway, he calls up Tressa and does his 'Dev' thing—"

Now Peri was sitting upright. "His Dev thing?"

Alicia smiled. "You know what a sweet talker he is. I mean, he's a great marketing director—he can sell anything to anyone."

Peri nodded. *Sure, of course. I know Dev. Except I don't.*

"The plan was for him to get some free insights from Tressa. That's all. It wasn't illegal. It was just— economical. Rodolfo is doing his best to keep us afloat. Once we get this contract, everything will be golden. Until then, I heard he's mortgaged his house to pay our salaries."

Peri reached for her notebook. "Tell me, Alicia, is Tim part of your merry band?"

"Um, yes." She blushed. "I swear he didn't do it."

"Didn't do what?" Peri leaned forward.

"Didn't hit your car, didn't shoot at you, OMG, he doesn't even own a gun." Alicia reached toward Peri, palms up in supplication. "You gotta believe me, Tim's a friend of mine. I was there when the police came in to question him. He was terrified."

"But his car certainly looks like it was him." Peri swiped at her phone, shoving the photo at the girl's face.

"But he couldn't have been driving it." Her voice grew louder, before settling. "Thing is, we all quit work at eight that night, we walk out to our cars, and Tim's car is missing. We look up and down the parking lot, can't find it. He calls the police, fills out a report. Next day, I give him a ride to work, and his car is back in the lot, only it's all beat up." She took a sip of her almost-forgotten tea. "Then the cops come and accuse him of shooting at you, and confiscate his car."

"Are you still giving him a ride to work?"

"God, no, he uses Uber." She looked at Peri as if she had just unearthed a dinosaur.

Peri nodded, tapping her fingers. If Tim worked until eight, he had an alibi for the car chase. Whoever did it was either trying to pin it on him directly, or simply needed a plain, dark sedan to do their dirty work. The impact of the car smashed into her memory, and she winced.

"Are you okay?"

"I'm fine." Peri shook her head. *Focus.* "Let's get back to you. What brought you over here in such a rush?"

Alicia stared into her mug. "I was on my way to work today. I don't live that far, downtown Fullerton. I got a phone call. Someone said I had to help them, or they'd hurt my folks."

"Help them how?"

"With this." She pulled a dark brown envelope from her backpack. "This was on the seat of my car—my car that was locked and parked in a security-guarded parking garage."

CHAPTER TWENTY-NINE

PERI TOOK THE envelope and emptied its contents onto the chaise. There were photos of Tressa, all sizes, all poses, all looking as if she didn't realize she was being photographed. It only took seconds for Peri to take a guess.

"You're supposed to plant these in Dev's office, yes? Probably hide them, to make it look like the police missed them the first time."

Alicia nodded. "They were specific about where to put them."

"Specific?"

"Dev's file cabinet, underneath the hanging folders."

Peri held up the envelope. "Dark. Would blend in with the bottom of the drawer. Yeah, cops might miss it." She tapped the envelope on her chin. "But only someone who was there would know where the cops searched."

Alicia grabbed at the photos and the envelope. "I have to do this, to keep my family safe."

"Whoa, slow down." Peri helped her stack the photos. "Yes, I want you to do this, but…we should do it in a way that points to tampering, not to Dev."

"Are you not listening to me? He'll hurt my family." Tears were now pooling in her dark eyes.

"I am listening. Someone told you to plant this envelope, and where." Peri patted her arm. "Nothing says we can't make it point away from Dev."

She sniffled. "Like how?"

"Lemme think. I don't want you to get into trouble, either. First thing is, we have to wipe the fingerprints off. The police will check. If yours are on it, they'll come after you. I suppose you could argue, if there are no prints at all, that puts the evidence in doubt. I mean, why would Dev wear gloves to handle his own photos?"

Peri went into the house and returned with two pairs of latex gloves, and two small, grey rectangles. She handed Alicia one of each.

"What's this?" Alicia asked.

"Art gum. Kind of an eraser, but it will pick up the oils from our skin." She put on her gloves, then emptied the envelope and handed Alicia a stack of photos. Taking one of the photos, she slowly and gently swiped the art gum across the back, stopping to blot occasionally. "You see? Soft swipes, front and back of each one. If it feels a little rough, stop and blot. Always careful. You don't want to wear a spot, or a hole, in the paper."

They sat in silence, working over each photo, until at last, Peri took the envelope and applied the art gum to it.

She held up the envelope at last. "There. Now we can put the photos back in, and you can take it to the office."

Alicia nodded. "I hope this works."

"Do you suppose I could come with you?" Peri handed the package to her. "I'd like to see if I can find anything else that would help Dev."

"Sure. I'd actually prefer not to be alone at the moment."

Peri jumped up. "Let me get dressed."

She emerged from her bedroom, in slacks and a polo shirt, hoping that Alicia hadn't run off without her. The girl still sat on the patio, patting her backpack, gazing at the garden.

"We'll have to take your car," Peri told her. "Mine's still being repaired."

The ride to Ro-Bet was quiet, apart from the low murmur of NPR on the radio. Peri watched the road, the scenery, and the traffic on all sides. Her stomach quivered, and skin tingled, waiting for the slam of a car, or worse—the pop of gunfire.

I really need to make that appointment with my therapist. She stretched her legs out, and swiped through the photos she'd taken at Dev's place, stopping at the pill bottle. "Alicia, did Dev ever talk to you about being sick?"

"You mean his rheumatoid arthritis? Yeah, he was private about it, but he's pretty careful with his health, watches his diet and takes pills for the neuropathy." The young girl whipped her car in and out of the sparse traffic.

"Neuropathy?"

"Yeah, it's when your hands and feet cramp or sting or stop working in general. Pretty common when you've got RA." Alicia shrugged. "I have it, too, only not as bad. We kind of bonded over that."

Rheumatoid arthritis. Peri pictured Dev's fingers on that cup of coffee, and how much they resembled Erik's gnarled hands. She had managed to escape the genetic curse. Dev had not been so lucky. She pressed Skip's number. "Call Detective Logan. They need to interview Dev again. He's got RA."

"So?"

"So he inherited the family arthritis, and I found evidence that he's got neuropathy from it. I'm betting that he can't grip a knife, let alone stab someone with it."

"Will do, Doll. Why does it sound like you're in a car?"

She hated when he guessed what she didn't want him to know. "I'm just going with Alicia Duarte to Ro-Bet." She glanced at Alicia, who was eyeing her back, shaking her head. "She's accompanying me to look through Dev's office again."

"Peri—" His voice scolded.

"I'm perfectly safe, not breaking into anything, just doing some legal snooping."

The silence told her what he thought about it. At last, he said, "We'll talk about this tonight."

"Love you." She ended the call, leaning back into the seat, and wincing at the ache in her hip. *I hope I find something to make this worth the fight I'm going to have with that man.*

They seemed to be traveling faster than the speed limit, but she didn't want to crane her neck to see the speedometer. Instead, she breathed, slow and deep. Looking up, she saw the office building to her right, as Alicia darted into the parking lot.

Getting into the company was easy with an employee. Alicia plucked a Visitor badge from the stack and handed it to Peri.

"Ordinarily, I wouldn't bother with this, but Rodolfo's never here on Saturdays, which makes Tim go all Security Guard on everyone. He's a pain."

"Is Tim usually a pain?"

"Totally." Alicia smiled, her hands waving. "No, I shouldn't say that. Tim's not a pain, he's just different."

"Don't worry, I've got a 'Tim' in my life, too. I'm not sure which makes him a bigger pain, his OCD or his Asperger's—sorry, his being on the spectrum."

"As far as I understand, Tim hasn't been diagnosed as anything, but he's got no filters on what he says, a specific way of doing everything, and a complete lack of flexibility."

"Yep, that's my Benny. Sometimes I get to the end of my rope with him, then I remember that he's trying to process things the only way he knows how."

"Exactly. Knowing Tim has kind of taught me to slow things down, in some ways. I'm always too quick to get things done." Her hands accentuated her words. "It's amazing that he works so slowly, but his part of the code was finished first. He's helping me with my part now."

As they opened the locked door, Tim stood at the other side.

He pointed at Peri. "Does she have authorization to be here?"

CHAPTER THIRTY

SKIP WATCHED THE freeway as Logan drove them to the Orange County Men's Jail. Peri's brother had been there for 24 hours now, without asking for a lawyer, making a phone call, or even inquiring about bail. There was something wrong with that.

"Ever spend time with Peri's family?" Logan asked.

"Parents are dead. The brother's hard to figure. Each time Peri hunts him down, he changes his name and moves." Skip shook his head. "She's a smart gal, but she can't leave this alone."

"Tough break. Family sucks sometimes. How are the girls doing?"

Skip laughed. "Yeah, speaking of families. They're actually both doing well, finally. Daria is moving to San Francisco, so she'll be a little closer. Amanda decided, after she broke up with the fiancé, to change direction. She's in Peru, doing a year with the Peace Corps."

"Wow, good for her."

"Yeah, you want 'em to be happy."

They pulled into the driveway at the reserved parking lot of the jail and produced their IDs. Skip nodded at the officer. He kept his wallet out, running his thumb over his badge.

"Steve, how much time you got left?" he asked as they cruised into a space.

"Five years is the earliest I can retire. How about you?"

"Technically, I'm eligible. I'd always planned to wait a bit, but I'm starting to wonder if I should let the younger guys take over." Skip got out of the car and clipped his badge to his belt, before picking up a folder.

"I hear ya," Logan replied, tucking his polo shirt into his khakis as they walked into the building.

The chairs in the waiting area had high backs and hard seats. Skip shifted around every couple of minutes, trying to keep his butt from getting numb. Behind the blah-green counter, he could see the clerks processing paperwork and answering phone calls.

"So..." Logan's soft voice jarred the stillness. "Think you might retire?"

Skip shrugged. "I'm still working the math, but depending upon what I get for the house, I can probably do it. Peri's closing her PI office, so it'd be nice to have time to do things together. Maybe travel."

"You? Travel?" Logan laughed.

"What's so funny?"

"When's the last time you took a vacation?"

"Two years ago, when Peri and I went to Paris." Skip grinned.

"And what did you tell me when you came back?"

"That I was never leaving southern California again."

Logan smirked. "So where are you planning to travel? San Diego?"

"Keep laughing. I'll wave at you from the RV on our way to the Grand Canyon."

A man's voice interrupted them. "Detectives, the prisoner is ready for you in Room 1233."

The two men walked through the door that stood between freedom and incarceration. As always, Skip was grateful that he could walk out at the end of the visit.

Dev sat in a small, drab room, at a bare wooden table, his shoulders slumped and his hands in his lap. Skip sat down across from him, while Logan stood in the corner.

"We met briefly, Dev," Skip said. "I'm Peri's fiancé. How are you doing?"

Dev glared at him. "I'm in jail for murder."

"Yeah, about that," Logan said. "We'd like a better description of how you did it."

"I already wrote it down." He remained hunched over the table, his voice flat. "She tried to blackmail me. I couldn't keep paying her. When I told her I wouldn't pay anymore, she went crazy, and attacked me. I got mad and picked up the knife. I don't remember the rest."

Skip folded his hands. "That's interesting. Detective Logan and I have a few more questions."

Logan pulled a photograph from the folder and laid it in front of Dev. "Do you recognize this?"

"No." Dev glanced at the photo. "I mean, yes. Sorry. It's the knife I used."

"Not just any knife, Dev," Skip said. "It's a chef's knife. It's found in a kitchen."

Dev shrugged. "So?"

"Now, it didn't come from the hotel kitchen, because they keep a careful count of their knives, and they're not missing any. It also didn't come from your apartment, since you have that nice wooden block with knives stuck in it, and they're all there. And we checked Tressa's place. No missing knife."

Logan picked up the conversation. "So naturally, we're curious. Where did you get the knife, and when did you plan to use it?"

"I-I, well, she brought it."

"Tressa brought it to the hotel room," Skip said.

"Yes. She was using it to threaten me. I told you she went crazy."

"You told us she went crazy after you said you wouldn't give her any more money." Logan tapped his fingers on the table.

"She must have brought it, to threaten me."

"Okay, then, Dev," Skip said. "How did you hold the knife when you stabbed her?"

Dev looked from one detective to the other. He spoke haltingly. "Like…you…hold a knife."

Skip stood and reached into his pocket, withdrawing a banana. He placed it on the table.

"I had the munchies, so we stopped at the store and got some snacks," he said, smiling. "Detective Logan here thought this banana is about the same size as the handle on that knife you used."

Logan pointed to the fruit. "Why don't you pick that up and show us how you did it?"

Dev scowled. "That's just stupid."

"Maybe we're in a stupid mood." Skip leaned against the wall, arms crossed. "Humor us."

"No. I gave my statement, that's all you need."

Logan walked around the table, picked up the banana and shoved it into Dev's hand. "We want to see how you handle a knife."

Dev tried to wrap his fingers around the fruit, but they wouldn't tighten all the way. It wobbled, so he steadied it with his other hand, until he could balance the end of the banana against his palm, holding it into place with his thumb. He propped it up and glared at the detectives.

"See?"

Skip held out a piece of paper. "Now. Stab this."

As soon as Dev moved it forward to stab at the paper, the banana fell from his hand.

Skip picked it up and looked at it. "Not even a bruise. Peri told me you've got RA."

"Who told her?" Dev's face reddened. "She has no right."

Skip glowered at him, but kept his voice steady. "And whose fault is that, Dev Chaplain? You never kept in touch. Every time she locates you, you move. You even changed your name. And this? Moving within five miles of her and not telling her? Confessing to a crime you couldn't have committed because you. Can't. Hold. A. Knife."

Logan rocked back on his heels. "You're a real piece of work."

Dev straightened, shooting daggers at the detectives through red-rimmed eyes. His fingers curled in an attempt at making fists, before he clutched his right hand in his left, rubbing the knuckles. After a tense minute, he turned and pounded on the door.

"Guard. We're done here."

Skip stuck the fruit back in his pocket. "Let's go."

"Oh, well," Logan said. "Some guys just can't handle their banana."

CHAPTER THIRTY-ONE

ALICIA SMILED. "HI, Tim. You remember Peri Minnie..."

"Minneopa." Peri helped her. "I accidentally spilled your tea yesterday."

He remained solidly in the doorway. "Why is she here?"

"I didn't get the chance to introduce myself. I'm a private investigator, looking into the murder of Tressa Velasco."

"Oh." Tim's eyes flitted back and forth as he processed the information. "Was she the blond lady Dev knew?"

"Yes. He's been accused of her murder, and I'm helping the police determine if that's true."

Tim frowned. "Why don't you ask Dev?"

"He is being..." Peri shrugged. "Uncooperative at the moment."

"Do you have a warrant?"

Peri tamped down her irritation. "Private investigators don't need warrants."

"Then absolutely not." The tall young man folded his hands. "I'll have to ask you to leave."

Peri smiled. "Why don't we call Mr. Betancourt to see if he gives his permission? I'm assuming he put you in charge of security on the weekends?"

Tim paled. "Someone has to keep the wrong people out."

"I don't want to get anyone in trouble." Her voice softened. "But Dev happens to be my brother. Although I'd prefer it if he was innocent, I'm honor bound to present any evidence that I find. I'd just like the chance to present it in context. Please, Tim."

The young man was frozen in place, staring at Peri. Alicia stood beside him, mouth hanging open. Peri wondered if either of the engineers would speak again, and if there was some kind of reboot procedure she should follow.

I guess I could kick-start them.

"You may go ahead and look," he said at last. "But you aren't allowed to remove anything from the office. Is that understood?"

"Of course. I would never remove evidence. I will simply report it to the police." She blanched a little, thinking of Dev's photos.

"Very well." He nodded at Alicia. "Keep her under surveillance at all times."

As they walked down the cubicles, Alicia continued to stare at Peri. "Why didn't you tell me who Dev was? Ohmygod, he's your brother?"

"I didn't think anyone needed that info," Peri told her.

"Are you mad at me, for lying about your brother?"

Peri shook her head. *If you only knew.* "Not in the least."

They stopped at Dev's office. Alicia put on her gloves and pulled out the envelope. "You won't tell anyone about this, will you?"

"Not unless I absolutely have to."

"What does that mean?"

"I mean, right now, I think the police will have a hard time tracing this envelope to Dev based on physical evidence, and I'm going to let them do their job. If revealing the truth would save you, or catch the killer, I'm not going to hold back. Understood?"

Alicia sighed. "I guess that will have to do."

While the young woman completed her task, Peri walked to Dev's file cabinet with the combination lock on it. Swiping through notes on her phone, she found the set of numbers and keyed them in. No response.

"Alicia, can you help me with this?" Peri showed her the note from under Dev's blotter. "I think this is the combo to his lock, but I'm not doing it right."

Alicia read it. "No, this can't be right. It's four numbers."

"I thought that was standard in aerospace companies."

"Sort of, except on our locks, the last number is zero." She tried a few combinations, with and without a zero, all without no success. "Sorry."

"Then what is this?"

"I'm not sure." Alicia studied the numbers again. "I don't think those are dashes between the numbers, I think they're periods."

"Does that mean something?"

"I'm just thinking, it looks like time. The first two would be 45.43, as in 45 minutes, 43 seconds. The second pair are 58 minutes, 25 seconds."

"Time." Peri paced, combing through her hair. "Time of what?"

"That I don't know." Alicia peeked over the cubicle wall. Tim was dawdling near the door, looking in their direction. "Can we go now?"

They left Dev's cubicle and headed toward the hallway. Peri glanced at the rows of cubbies. A small movement caught her attention. She looked back to see fingers wrapped around the side of a wall.

CHAPTER THIRTY-TWO

TAPPING ALICIA'S ARM, Peri nodded toward the cubicle. Alicia turned, narrowed her eyes, and chuckled.

"James?"

The compact man peeked around the wall. He smiled, thin-lipped and tentative, as his ears turned red.

"Hey, Alicia."

"What are you doing here? Have you gotten your code integrated yet?"

"Almost." He walked out of his office. "What are you doing here?"

"Us?" Alicia looked at Peri, eyes wide.

"I asked Alicia to show me around," Peri said. "I'm still investigating."

"Shame about Dev," James said. "But it doesn't surprise me that he'd kill that woman."

Alicia winced, but Peri touched her shoulder lightly. "Why? Did he strike you as violent?"

"No, maybe not violent." The young man ran his hand through his hair. "But Tressa was a beautiful woman. She might make him do something he wouldn't normally do."

"You knew Tressa?" Peri asked.

"Oh, no, no." He backpedaled faster than a Bugatti in reverse. "Dev had photos of her. She was smokin'."

"She was, huh?" His schoolboy description of a woman, reduced to her parts, made Peri want to pat him on the head, condescendingly, before she backhanded him. "Last time we met, you told me Dev wasn't very sociable. Why would he show you photos of Tressa?"

The iciness of his glare was supposed to make her shiver, but Peri didn't feel the cold. "You ask a lot of questions."

"I'm good at my job." She rested back on her heels and smiled at him, noticing the creases at the corner of his eyes. He was older than she'd originally thought. "I'll get to the truth any way I can."

Alicia pulled at her arm. "We should be going."

"Sure." Peri turned and moved toward the door. She looked back, grinning, at the young man still glaring at her. "Don't work too hard."

They walked toward the elevator.

"Alicia," Peri said, picking her words with care. "Do people…take a lot of photos in here?"

"Oh, no, that's against company policy. Photos might mean espionage, and that gets you fired."

Peri's stomach turned over. Maybe Dev was a spy. "So there've never been photos taken in the lab."

"No—except for that TV crew."

"What TV crew?"

"The news team that came out and did a special feature on us. Startup business that invents something incredible, humble owner, all that."

Peri pulled up the photos on her phone. "Do these shots look like part of that feature?"

Alicia scrolled through the photos, studying them, and nodding before handing the phone back.

"They were definitely taken the same day as the news story." Alicia pointed at the phone. "I remember wearing that blouse, and I had just gotten my hair cut and dyed."

Peri felt her stomach relax. Learning Dev was a spy would be too much at this point. She was barely certain he wasn't a murderer.

"Wait," Peri said. "How long was that segment?"

"About 5 minutes."

"Darn, I thought maybe the times on that note corresponded to times on the film."

"Yeah, not long enough." Alicia strolled into the elevator, and stopped. "Unless it wasn't minutes and seconds, but seconds and fractions of seconds."

"Where's that film?"

"The news channel has it." Alicia smiled. "But I know who can get us a copy of the unedited stuff."

"Call them," Peri said, as the elevator doors closed. "We need to see that film."

Chapter Thirty-three

THE NEXT MORNING, Peri called her assistant. "Hey, Benny, want to run an errand with me? I can bring you up to speed on the case."

"I thought it wasn't a case, Miss Peri."

"Yeah, well, it's kind of a case. Now. It's a case now. The local TV station has a video I need, and they've agreed to share it with me if I pick it up."

"I have to be back by 3:30 sharp." He sounded stern. "Sam and I are going to a musical tonight, at the Maverick Theater, and I have to get ready."

"Absolutely. We're just going to Orange. Get over here, quick."

Peri knew that nothing happened quickly in Benny's world, but it didn't hurt to try to nudge him along. Forty-five minutes later, the black Caddy floated into her drive. Dapper as ever, Benny stepped out in a vintage black and gray bowling shirt, with charcoal gabardines and cream Nubucks.

"Looking good, Mr. Needles," she told him.

"You have to walk faster." He opened the passenger-side door. "I mean, thank you, Miss Peri."

She slid into the passenger side and checked her watch. "Yes, you're in a hurry, but we've got over five hours to go to Orange and back."

"Why do we have to go?" Benny slowly backed out of her drive, stopped to change gears, and proceeded forward, crawling toward Chapman Avenue. "Couldn't that guy send you the file, like, over the internet?"

"He tried to email me the file this morning, but it was too big. And before you ask, he didn't feel any kind of file sharing cloud was secure enough to pass the information."

"What's a file sharing clown?"

Peri smiled. "It doesn't matter. I'm picking up a USB drive. Five minutes, in and out. Ten, tops."

"No more than ten." Benny paused at the stoplight, and reached down to adjust the volume of his 8-track player. Dean Martin crooned a little louder. "Now you have to be quiet so I can concentrate."

They began the slow roll to the city of Orange, down one of the main streets of the north county. The freeway would have been faster, but Peri dreaded getting on a freeway with Benny behind the wheel. His insistence on driving ten miles under the speed limit might get them killed.

Half an hour later, Peri directed him into a sizeable complex of square, functional office buildings. The facades had a quirky uselessness about them that screamed toddler design.

Benny parked in a corner space and smiled. "The perfect spot. Just enough shade, no one on the passenger side."

Peri opened the door. "I'll try to be back before anyone parks next to us."

"Just hurry." He looked at his watch. "It's already ten-thirty."

Rolling her eyes, she hopped out. *I've had sorority sisters take less time than you to get ready. And they were freakin' princesses.*

Suite 4 was a bland white door in the brick façade. She entered a small foyer, with a laminate counter and two chairs. It was too much furniture for the space. A clay pot sat by the door, full of dirt and a brown stick that was probably once green and leafy. Behind the counter was a wall with another bland door on the right. There were no pictures, nothing but white space, decorated with scuff marks.

"Hello?" She called out. No answer. "Dan? Hello? Anyone?"

No one responded, but the office felt occupied. She could hear the muffled sounds of movement. Looking up her contact again, she pressed Redial. She heard ringing from behind the door.

"Dan?" She sat on the counter and swung her legs over.

The phone had stopped ringing by the time she entered the station. It was like stepping into Oz. What seemed like it would be a small office space yawned before her, wide and cavernous. To her left, the news team desk, emblazoned with the station logo. To her right, a room with a large window, through which she could see the reflection of monitors and boards with rows of switches and buttons. In between the two, a network of lights, cameras, and miles of cable, snaking their way across the floor.

She kept moving forward, hiking through the forest of technology. The window to her right seemed a good place to start. From watching TV, she guessed it was the control room. She turned the doorknob slowly, cracking it open.

Dan was inside, face down on the floor.

CHAPTER THIRTY-FOUR

PERI RUSHED IN and turned him over, putting her fingers on his wrist. His pulse was there, thumpa-thumpa, but she had no idea whether it was strong, or weak. She was just happy to feel it at all.

Pulling out her phone, she hit the Emergency number. "I'm at KNOC on Grand and there's an unconscious man here. My name is P—"

Strong hands gripped her mouth, across her nose, and dragged her backward. She struggled for breath, and flailed, trying to free herself. Her assailant never spoke. His arms clamped her head against his shoulder, his mouth near her ear, his foul breath wheezing. She tried opening her mouth to allow his hand in, where her teeth could grab flesh. His grip was too rigid.

Her gutteral roar became a muffled scream that escaped through his fingers like air leaking from a balloon. Breathing in came hard, and her head swam. She could feel a darkness creeping into her mind, and thrashed about manically, pulling the stranger forward. His hands loosened for a half-second, enough time for her to draw in a breath and swing her elbows back.

She made contact with his right side, and felt a thwack as elbow met ribcage. He gasped and let go. Peri turned, and saw a figure in basic black sweats and a striped ski mask.

They were interrupted by a shrill voice, shouting, "Miss Peri? Where are you? We have to go. Hey, what are you doing?"

As the assailant looked up, Peri swung the back of her fist toward his covered face. Her knuckles drove into his cheekbone, sending him flying across the floor. He scrambled away from her, to the door and out. She chased him across the studio, stumbling over wires and around cameras, to the front door, where he leapt the counter and fled across the parking lot.

A security company sedan pulled to the front of the business and stopped as Peri ran out. She pointed to the figure running through the parked cars. "Get him—he attacked me!"

Two uniformed guards got out of their vehicle and strolled over to her. "How can we help you, ma'am?" the tall one asked.

Peri again pointed, wagging her finger a bit. "You can go catch that S.O. B. who just tried to strangle me. He's probably the same guy who knocked Dan out."

They looked at the escaping man. They looked at each other. Tall Guard turned to Peri, while the other one walked away, talking on his radio.

"Ma'am, he's gone, but we'll get him. Why don't you tell us what happened, and show us to this Dan fella?"

Grudgingly, Peri led them inside to the sound booth, and the man on the floor, who was now moaning.

"Are you Dan?" Peri asked.

"Are you Peri?" He tried to prop himself into a sitting position, but grabbed his head and lay back down.

"Ow, I was in here working…suddenly I feel a pain in my head, then nothing."

Tall Guard knelt beside him. "Paramedics are on the way. Lie still."

Dan looked up at Peri, his hands rummaging around his pockets. "I think he took the drive."

"It's okay. You can make another." She knelt on the other side. "I'm just glad you're alive."

The paramedics arrived and worked on Dan, while Peri conferred with the guards.

"I didn't get the greatest look at him," she said, rubbing her knuckles.

"And yet, you managed to hit him in the face, according to your statement." Tall Guard did not sound convinced.

"First of all, he was wearing a ski mask. Black with red stripes. Second, I had been choked. A lot. I was pretty close to blacking out." She turned to Tall Guard's partner, an Asian man of normal height. "I can tell you he was shorter than me, that he had a lot of upper body strength, and that he doesn't like it when girls fight back."

The partner nodded, but Tall Guard scowled. "Maybe he saw us coming."

Peri tried not to roll her eyes out loud. "That's it. You frightened him off, and saved the day."

"Miss Peri, we need to leave. I cannot be late." Benny tapped his foot.

"I'm coming. Gentlemen?" She nodded. "If you require any more answers, I did leave my contact information. I'm always happy to help."

She looked back at Dan, now sitting up, still holding his head.

"Dan, are you all right by yourself? Do you have anyone who can meet you at the emergency room?"

"I do, thanks." He managed a small grin. "My boyfriend is on his way."

"Miss. Peri." Benny's stern voice clipped each word.

She turned and walked with him to the door. "Yes, I'm coming. So sorry I had to get attacked and spoil your schedule."

They got into the car, Benny shaking his head. "I don't think this is going to work, Miss Peri." He turned on the ignition. "I cannot be your assistant and be Sam's friend. I am going to have to stop being Sam's friend."

"What? No, Ben, that's no solution. This case is truly my last one, and I only took it because he's my brother and he's in trouble. Sam seems like a very reasonable girl—I'm sure she understands when you have to help me." Peri rubbed her neck gently, checking the spots that were still sore. "But don't break up with her on my account."

"Stop talking. I'm driving now."

Peri sat back and folded her arms. *If anything, Benny's consistent.*

CHAPTER THIRTY-FIVE

BACK AT HOME, Peri scrolled through Dev's photos again, looking for some sign of importance in any of them. She focused on the ones from the flash drive, praying for context.

Rodolfo smiled for the camera, one hand holding a small white tray containing a smaller black object, and in the other hand, a shiny piece of paper. Peri zoomed in—it was a certificate of excellence for their innovation, from the American Society of Engineers. She recognized Alicia in the background, holding a folder. No one else was in the photo, apart from someone in the laboratory wearing a white coverall with a hood and mask.

They call them clean suits, I think.

She flipped through the next photo. It looked like the previous one. Peri split the screen to look at the two. Rodolfo was smiling. Alicia was studious. The figure in white was still leaning over a computer—or was he?

The differences were subtle. In one photo, his hand was pointed up, an object in his fingered gloves. In the next, his gloves were pointed away from the camera, toward the computer. Peri enhanced that corner of the images. The object looked like a USB drive, but the image was fuzzy.

Going back to the first photo, she clicked on the details. It was taken a day before Tressa died. The time stamp said 02:45.43. She looked up the note with the mystery numbers. If Alicia was right, the first pair was "45.43."

She swiped through the images until she came to the last one. It was time-stamped 03:58.25, matching the last pair on the note. These were the two photos that were important. But why?

Peri sat back. There were no other differences, so it seemed reasonable that Dev wanted to document the person in white—but who was it? Did he know? And who else could she turn to for help?

Rodolfo and Alicia were plainly in the picture, so they could not have done it. But they could still be helping whoever did. That left James, Tim, Emily, and everyone else on the payroll. Dev held the answers. Too bad he wasn't talking.

Her phone played a tune, so she grabbed it. "Hey, Skipper."

"Just thought you'd like to know, they've released your brother from jail. Lack of evidence."

"Great! So, he's back at his apartment?"

"No, he actually checked into a hotel. Not sure why, but we have an officer keeping tabs on him. He's not quite off our list of suspects yet."

"Maybe now he'll talk to me. Which would be lucky timing, because I've discovered something, but I need someone to interpret it." Peri snapped her laptop closed. "Want to come here, or should I meet you somewhere?"

He chuckled. "You are a bulldog on a case. Meet me at Logan's office. Let's share everything we've got."

"OK—wait, I still don't have a car. Let me call Allen, see when it will be done."

"Where's your assistant?"

"He had an…engagement."

"Damn, girl, what are you paying him for?" Skip teased.

"I'm not paying him very much right now, since he's just driving me. And I do keep telling him I'm not on a case and he's not working for me. Can you pick me up?"

"Your wish is my command."

Fifteen minutes later, he pulled into the driveway.

She settled into the passenger seat with a long sigh. "Bad news. Allen says the adjustor didn't notice they'd clipped my gas tank."

"Uh-oh," Skip said as he backed his car out onto the street.

"Uh-oh is right. They called him back out, had him re-inspect the car. Totaled. My car is totaled. I can't believe I have to see what they'll offer me to replace it, go out and shop for a new car—I'm just so…so…Arrrgghhh."

"I know." Skip reached for her hand. "See if your insurance will pay for a rental. If not, Benny and I can squire you around for as long as you like."

"I feel like I've just been put in travel jail. No more freedom to move about the country." She rubbed her temples with her fingertips. "Speaking of jail, where's my brother holed up?"

"An Extended Stay on Imperial Highway." Skip watched the road as he talked.

"How are you going to keep him from leaving the area?" Peri smiled. "Tell him to stay in town, like the cops on TV?"

"We can't do that." He shook his head. "But if he leaves, we can find out where he's going pretty easily."

She leaned her head back and looked at the rows of houses on the avenue, set back on a wide swath of public grass, and peeking over walls of stone. "I wish I knew whether he'll run or not. I should be able to guess what he'd do."

"You can't. Accept that, and treat him like a client— or a suspect—and you'll be happier." He shrugged. "At least, you'll be more at peace with whatever comes."

"You're right. This all happened at the worst time."

Skip pulled into the civic center parking lot and stopped. He leaned over and kissed her cheek. "True. But now you've got me to help you."

CHAPTER THIRTY-SIX

DETECTIVE LOGAN WAVED them into his office. "I've been in touch with Fullerton PD and the FBI, and discovered Tressa Velasco was under surveillance for possible espionage."

"Do tell." Peri sat down and leaned forward, trying to read his notes upside-down.

"Turns out, she was eager to climb the company ladder, and began by giving her manager the scoop on competitors' products. He rewarded her with bonuses. Then she brought him actual designs, blueprints, etc. She received promotions. Every delivery came with a reward.

"Nobody minded, until the day came when the corporate bosses pushed back, and told her manager she wouldn't be getting any more perks. He got scared—what would happen if he stopped giving her what she wanted? Espionage and theft were now part of her job description."

"What happened?"

"She got mad, stopped volunteering, but they all knew she was still shopping for secrets. According to her boss, she said, 'If you can't afford them, I can find someone who can.'"

"Wow," Peri said. "Why wasn't she fired?"

"Because she wasn't stealing from Howard Aerospace—yet. They were watching her carefully. If they couldn't catch her stealing from the company, they hoped to find out who she might sell to if she did take something from them." Logan held out a piece of paper to her. "Which is what they were hoping to get on this thing with Ro-Bet."

Peri reached into her tote and pulled out her laptop, and an envelope. "I found photos, plus this flash drive in Dev's apartment. Actually, Benny found them, in the bedroom closet. I downloaded the flash drive contents."

She opened her computer and displayed the gallery of pictures, carefully avoiding the disapproving stares of the two men. The trio studied the photos, Peri pointing out the actions of the figure in white, and explaining the news segment where they came from.

"We can see from the photos, only two people with alibis. Perhaps one of them saw who it was."

"Yes, but who do we trust?" Skip tapped at the screen. "Are we sure these people aren't working together?"

"True," Peri said. "Alicia told me that the company needs to start making some serious money. Rodolfo mortgaged his house to make payroll."

"Ideally, if we could get that computer," Skip said. "Jason could find out who was logged in at that time."

Peri shrugged. "If their lab computer requires a login. I didn't get to see anyone actually using it, so I don't know their protocol."

"First, I want to see the video these stills came from, for context," Logan said. "Let me call the TV station and see if I can get the whole footage."

"Here's the thing." Peri grimaced. "I had arranged to get the footage, but when I went—"

"Peri—" Skip began.

She held up her hand to stop him, before explaining the trip to the station, and subsequent struggle with the masked intruder. "You can't say this was my fault. I was invited to the station specifically to get that video."

Skip shook his head.

She sighed. They would be discussing this later.

"You two can sort that out on your own," Logan said. "In the meantime, Peri, if you could get those photos and USB stick to Jason, he can take a closer look."

Peri tapped her phone against her palm. "Maybe I could get some information from Alicia without revealing anything more. Lab protocols, who works with what, in general."

Logan nodded. "If you can, we'd learn whether that computer would tell us anything."

She felt Skip's hand on her shoulder. "Just be careful."

"Always." She smiled.

The phone rang as she squeezed Skip's hand, and moved toward the door. Logan's voice was background noise, answering.

"Peri." He interrupted her exit. She turned and he put his index finger in the air, signaling her to wait. A few more affirmative grunts, and he hung up. "That was Detective Berkwits. Art Gibbons was found dead in his kitchen. Bludgeoned, pretty gruesome."

"Tressa's fiancé?" Peri asked.

He nodded. "I hate to tell you this, Peri, but your brother was passed out in the living room with a baseball bat next to him."

She said the first thing that popped into her mouth. "God. Dammit."

CHAPTER THIRTY-SEVEN

BEYOND THE NORTHWEST corner of California State University, Fullerton, is an enclave of stately homes, too old to be called McMansions, but fitting the description perfectly. The houses are carved into the hill, along streets that curve back and forth, creating a high-end maze for drivers.

Peri and Skip pulled into the large, circular cobblestone drive of the topmost home, a gleaming white stucco edifice with wide iron gates. Logan and Powell drove in ahead of them. A five-car garage sat apart from the house, in addition to the attached one that looked big enough for two more vehicles.

Neighbors stood across the street with their dogs and coffee mugs, watching the show. Logan caught Peri's attention as he walked toward the front door. He nodded and raised a hand. Peri reached down to release the seatbelt before Skip could put the SUV in park.

"Whoa, there, Zenyatta." Skip took her hand. "At least let me slow down before you jump out."

"Sorry. Got a little ahead of myself."

He finished parking, leaned over, and kissed her. "Go on. I'll join you."

She kissed him back and leapt from the SUV, trotting to greet Logan on the porch. "You must have flown here."

"Prepare yourself. Berkwits says it ain't pretty."

She followed him through the marbled entrance, noticing the sunken living room ahead, then taking a left turn toward an expansive chef's kitchen. The color scheme of this house was light walls, cherry wood cabinets, and cool blue furniture.

"Wow, he was sitting pretty."

"No joke." Logan craned his neck, surveying the entire room. "I could cash out my entire net worth and not come up with the down payment."

Peri nodded toward the legs on the floor, jutting out from behind the immense island. "Wonder who inherits it."

"I dunno, but they're going to have to re-grout." Detective Berkwits stood next to the body, which was mostly hidden by a white sheet. The legs and arms could not be contained, and were splayed out on the dark blood-stained tile.

"Smashed in the face?"

He nodded. "Repeatedly and with great force."

She shook her head, reached into her tote and pulled out gloves.

"What are you doing?" Logan asked.

"What, these?" She held her hands out. "Just protecting the scene in case I accidentally touch something."

"Don't believe her for a minute." Skip walked into the room. "She'll be rifling through the drawers if you don't watch her."

"I thought we were working together on this." She pointed a finger toward the body.

Skip mimicked her motion. "We aren't working on *this* at all."

"If you crazy kids could take the fight outside, I have to get some work done here." Logan barked the words, but Peri could see the smile tugging at his lips.

She took out her phone and catalogued everything she saw. Pristine, beautiful kitchen, dark red wood cabinets with veined quartz countertops. The appliances gleamed in black stainless, and the backsplash tile captured the warm neutral colors while adding ocean blue to the mix. Nothing was in the spotless sink, nothing was out of order.

It looked like a model home.

Paper at the side of the refrigerator caught her eye, so she investigated. Several post-its, all the same color and size, were in perfect rows. She snapped several photos of the display. Afterward, her focus drifted to a drawer next to the fridge.

"Peri, what are you doing?" Logan asked as she opened it and looked inside.

"Hmm?" She pushed miscellaneous items around. This was the junk drawer, a requirement of every American kitchen, where oddities came to die. "What am I doing?"

Logan was looking over her shoulder. "Yes, why are you snooping in other people's drawers?"

She pulled out a small plastic card and held it up. "Looking for stuff like this."

It was an employee badge for Ro-Bet Engineering, exactly like the ones she'd seen on Alicia, Rodolfo, and the rest. The photo was of Art Gibbons. The name said "Tim Neal."

"Isn't he the guy who owned the car that chased you?" Logan asked.

Peri studied the photo. "I suppose they sort of look alike. Both tall, gangly, light hair, light eyes. Probably the only way to tell them apart is—"

She scurried to the body and glanced down, pointing. "Hands. What do you remember about Art Gibbons' hands?"

Skip knelt and carefully lifted one of the victim's fingers. "Gibbons' fingernails were long and yellow. These nails are chewed down to the nub. Looks like they've been that way for a long time." He stood. "That's not Art Gibbons."

"No, but it just might be Tim Neal." Peri said.

CHAPTER THIRTY-EIGHT

TWO YOUNG MEN in dark uniforms entered, carrying a stretcher.

"Got a spare body bag with you?" Peri asked the EMTs.

"No bag," Berkwits said. "Don't want the neighbors to be spreading this around on the gossip chain just yet. I, too, was suspicious about whose body this is. We should have found the vic's wallet or cell phone in the house, but there's nada. So I had officers locate Gibbons. He's at the station now, alive and well."

Skip nodded. "It's possible whoever did this thought they were killing Art. We should let them continue to think that as long as we can."

"And we're going to try to load this guy out like he's still alive." Berkwits gestured to the body. "Keep the face hidden, put him in the ambulance, run the sirens."

"Such smarty pants." Peri smiled. "Okay if I talk to my brother?"

Berkwits and Logan exchanged glances. Berkwits shrugged.

"Go ahead," Logan told her. "They took him to the CSU van for processing."

"Wait a minute." Skip encircled her arm with his hand. "What were you investigating over at the fridge?"

She pursed her lips. "Nothing. It's just that Alicia Duarte's number is on a note. No name. It wouldn't be like me to let that slide."

He released her. "I realize you don't listen to me, but please be careful."

"It's always my intention." She blew him a kiss before exiting the house.

The black crime scene unit was parked in a near corner by the garage. Fullerton's crime scene processor was a tall, ruddy-faced woman, with her burgundy hair pulled into a neat bun. Peri guessed her to be in her early thirties. She was grabbing a tablet from her front seat when Peri approached and introduced herself.

The woman looked up and nodded. "Jeanine Olmos."

Peri pointed to Dev. "I'm helping the detectives with this case, and I have to ask this man a few questions."

"Knock yourself out."

Dev sat at the edge of the CSU van, holding his hands out for swabbing. A paper bag was folded next to him, and he wore an oversized "Fullerton PD" t-shirt. Peri fought back the urge to slap him as she approached.

If I want to help him, I have to be patient and kind.

"What the hell is wrong with you?"

He lifted his chin and looked her in the eyes. In a few short days, he had aged ten years. "Sorry, Sis."

Peri's heart softened. "Tell me what happened."

"I got a text, said it was from Art, said he knew something about Tressa's killer. Wanted to talk to me about it before he went to the police."

"Why you?"

Dev shrugged. "Art and Tressa and I were close at one time. We met at University of Arizona, then briefly worked at the same company. So I drove to his house. When I tried to knock on the door, it swung open. I went inside. I saw his legs sticking out from behind the kitchen island. There was a bat on the floor. I heard footsteps behind me, so I grabbed it, then felt a pain in the back of my head and everything went dark."

"So now your prints are on the bat."

He hung his head. "I'm stupid."

"No, you did the logical thing. You picked up the bat to defend yourself." Peri rubbed her forehead. "Logical, and probably calculated."

"What was calculated?" Logan walked up.

Peri told him what Dev had just explained. "If you're looking to make someone a suspect, find a way for them to handle the murder weapon."

"I'm sure the Fullerton PD will run all the tests," Logan said.

"Dev, will you talk to me now?" Peri turned back to her brother. "Why the confession? Why refuse to see me?"

"To keep you safe, not that it did any good."

CHAPTER THIRTY-NINE

PERI STARED AT her brother. "I don't understand."

"I was—contacted—by someone who said if I confessed, they wouldn't go after you."

"Me?" Peri laughed. "I'd like to see them come after me. The gal with a fiancé on the force. Dev, next time, talk to me."

"And I thought if I confessed, you'd stop digging, or at least you wouldn't be good enough to figure out I didn't do it."

Logan chuckled. "Do not underestimate the Placentia Police Department. And never doubt your sister's stubbornness."

"Time to come clean," Peri told him. "Where did the knife come from?"

"I was in the back of the squad car. They had cuffed my hands in front, because I couldn't keep my arms behind my back and sit in the backseat. I got a text."

"I thought they took your phone."

"They did, but I've got a smart watch. It displays my emails and texts." He lifted his arm to show her. "The text said to ask to use the restroom at the station, and not to say anything if I wanted you to live. In the restroom, another text came. Said to look behind the toilet. There was a knife."

Peri looked at the detective. "Satisfied?"

Logan shrugged.

"Tell me about these." Peri took out her phone, and scrolled through her photos. She showed the stills from the video shoot to her brother. "I found photos, plus a flash drive, at your place. What do they mean?"

"The photos are just pictures from when I lived in Arizona." Dev shook his head. "I don't know what's on the flash drive."

She scowled. "I'm going to find out, Endeavor."

"I seriously don't know. Tressa gave the flash drive to me. Said to hang onto it."

Peri sat back on her heels. "Interesting. They're pictures of your workplace, but Tressa knew more about them than you do."

He shrugged. "I suspected she was seeing someone else at Ro-Bet. She was dodging my calls. I was honestly surprised when she wanted to meet me at the hotel."

Detective Berkwits approached, phone to his ear. He nodded at the detective, and gave Peri a small grin.

"That was Officer Darden," he said as he ended his phone call. "Someone called in an anonymous tip, that we could find motives for both murders in the bottom of Dev's file cabinet."

Peri opened her mouth to say she knew what they were and how they got there. She remembered her promise to Alicia and bit her tongue.

"What did you find?" Logan asked.

"Candid photos of Tressa Velasco. Nothing risqué, invasive, but definitely nothing she would have been aware of."

Peri tried to look surprised. "But we already proved Dev couldn't have stabbed Tressa."

"Have we?" Logan said. "I just heard him say he picked up a bat to defend himself. If he can't grip a knife, how can he grip a bat?"

Peri looked at her brother. "Dev?"

"It's not like I can hold it tightly. I picked up the fat end that I could close my fingers around." He looked up at the detective. "I was going to swing the narrow end."

"Fair enough," Peri said. "The police will know by the fingerprints. How about this question—were you selling company secrets to Tressa?"

"What? No." He glared at her.

"That's not what we hear," Berkwits said.

"I don't care what you hear. I don't betray my company." His voice got louder with each word. "I'll have you know, I have a top secret clearance. Every piece of my life scrutinized, a lie detector test, the works. I signed a contract."

"Okay, okay," Peri said. "Was Tressa trying to get information from you? Especially that new translator-thingie your company has?"

"Oh, the UTran." Dev shifted in his seat. "Of course she was trying. Here's the thing, when Rodolfo heard that I knew Tressa, he wanted me to get information from her about how her project met their software certification requirements. Rumor has it, they were able to cut a few corners and still make the grade. It wouldn't surprise me if she thought she could make a deal."

"But you wouldn't have?" Berkwits asked.

"Nah, my plan was to get as much intel from her as possible before she came right out and asked for our algorithm. When push came to shove, I'd shove back."

"So the deal was never about money," Peri said.

"Of course not. We never discussed money."

"These corners that were cut," Logan said. "I have no idea what software certification is, but would Art have taken advantage of them?"

"Only if Tressa told him. He worked on another project."

Peri ran her hand through her scalp. "Unless…unless the corner-cutting goes higher up in the company food chain. Like, all the projects get away with it."

Dev shook his head. "Maybe, but not all projects require certification. It depends upon the customer."

"Then why does Ro-Bet need it?" Logan asked.

"To make our product more attractive to the big aerospace companies. We get everything certified, we can sell to anyone. And of course, the cheaper we can get it done, the better."

Jeanine held up her hand. "Sorry, folks, he's got to go with those lovely uniforms over there."

"Don't worry," Peri told him. "We'll work this thing out."

She returned to Skip's car, praying the bat had someone else's fingerprints, anything that would clear her brother.

"Looks bleak, Doll." Skip was behind her, his hands caressing her shoulders. "But you'll get through it, along with your brother."

"At least he's being more talkative now." She turned to him. "I'm still mad at him, but I feel more like fighting for him than when I started. That's a good sign, right?"

"That is a good sign." He kissed her forehead. "Why don't we get some food and talk about our next move?"

"Sounds good." Peri looked over at the CSU van. She shook her head, brow furrowed. "I don't like this."

"Yeah, if that's Tim Neal, what was he doing in Art Gibbons' house?"

"No, worse than that. From what Dev told me, I think there's an officer involved."

CHAPTER FORTY

BENNY STOOD IN his bedroom, regarding his tie in the mirror. One of the corners was higher, he was certain. He looked at the framed photo of Dean Martin on the dresser. Dino's skinny black tie was perfect. Benny wanted to be perfect.

"Sam?" He walked down the stairs to the living room. "Sam? Could you help me with my tie?"

"What's wrong with it?" She glanced up from her magazine. "It looks fine."

"I don't want it to look fine. Fine is for people who don't care." He pointed. "This side is higher than the other."

She walked closer, squinting. "Well, I don't see it, but you should be comfortable." She reached out and manipulated the thin red line of silk. "See if that's better."

He turned to a mirror on the opposite wall and studied his reflection for a long time. "Yes. Yes, this is good. Perfect. The perfect Windsor knot."

"I'm glad. Let's go pick Peri up."

Benny stared at her. "You...you want to go with me to pick Miss Peri up?"

"Well, sure, I thought that's what we were doing. Take her to the rental place to pick up her car, then you and I head to the TV station." Sam frowned. "That's why I met you here."

"Yes, but I was going to take Miss Peri to her car, then come back and take you to your interview." He fidgeted, shifting from one foot to the next.

"You could do it like that, I guess." Sam smiled. "I just thought we'd save time by combining trips."

"Oh, no. No." Benny shook his head. "Miss Peri is my job. You are not my job. I can't mix them."

"I understand. My interview isn't until noon, so we have time." She patted his shoulder. "By the way, why wouldn't Peri just take an Uber to get her car?"

"*Uber?*" He stared at his friend. "*I* am her assistant. She calls *me* when she needs a ride, not some fancy phone thing."

"Of course, Ben. I wasn't thinking."

He picked his keys from the basket, opened the front door, and stopped. Turning, he told her, "I know I'm different, Sam. I have to do things the way I have to do things. I can't mix things up."

"It's okay. I'm flexible enough for the both of us."

He jingled the keys, feeling the metal jump in his palm, cool and sharp. "It's not okay. It's hard."

"What's wrong?"

"I can't talk now. I have to pick up Miss Peri." He strode out the door, and down the path to his Cadillac. The shiny black fins stood sharp, cutting through the air around them. Brake lights poked out from each fin, held in tubes like missiles ready to strike.

No one tailgated the Caddy.

He slid onto the red leather bench seat and turned the key that made the car purr. Easing backward out of the driveway and onto the quiet street, Benny headed toward the house of his sometimes-boss.

Driving took immense focus, but this trip was more difficult than usual. He liked Sam, liked her a lot, and not just because her dad named her after a Dean Martin character from a movie. Sam Hollis was strong and smart and easy for him to get along with. She never did anything unexpected, like Miss Peri did. He didn't have to work at keeping up.

But it was hard to have a good friend, and a job. Some days, it felt like his brain might split in two. Miss Peri said that Sam was important to him. True, he enjoyed being with her. They'd done a lot of things he wanted to do, but hadn't been brave enough to do alone.

I wish I knew how to put Miss Peri aside and have fun with Sam, then stop thinking about having fun with Sam when I have to work for Miss Peri.

CHAPTER FORTY-ONE

PERI WAS SITTING on her front porch when he arrived. She leapt up and trotted to the car.

"Thanks, Ben. The shop isn't too far from here."

He frowned. "Miss Peri, you didn't even wait for me to open the car door. Don't you have good manners?"

"I thought you'd appreciate it if I didn't make you wait." She lowered her tall frame onto the passenger side. "You probably have other things to do today."

Benny pounded the steering wheel. "But it's all wrong!"

She leaned away, staring at him. "Okay, what kind of bug you got up your butt today?"

"I don't have any kind of bug, and that's just gross."

"I mean, what's the matter?"

"It. It's all wrong." He turned off the engine. "Everyone's trying to help me. Sam wants to save time, riding with me to pick you up. You want to save time jumping into my car when it's barely stopped. No one is listening to me."

"I apologize." She folded her hands in her lap. "I want to listen. What do you want me to hear?"

He closed his eyes, quieted himself, then opened them and faced her, staring at her hands. "First, I cannot

175

mix my work and my friends. If I am doing something with Sam, I cannot answer your phone calls. I need a schedule, just like my schedule for visiting Matt Helm."

Matt Helm was a large orange cat whom Benny had adopted, but didn't want to actually live with. Phil and Nancy Nickels, Benny's friends and financial administrators, were kind enough to give the cat a home and let him visit whenever he wanted.

"Okay, it's a little inconvenient," Peri said. "But I'll adjust. Anything else?"

"I still need..." He struggled for the correct term. "The rituals. I need to hold doors open, and say 'hello, how are you,' and hear 'I am fine, how are you,' and 'thank you for driving me.'"

"Sounds fair. How about we agree, that if neither of us is being chased by bad guys, we always have time for a proper hello?"

He nodded.

She waved her index finger between them. "Want to start this thing over again?"

"Yes, please."

Peri got out of the car and walked to her front door. She turned and looked at him. The driver's side window rolled down and a small, chubby palm motioned her back.

"All the way into your house."

She rolled her eyes, dug her key out of her purse and unlocked her door, entering and closing it behind her. Thirty seconds later, he was on the porch, ringing the doorbell and rapping his knuckles five times. She opened the door.

"Hello, Benny, how are you?"

"I am fine, Miss Peri. Are you ready to go?"

"Yes, thank you." She stepped out. "And thank you for taking me to get my rental car."

They walked to the Caddy, where he held the door open for her. As she got into the passenger side, he said, "Thank you. Now we can go."

He got in, started the car, and cruised down the street, out of the neighborhood, and off to the rental facility. He was extra careful on these quiet streets, to drive slowly and look for children—or adults—who might run in front of his car.

"Is there any way of getting the car *near* the speed limit?" Peri's voice whined at him.

"Shh. No talking when I'm driving."

She pushed back against the bench seat, and he felt it bounce on his side. He guessed that she was mad, but at least she stopped talking. Twenty minutes later, he pulled up at a lot full of shiny cars, from SUVs to the smallest compacts. A rectangle of a building sat at the end, flat roof, sharp corners, glass and stucco.

One of the employees was outside with a clipboard, checking in a return. Short, neat, and polished, from his jet-black dress shoes to his perfectly styled hair, he snapped his head up at the sight of the immaculate 1959 black Coupe deVille, gliding to the curb.

"Good morning." He stopped writing and walked over to greet them as Benny was getting out of the car. "That is one beautiful machine."

Benny squinted, nodding his head as he walked around to open Peri's door. "I know."

"Thank you again for the ride," Peri told him, stepping out into the sunlight. "I promise to put a work schedule together for you today, and we can review it tomorrow."

"Thank you for understanding. I don't know—" He stopped, faltered. If he said it aloud, it wouldn't be a wish anymore.

"Don't know what?"

He stared at his car, tapping his thumb on the roof. The blush rose in his neck, to his cheeks. He felt hot and molten all over, his voice soft and crackling. "I'm not sure if Sam will ever like me. You know, *like me* like me. Maybe we will always be friends. But I don't want to mess it all up because I can't work for you while I spend time with her."

"I understand." Her voice sounded kind, like his mother. "I'd never want you to break up your friendship over your job with me. Even if you do end up just friends, friends are as important as lovers. You love them in a different way, that's all."

"I do l-l-love her, but I'm still not sure which way."

"Doesn't matter, Ben." She patted his arm. He flinched, and looked in her direction. "At the end of it all, love's the only thing that matters. Jobs, things, they don't mean anything."

He nodded. "See you later, Miss Peri."

"See you later, Ben."

Back in the car, he pressed softly on the accelerator, and threaded the big black Caddy through the parking lot. He managed one glimpse of Peri in the rearview mirror before turning right, down the side of the building, where he stopped and waited his turn to join the traffic on the street.

CHAPTER FORTY-TWO

PERI'S FIRST STOP was the police department. She needed to talk to Detective Logan. He was in his office, at his desk.

"Pretty heavy charges, Peri," he said. "I don't mean to be the bad guy, but how can you tell that your brother is telling the truth?"

"Fair question. I wish I could say because I know him so well, but that's not true." She shook her head. "I've never seen him look the way he did at that crime scene. Like he'd run out of options. I think he had no other choice, except be honest with me. For once."

"And which officer would you suspect?"

"I don't want to suspect anyone, especially law enforcement. But I think, if Jason could look at Dev's texts, we might find out. I mean, who else could hide a murder weapon there?" She tried to read his expression, but it was as flat as Skip's usually was. Good cops had good poker faces. "Just check the texts. Verify what he told me."

The detective stood. "Let's see where Jason is, processing-wise. Hopefully, he can pause what he's doing to take a look at Dev's phone before we have to return it."

"Thank you, Steve. Of course, I'd rather find out it was someone else."

"Me, too."

They walked down the hall to Jason's lab, where they could see him hunched over his desk, his fingers flitting across a keyboard.

"What's been processed," Logan asked, "And what's next on the list?"

The younger man pointed at various equipment around the room. "DNA on the knife is all victim. No prints of any kind, but a weird substance on the handle. You'll never guess."

"Let me try," Peri said. "Bleach? Chloride? Sodium Hydroxide?"

Logan stared at her, one brow arched in a question.

"Give the lady a gold star," Jason said. "Toilet bowl cleaner."

"I cleaned enough houses to know my toxic chemicals." Peri stared back at Logan. "So Dev was telling the truth about that."

"Okay, I'll give you that one." He turned to Jason. "Have you done anything with his phone?"

"Not yet. It's next on my list."

"Pay particular attention to the texts." Logan grimaced. "Especially the ones after we put out the BOLO on him."

"Did you get a copy of the videotape yet?" Peri asked.

Jason shook his head. "No. Dan hasn't returned to work yet, after the attack, and no one at the station is answering my calls or my emails."

"I guess we could get a subpoena," Logan said. "I thought we had a friendlier way of getting this done."

Peri turned to him. "We have the photos. They've got dates and timestamps on them. Can we use them?"

"Sure, we'll use them, but if we had the full tape, we'd have context."

"Yeah, you're right." She closed her fist around her rental car keys. "We need the texts, need the tape, need, need, need."

"I'm working as fast as I can," Jason told her.

"And you do a damn fine job." She smiled. "I'm just wishing this was over."

She slung her tote over her shoulder and nodded her goodbyes. The air outside felt warmer than when she'd gone into the station. June was that way—the sun, the wind, and the clouds were always playing hide-and-seek.

Next on Peri's list was another talk with Alicia. She'd have to be discreet, in case the girl was working with whoever was in those photos, potentially stealing data, potentially killing people. Too bad she didn't know what was going on in the photos on that flash drive.

Who am I kidding? I'm no techno-whiz. I wouldn't understand what was on that drive if it bit me.

She checked her watch. Noon. It would be a few hours before Alicia would be winding down her work day. Maybe she'd like to meet for a drink.

"But first, I need to call the therapist." At a traffic light, Peri dialed her number.

She answered on the second ring, sounding a little snippy. "We are not going to make progress if you keep cancelling your appointments."

"My apologies, Dr. Andrews. I'm dealing with a family emergency. Crisis. Emergency crisis."

"All the more reason you should be in my office."

I thought therapists were supposed to take away your guilt, not add to it. "Look, I am not getting a lot of time to sit in your comfy chair and reframe my trauma, okay? Pencil me in for Friday, and I'll call you if there's a problem."

After that, calling Alicia was almost a pleasure.

"Ohmygod—Peri, did you hear about Art?" The flood of words poured out of her.

"I did. I was wondering if you had time for a drink after work? I have questions."

"Absolutely, I'm so squicked out, I could def use some alcohol. Where can I meet you? Do you know Brian's on Placentia? I can go there. What time? I get off at three."

Peri drove on, waiting for the girl to take a breath. "Brian's will be fine. Meet you there around four."

CHAPTER FORTY-THREE

SAM ADJUSTED HER polka-dot headband as she studied herself in the guest bathroom mirror. "Benny, are you certain you want to come with me? TV interviews are unpredictable. It could take a long time, or we could be over in 5 minutes."

"It will be okay." He raised his voice, so she could hear him from the living room. "We will eat afterward. If it's 5 minutes, we will have lunch. If it's longer, we will have dinner."

She joined him in the living room. "I realize how much you hate a loose schedule like this, and I don't want you to be bored."

"Oh, I won't be bored, I have plans." He fell quickly silent, and stared at the ceiling.

"Plans?" Sam fastened her green patent-leather belt. "What kind of plans?"

Secrets were hard to keep. He tried to keep from fidgeting, but her casual questions sharpened his guilt. "I have to help Miss Peri."

"Help her do what, exactly?"

Looking down, he shifted from one foot to the other. "You're going to the TV station that I drove Miss Peri to, remember the day I was almost late to the theater?"

"You weren't late, you were two hours early."

"But I was almost late. She was supposed to get some kind of video of some kind of interview, and instead the man she was meeting got drugged and she got choked and they stole the information."

"Yes, I remember that."

"She never got the video." He shrugged. "If I go with you, maybe I can get it for her."

"Why?"

"I told you. To help Miss Peri."

"Are you working the case with her?"

He shifted his weight again, and rubbed his fingers together. "Maybe. Not as much as before, but this case is different. She told me so."

Sam picked up her purse and walked to the door. "I really appreciate you taking me to the station, but I don't think you have to help Peri get her video."

"But I *do*." He pouted. "Miss Peri has always helped me. She kept me from getting into trouble when Auntie put that hand in my freezer, and she gave me a job when the judge said I had to work to get out of jail. She helped when my house burned, and that stupid boy was inside. She is my friend. If I do not help her, then I cannot be a friend back."

Sam nodded and smiled, before giving Benny a quick, firm hug around his shoulders. "You're right. You're a good friend. If you need my help getting the file, just ask."

They headed outside to the car, where Benny insisted on holding the passenger door for her. Once safely installed in the long, black rocket, they began the slow journey from Placentia to Orange, past the rows of square, industrial buildings selling windows, tile, and paint on Kraemer Boulevard. Once they crossed the 91 freeway, the boulevard began a new life as Glassell Street, hosting old, quaint houses with front porches and flower boxes. Dean Martin crooned to an easy beat, matching their unhurried pace.

At long last, Benny pulled into the parking lot, and settled on a spot that would get shade from a small tree, without dropping leaves or flowers. He hoped it was not a favorite among birds. It only took one attempt to get the Caddy straight and equally spaced within the lines.

I can't do that with Miss Peri along. She makes me too nervous. He turned off the engine and looked at Sam, who had fallen asleep. "Sam. We are here."

She stretched, pulled the car's visor down and checked her makeup for smudges. Satisfied, she nodded at him. "Let's go."

A hefty young woman sat at the counter in the reception area.

"I'm Samantha Hollis and I have an appointment with Jay," Sam said, and pointed to Benny. "This is my associate, Benny Needles. He'll be accompanying me today."

The young woman gave her a sign-in sheet, and picked up the phone. Benny could barely hear her talking. He pushed his hands together, running each finger along its counterpart, massaging and rubbing. If he couldn't get into the back offices, his plan would fail.

"Sir? Sir?"

He looked up to see the receptionist handing him something—a Visitor's Badge on a lanyard. "Oh, good!

I'm so happy it's on a lanyard. I hate to get pin holes in my clothes."

The receptionist motioned them to take a chair, then returned to staring at her computer monitor. Benny could see, in the reflection of her glasses, a deck of cards on the screen. *Solitaire—what a silly game.*

A slender man of average height, impeccable grooming, and a noticeable coat of makeup, popped out of the side door. "Samantha? I'm Jay."

Sam stepped up, shook his hand, and made the introductions. No one minded if her "assistant" accompanied her backstage, so Benny tagged along, looking around and trying to remember where he found Miss Peri during their last visit. He hated this big room, with all the lights and the cables going everywhere.

Jay steered Sam left, chattering so much, Benny wondered how she was going to get him to shut up so she could talk. He glanced to the right and saw the room Peri had been in. It had a big window, and he could see a man with fuzzy red hair and a big beard. He looked like a Viking.

The man's head raised, and his eyes met Benny's stare for the briefest wisp of time, before Benny turned his eyes away. Other people's eyes, especially strangers' eyes, bored into him like a hot poker. Even with Sam, looking her straight in the eyes required preparation.

The door to the room with the window opened, and the Viking man bounced down the steps, taking two at a time. He carried two small black boxes and a tangle of cords as he strode toward the stage. As he passed by Benny, he gave him a quick pat on the back.

"How's it going?"

Benny stepped to the side, annoyed by the touch. Viking man was so wide and tall, his employee badge nearly smacked Benny in the nose. Benny looked at him, and back at the open sound booth door.

I might as well get the file myself.

CHAPTER FORTY-FOUR

NO ONE NOTICED him crossing the room, ascending the steps, and closing the door. It was quiet, as if even his footsteps were silenced. *This would be a great room to sleep in,* he thought. Searching the room for a computer, he found one in the far corner, away from the window. He tapped the mouse and the screen lit up. The first thing it asked for was an employee ID.

Benny scoured the space around the keyboard, trying to find a scrap of paper with someone's name and number on it. There was nothing. He closed his eyes, but a vision of Viking man's badge in his face, made him open them again. *The man's employee badge.* He closed his eyes and replayed the swinging badge, over and over. It took him a minute to remember, but the silence of the room helped his focus. There were numbers, and a letter. As he remembered, he typed.

The computer liked his answer, and leapt into service. He read the names of all the files and folders on the desk top, looking for any word he might recognize. Under "June Programs," he found a folder marked "Ro-Bet." There were video files in the folder.

He pulled a USB flash drive from his pocket, one shaped like a man in a tuxedo. Sam had given it to him, so he could transfer some Dean Martin movies onto his computer. He pushed the drive into the computer's USB port, selected the folder, and requested Copy.

"Looks like everything's working." A strange voice jumped into the booth. Benny turned and saw lights on the board that he had not seen before. Remaining back in the shadows, he peered out the window and saw Sam and Jay, with Viking man. They were adjusting small microphones on their clothes, and Jay was sticking a wire behind his ear.

"How's that feel?" Jay asked Sam. "Tell Eddie if it's not comfortable. We want a good interview."

Sam smiled and nodded to Eddie. "Feels okay. I've been miked before."

Eddie took a few steps back. "Let me get to the booth and I'll check sound levels."

Benny snapped back to the computer screen. It was 80% complete. *Oh no no no, he's gonna get mad when he finds me, what was I thinking?*

He took two steps toward the door, then two steps back to the computer, the sweat beading around his hairline. Eddie was almost to the stairs. Benny looked around for a place to hide, but saw nothing. As his gaze swept across the window, he saw Sam look up. He waved and shook his head, trying to get help.

"Oh, Eddie." Her strong, clear voice rang across the room, making him stop and turn. "I think there's a loose wire here."

Swinging left, Eddie flipped a reverse and returned to her. "Not a problem. Better catch it now instead of when I'm already in the booth."

Benny turned back to the computer and counted the percent, from 89 up, his foot tapping like a speed demon. At "Copy Complete," he grabbed the drive and bolted to the door, opening it slowly and peeking around to see if Eddie was on his way back. He couldn't quite see him, but from the booth, he could hear Sam's voice, telling him to move the box a little to the right.

She's stalling for me. He smiled as he slipped down the stairs.

Eddie rushed past him, patting him on the shoulder again. It was not as annoying this time. His skin was tingling and his head giddy from his escape. He barely felt the man's touch.

"Hey, there are seats over to the left if you want to watch your friend's interview," Eddie said as he dashed into the booth.

"Thank you." Benny took a silk kerchief from his pocket and dabbed his temples. He ambled to a seat, his hand in his jacket pocket, rubbing the edges of the tuxedoed drive. *Miss Peri is going to be so happy.*

Sitting back in the lightly cushioned chair, he folded both hands in his lap, rubbing his fingers together. Now it was time to forget about Miss Peri and his mission, and focus on Sam and her interview. He stifled a yawn. *How did people do two things at once? It was exhausting.*

CHAPTER FORTY-FIVE

BRIAN'S ORIGINAL SPORTS Bar in Fullerton was quiet at 4 pm, so Peri pulled into a mostly empty parking lot. The door was open, letting all the air conditioning escape onto the tiny patio.

Windows in front were large enough for her to see shadows moving inside—even the door was glass. However, the simple black curtains and painted advertising kept the outside world from truly seeing in.

Inside was wood, wood, and more wood, with large-screen TVs in every corner of the ceiling, and a mirror behind the bar. The remaining wall space was crammed with sports memorabilia, a few concert posters, and a moose head.

Brian's was a throwback to what bars used to be, before smoking became illegal and weed got the green light. Still, crowds jammed the place on Wednesday nights for two-dollar schooners. No one cared about being a hipster when cheap beer was on the table.

Peri found an empty bartop against the back wall, under a giant TV screen. As usual, Garth the bartender was zipping around the room, picking up a tab, dropping off a pitcher, and clearing plates, all with hyperactive ease. Sliding onto the tall seat, she waved at him.

He sailed over, giving the wood table a quick swipe with his towel. "White or red?"

"Water at the moment. I'm working." She looked up at the door. "And an order of fried zucchini."

"You got it." He left her to alternate between staring at the entrance and checking the time.

Alicia rushed in ten minutes late, searching the room in an almost panic. Peri raised her arm to get her attention. The girl frowned, squinted, and raced over.

"I'm so glad you're here, sorry I'm late, I was afraid I was being followed again, but I shouldn't be, right?"

At last, Alicia ran out of breath, or words. It was difficult to tell which.

Peri pushed the basket of zucchini toward her. "Want a beer or something?"

"I'm not really hungry." The young girl shook her head, as Garth approached. She took a wedge of zucchini and picked the breading away, before dipping it in the ranch container. "Maybe a little. And can I get a Stella?"

"Why don't you add a Bass and an order of sliders to that," Peri said.

Garth nodded, smiled, and disappeared.

Peri let her get settled in, eat a little, relax. Alicia closed her eyes as she chewed. She opened them in time to see Garth place a frosty mug in front of her, and grabbed it with both hands. One long pull later, she looked at Peri as if it were the first time.

"Sorry, I guess I forgot to eat lunch today."

Peri squinted at her. "How does that even happen? I've never forgotten a meal in my life."

Alicia laughed. "I was a picky eater growing up, and I guess I just never got into the three-meals-a-day groove."

"Speaking of meals, you mentioned going to happy hours with other employees. Anyone in particular?"

"No, everyone, really. Well, except for Rodolfo, he's married."

"How about Emily?"

"Yeah, she comes along." Alicia made a sour face. "She's kind of a pill. Bosses Rodolfo around a lot."

"So...Rodolfo is married, but Emily bosses him around...any rumors?" Peri leaned in.

Alicia shrugged. "Only a million of 'em. He's having an affair, she's his illegitimate daughter—blackmail is a front runner."

"Blackmail. What would she have on him?"

"I have no idea, and it doesn't make sense anyway. He's always broke, from trying to save the company."

"Would Emily have any reason to go into the lab? Like, wear the clean suit and do stuff?"

"No, not her. She doesn't even understand what we do, and she makes fun of anyone in the white suit, especially Tim."

"Tim Neal?"

The young girl nodded. "She constantly talks trash about him, especially when he's around to hear it. I always tell her to knock it off, but she ignores me."

"You like Tim?"

"He's okay. I mean, I'm pretty sure he's on the spectrum, but so what? He def processes stuff differently than almost anyone ever."

Peri grinned, thinking of Benny. *Not anyone.*

"But he's never mean." Alicia took another zucchini wedge. "And he's uber helpful. Emily's just a bad witch."

"She doesn't sound like someone I'd want to hang with," Peri said. "Did Dev come to happy hours with you?"

"Lots of times. A couple of times, he brought Tressa and Art."

"Wait—you knew Tressa and Art?" Peri frowned. "Didn't you tell me you didn't know the victim when I interviewed you before?"

Alicia blushed. "No, you never really asked me if I knew her. I just didn't tell you that I did."

CHAPTER FORTY-SIX

PERI LEAFED THROUGH her notes. *Damn. I slipped up.* "Okay, want to tell me about how you met Tressa and Art?"

"Through Dev." Her hands pushed, palms up, in a classic *duh* gesture. "They came to a couple of happy hours."

"And did you talk to them a lot?"

"The first time, yeah. I mean, they're a little more Dev's age, but I don't care. We had a lot in common, being software nerds. The second time..." Alicia looked up, tapping her index finger on the rim of her glass. "The second time they didn't stay long."

"Their excuse?"

Alicia shrugged. "Tressa mumbled something about a headache, which was a pity, because James had just shown up."

"So?"

"So James does fewer happy hours than Tim does." Alicia rolled her eyes. "He thinks he's sooooo much more sophisticated than anyone in the room. Beer's not exotic enough. Chips and salsa are pedestrian. Ugh."

"Why would you want him there with Tressa and Art?"

195

"It's mean, really. I kinda feel bad about it. I was trash-talking James to Tressa at the previous meetup. I wanted her to meet him, so we could trash-talk him together."

"You must have liked her." Peri smiled.

Alicia took another big swig of beer, her eyes teary. "And Art. I didn't know them well, but it's so awful. Who could have done this? I mean, it wasn't Dev. He could never."

"Never say never, it'll bite you in the butt." Peri slid her own mug closer, finally picking it up for a sip. "But no, I don't think he could have done it either."

The young girl ran her finger around the rim of her glass. "I probably shouldn't tell you, because I liked Tressa, but there were rumors...that she would do anything to get to the top. Sleep with a boss, present someone's ideas as her own..."

"Steal another company's technology?"

Alicia shot her a glance. "Maybe. But I don't think Dev would help her."

"Hey, not saying he would." Peri sat back, hand to her chest. "I heard she was manipulative, seductive, and relentless. Which one of the guys—or gals—in your company would that work on?"

"Well, not Rodolfo. This company's his life." She counted on her fingers, looking at the ceiling. "Not Dev. I've never really watched Emily around Tressa. Tim was kind of a goofball around her. Actually, Tim is just a goofball. James didn't get the chance to even meet her."

Peri nodded. "How much testing is done in your lab? Does everyone wear suits when they're in there?"

"Oh, yes, it's a clean room. We learned early in our testing, some of the components can't handle dust, hair, extreme temperatures, that kind of stuff." Alicia cocked her head. "Why are you asking about the lab?"

"It's my job to be nosy. Check under all the rugs, behind all the curtains, so to speak." Peri sipped her beer again. "Can you talk about the day of the filming? Who was interviewed, who was filmed working at the various stations, like in their office, or the lab?"

Garth returned with pulled pork sliders and two plates. Peri took one of the small sandwiches and loaded it with extra sauce and pickles. She waited for Alicia to break the silence, and hoped for the truth, or at least Alicia's perspective of it.

Alicia picked at the slider on her own plate, tearing off a chunk of bun and sniffing it before putting it in her mouth. "So, that was the day Rodolfo and his wife had a big fight, first thing in the morning."

Peri sat back and swallowed her eagerness. "Fight, huh? What about?"

"I didn't hear all of it," Alicia said, putting down the sandwich and setting her hands free to help with the storytelling. "And I didn't see it. I was in the reception area, trying to fix Emily's computer, which is old and she downloads crap onto it, so she gets viruses and lucky me gets to clean it all up. Suddenly, I hear voices in Rodolfo's office, and they're getting louder and louder. Of course, I recognized them.

"Mrs. Betancourt was saying that they had worked too hard to hand it over to a bigger dog, and Rodolfo was telling her it wouldn't be like that, he had an idea for them to get what they wanted without giving up what they already had. Then she says, 'This. Was. My. Dream,' all snippy-like, and Rodolfo screams, 'Which is meaningless when we can't even make payroll,' and then I heard a smack, like someone pounded on something."

"Sounds like the company is on the edge of folding. Aren't any of you worried?"

"More like scared to death, but my resume is updated and ready to go. I managed to save a couple of months' salary, and I've got friends working at several companies in the area." She picked up her slider and took another dainty nibble. "I may have to relocate, but I'm young and single."

"Still, you'd think your company would be on an upswing. All that hoopla about your fabulous invention. Even getting that, what is it called—software certifying? I don't understand why that's such an impediment, or why the company can't shell out the money to get it done. Surely, it'll pay for itself."

Alicia averted her eyes, pursing her lips and moving her plate around on the table. "Yes, absolutely."

She's hiding something, and she's not good at it. "Look, I'm not trying to be mean, here. I'm only trying to help Dev. I think you'd like to help him, too."

The young woman froze. In excruciatingly slow motion, her eyelids lifted, her chin raised, and her eyes met Peri's.

"Here's the thing," she said at last. "It doesn't really work."

CHAPTER FORTY-SEVEN

"WHAT? HOW IS that possible, with all the hype?" As soon as the words left her mouth, Peri realized their foolishness.

"I mean, it probably will work, given enough time. But at the moment, it can open channels between two non-identical devices, then it crashes."

"Can you say that in English?"

"It's like opening an app on your phone, having it log you in, then the application aborts. Every time."

"Oh, I have several of those," Peri said. "So, help me out here, Alicia. Your bosses do realize that their fab device is a dud, right?"

Alicia nodded. "They should."

"So what exactly do you think they were talking about giving to a bigger dog, or trading for something they could use?"

"It's got to be the UTran, even if it's buggy. Rodolfo still believes in it, thinks it'll work. We just have to work harder to find the error in the code. Problem is, they have no money to pay us overtime, so we spend 8 hours a day modifying, testing, modifying, testing, and going home." Alicia's fingers massaged the air to demonstrate.

Peri absorbed as much of the girl's techno-speak as she could. "Help me out here. How many of you do this modifying and testing? What is actually happening?"

"So right now, it's me, Tim, and James. We have a main file, like a Word document, only instead of words that people understand, it's got instructions that only a computer understands. Each of us has our own branch of the main file. I have the instructions for the data that goes out, James has the part for the data coming in, and Tim does what we call the protocol handshaking—getting two systems to talk in a common language." She met Peri's eyes. "Tim's the furthest along. He's much better at programming than he is at peopling."

A bad feeling crept into Peri's gut. "Tim built the part that works?"

"As far as we know, yes."

"I'm not an engineer, but why are you and James working on the input and output? Wouldn't it make sense that if you got the data out part working, you would be able to get the data in part going, too?"

"True, but it's been such a tough problem, they split it up so that two people could essentially work at the same time." Peri opened her mouth, but Alicia held her hand up. "And no, we couldn't work together on a solution. James is brilliant, at least according to him, but— difficult, if you ask me. He gets stuck on doing things his own way. Ever have to work with someone like that?"

A distinctive voice caught Peri's ear. "Miss Peri, I found you."

She glanced over to see Benny's short, round form scurrying to her table. "What's up?"

"I got something for you." He held out his hand and opened his fingers, to reveal a USB flash drive in the shape of a fat man in a tuxedo. "But you have to give it back when you're done. It's mine, from Sam."

She picked it from his palm. "That's nice, Ben, but what's on it?"

"That stuff you wanted when you went to the TV station and almost made me late for the theater."

"What? How did you get this?" She held it up, alternating her focus between her friend and his gift.

"I knew you wanted it, and I thought about all the times we got evidence."

"You didn't do anything illegal to get this, did you?"

"No, unless you count going into a room where you weren't invited and searching on a computer that isn't yours." His words sounded like sarcasm, but Peri knew better. Benny was being earnest. "I didn't steal anything. It's still there on that computer—I just copied it."

"I'd like to scold you, but I'm impressed. Thank you. I can't fault you for breaking in, even though you shouldn't have."

"Oh, I didn't break in. Sam was there to be interviewed. They are filming something about the country club, and wanted her to talk about being head chef. I just came to the station with her. It's what friends do, right?"

"Exactly." She turned to Alicia, noticing that the young girl had pushed back from the table, eyes wide and skin pale. "What's wrong, Alicia? You were the one who told me about this footage."

"I just, I—gotta go." Alicia grabbed her things as she stammered, and bolted toward the door.

Benny pointed to the young woman rushing out. "Miss Peri, shouldn't she stay?"

Peri looked at Benny and shook her head. "It's okay. She's always free to go."

CHAPTER FORTY-EIGHT

"THANKS, GARTH." PERI paid the check and rose. She looked at Benny. "I'm going to review the files on this, then take it to the police, okay? I promise to return it."

"Do I have to go with you?"

"No, I'll take it from here." She nodded toward the front door. "Let's go."

Outside, Benny stopped to pull out his retro Ray-bans, shielding his eyes from the afternoon sun. Peri followed, adjusting her own shades.

That's when she saw the car, parked at the curb. The shopping mall did not allow curb parking, apart from dropping off or picking up passengers. Nevertheless, a silver sedan with tinted windows waited to her left.

Chills rippled down her back, accelerating when she heard the sedan's engine rumble to life. It had a healthy, muscle-car quality to its sound, despite its plain exterior. Benny stepped from the curb as the car's engine signaled a change in gear, rolling forward.

Peri took his arm in a firm grip, pulling him back, and turning them both toward the door. "I forgot my receipt."

He pulled away, but walked with her. "I don't need your receipt."

Once they were inside, she dragged Benny to the corner. "Did you notice if that car was parked by the curb when you came in?"

"Oh, no, it wasn't. It followed me from the TV station, back to Sam's house, and then here."

Peri's eyes widened. "Didn't you think that was unusual?"

"Yes. But I thought I'd tell you about it if they were still here when we left." His expression was neutral, unconcerned. "They're still here."

She laughed, to avoid strangling him. "If I had to guess, I'd say whoever is in that car wants your USB, and possibly our bodies hanging from their grill."

"But why, Miss Peri?"

"Because there is something else—maybe something big—about these murders, something I still haven't put together. I'm betting that film footage will give me the missing piece." She looked around. "I was going to take this home, but I think we should go to the police station instead. We just have to find a way to get out of here safely."

"Problem?" Garth had looked up from restocking glasses behind the bar.

Peri walked over to him, keeping her voice low. "We have a situation. Basically, there's a car outside that would like to run Benny, and-or-me, over. I'd rather go to the police station, but I don't know if we can make it to either of our cars. And I don't want them coming in here to get us."

"Oh, don't worry about someone trying to cause trouble in here," he said. "We can deal with that."

"I have no doubt." She smiled and patted his shoulder, looking at the other exit, in the back of the room. "In the meantime...I wish one of us had thought to park in the back."

"No prob," Garth said, getting the attention of a cute blonde. "Shauna? Come here a minute."

Shauna, the other server on duty, walked over.

"Can you cover things for, like, ten minutes?" Garth asked. "I need to help Peri and her friend out of a jam."

"Benny Needles." Peri pointed to Benny. "He's helping me on a case."

Benny smiled and stretched himself a little taller. Garth grabbed his hand and shook it, leaving him to alternate between staring at his palm and Garth. "What are we doing, Miss Peri?"

"We are hiding from the people in the car that followed you. Garth has graciously volunteered to drive us to the police station."

Benny scowled. "I can't ride in a strange car."

"Do you have a better idea?" Peri tucked her fist against her hip, pointing the other hand toward the front door. "Because I can't leave you here to be squished by that car outside, which is what they're going to do as soon as you step off that curb."

Benny's face softened into a pout. "Well, maybe I can ride in a strange car. But I don't want to."

"I understand that. Sometimes we have to do things we don't want to do, to keep ourselves or our friends safe."

"Or our family?"

Benny. So literal. "Yes, or our family."

Garth reached under the bar and got a Dodgers baseball cap. "Let's go."

As Garth opened the door, Peri held her arm across to block him from stepping out. She peered around the doorframe at the parking lot and everywhere a car could sit, unperceived. "Seems to be clear, but would you mind driving up to the door? We'll be vulnerable in the open."

Garth loped across the lot, to a sleek ruby-colored Mustang parked strategically alone in the back. It had a husky engine noise, that advertised Quiet But Quick. He pulled alongside the bar's exit, passenger side along the curb.

"You get shotgun," she told Benny, and slipped into the back seat.

"Police station?" Garth confirmed.

"As close to the curb as you can get," Peri said.

CHAPTER FORTY-NINE

"YOU ARE DRIVING too fast." Benny tugged on his seatbelt.

Garth chuckled. "We aren't even in Drive yet, my man."

Benny looked around. "Oh. Okay. But this car looks like we'll drive too fast."

"Benny." Peri used her no-nonsense voice. "We are in a hurry. Garth will be safe."

They pulled out of the back lot, onto Palm Drive. The speed limit down this short, narrow street lined with cars was a risky 35 mph. Garth reached that speed quickly but didn't exceed it by much. As he turned right onto Bradford, she looked out the rear window.

The silver sedan was there, closing the distance.

She glanced forward, to the traffic light on Yorba Linda Boulevard. A panel van turned out of the bank parking lot on the left. Garth slowed. The van rolled into the left turn lane as the green light changed to yellow.

"Go straight." The unease in her gut pushed up to her voice. "Like, now, Garth."

The little ruby car burst forward, beating the red by the blink of an eye. Benny grabbed the console and gasped.

"Too fast!" was all he could get out.

Peri looked back and saw the sedan run the red light behind them. A round black muzzle appeared from the driver side window. "Benny, get down as low as you can. They have a gun. Garth, whatever it takes, get to the station."

"I'm getting wrinkled." Benny sat up and ran his hands down his shirt and trousers.

"Wrinkled or dead, Ben. Get down now." Peri barked hard enough to make him cower before flinging herself across the back seat.

The Mustang flew down Bradford Street, past both shopping centers, toward Valencia High School. Peri could see Garth simultaneously checking his rearview mirror, and the street ahead. Her body slid back and forth as the car roared around the corner. Centrifugal force sucked her against the leather seat, as Benny whined and fussed from his folded position, being pounded against the door.

"This is not good, Miss Peri." His high-pitched squeal barely registered with her.

"Hang on, Ben." She ransacked her brain for something to give him courage. "Pretend you're Matt Helm."

"Matt Helm would be driving."

Garth interrupted their argument. "We're on Alta Vista—which street to the station?"

"All America Way," Peri said, as explosive sound erupted in her ears, and pebbled glass rained on her. "Punch it!"

Benny screamed.

"Almost there, my man," Garth told him, and whipped the steering wheel to the right.

The car's weight swung so far left, she thought they might flip over. She pushed her feet hard to the right, in a vain attempt to keep the car from rolling, and prayed Garth's car could keep all four wheels on the road.

"Are you okay?" Benny's face peeked around the seat, at the same moment a cracking splat sound bounced from the front windshield, leaving a bullet hole.

"Get. Down." The last thing she needed was for Benny to get shot. Her body yanked upward and back, knocking the top of her head on the padded side, then immediately was thrown in the opposite direction.

"Sorry," Garth yelled, and downshifted. The car slowed, as Peri watched his hand reach for the shifter, a woodgrain knob that reminded her of the 70s. His hand was shaking.

There was a yelp of tires on pavement, and she smelled smoke from the rubber. Garth had overshot the entrance and fishtailed in an attempt to get back.

"Sorry," he repeated, and launched the car into the parking lot. "That was close."

"They still back there?" she asked.

He shook his head. "All clear."

Peri sat up and brushed the glass nuggets from her clothes. "You can sit up now, Ben. Smooth your wrinkles out."

He rose, silently preening, but Peri could feel him giving her side-eye, even if he couldn't actually see her. Garth pulled up to the Civic Center, stopping in one of the spots marked for elected officials.

"Hope I don't piss anyone off," he said, with a sly grin.

"I don't care if you do." Peri nudged Benny, who leapt from the car like it was on fire. "I am so sorry about the damage to your car. I'll pay for it, of course."

"No worries," Garth said. "That's what insurance is for."

"God, no, don't do that. Your rates will go up." She pushed the seat forward, wrestling her body from the back, before turning to him. "Are you okay?"

His smile reassured her. "I'm fine. I always wanted to be in a James Bond movie."

She laughed as she stood. "Well, that was some badass driving."

"Any time you need me again, I'm up for it." He rolled the Mustang from the parking space and cruised away.

"Why are we here?" Benny asked. "How are we going to get back to our cars?"

"Don't worry, we'll get a ride with someone." She pulled him toward the police department door. "I want you to stay safe. Besides, you can help us with this file you gave me."

"Me? I don't know anything about that file."

"No, but you notice unusual things. I think we'll have to look at this video in terms of what isn't normal."

CHAPTER FIFTY

EVELYN WAS ON duty, and gave Peri her normal glower. Peri held up her cell phone, pointed a finger at the keypad and asked, "Should I call the Chief?"

The desk clerk frowned, but admitted Peri and Benny inside the station. Benny trembled next to her. Turning to him, she whispered, "It's all good Benny. You're a hero. Chief Fletcher will thank you."

He smiled, blinking nervously, and followed her through the hallway into the Chief's office. Fletcher was at his desk, glancing from his computer monitor, to a paper, and back again.

"Sorry to interrupt," she said.

"No problem, Peri, what's up?" He turned the paper over, and clicked the screen off.

"I think we've got the video from the TV station." She pulled the USB drive from her pocket.

"Are you sure it's on that drive?"

She glanced at Benny, who had positioned himself against the wall, halfway through the doorway. "Benny, did you view this file before you copied it?"

He stared, wide-eyed, at the chief. "No. I saw a folder marked Ro-Bet and I looked at the folder and the files were all video files, and so I copied the folder."

Peri sighed. "Sorry, Chief, I wanted to review the files first, but we were being followed by a strange car."

"No, Miss Peri. We were chased and shot at and Garth drove too fast."

"When was this?"

She gave the Chief a brief explanation, and tapped the desk. "Whoever was in that car thought we have the right files, whether we do or not."

The Chief stood. "Let's go see if we've got 'em."

Jason was in his lab, flitting from a microscope to a monitor. He stopped when he saw his commanding officer enter. "Chief, I'm just finishing the evidence on the Velasco case. Got the coroner's report this morning, wanted to look it over before I wrapped it up."

"Ooh, what did Blanche say about the victim?" Peri asked.

"We'll leave the coroner's report for another time," Fletcher said. He held out the USB. "Take a look at what's on this."

"Sure." Jason plugged it into one of his computers and read the screen. "A folder called, 'Ro-Bet.' Lots of videos in it. WMVs, MP4s, looks like every video is in each format."

"Do the names of the files sound like anything?" Peri looked over his shoulder.

"Not really. They're numbered. Probably has something to do with the camera."

"Maybe the create date would give us the order," said Fletcher.

"Let's try it," Jason said, and clicked on the earliest file.

A blur of bodies appeared on the screen, muffled voices asking where they should stand. Alicia came into focus first, smiling at the camera, the glass windows of the test lab in the background. Someone walked past— Dan was approaching her, holding a clipboard. More muffled voices, until Alicia's was heard, clearly, saying, "Seriously, a clipboard? Who uses that anymore?"

"Then go get what you usually use to—do whatever it is you do," said Dan. "I want you to stand in the background and look like an engineer."

Alicia glared at him. "I don't even know what that means. 'Look like an engineer'."

"Then don't be in the background."

"I'll get my tablet," she told him. "And by the way, you're a real butthead when you're working."

Peri laughed. The three men looked at her. "What? That was funny."

The video ended, so Jason clicked on the next oldest. Tim was facing the camera, eyes wide and darting around the room, avoiding the lens. Emily entered the frame and touched his arm. He jerked away, scowling.

"Tim," she said. "Go back to work. You don't have to be on camera."

He dropped his head and stared at the ground.

Emily looked at the camera. "Dammit, turn that thing off so I can get him out of here."

"Wow," Peri said. "I noticed he was different when we met, but I've never seen camera-shy like that before."

"Is he—is he more different than me?" Benny asked.

"You're a more polite, nicer different than him," Peri said, thinking it was mostly true. "And unfortunately, he was killed yesterday."

"Oh, that's too bad." Benny shuffled from one foot to the next. "Because I would not like to be in a video, either."

Her conscience gave her a pinch. "I'm sorry that I spoke ill of Tim. I was trying to make an observation about him, and it sounded harsh."

"Look at that man in the suit." Benny pointed to the monitor, where Jason was playing the next file. The camera had zoomed in on Rodolfo and Alicia. At the right side of the frame, there was a man in the lab behind them, wearing a clean suit.

"What about him?" Peri asked.

"He has nasty fingernails." Benny held up his right hand. "I have manicures now. Sam and I go together. See how smooth my nails are?"

She pointed. "Pause it. Jason, is there any way to zoom in on those hands?"

"Yeah, but it may not be the greatest resolution." He sat at the keyboard and worked his magic, until an enlarged screen shot popped up.

Peri sat next to him, nose to the screen, studying. The hand was fuzzy, but she could see the nails were long and yellow. It was like Art's hand, and yet something seemed off. She ran her own nails through her hair, feeling them scratch against her scalp.

"Can you identify the man?" Fletcher asked.

"Wish I could." She shook her head. "Art Gibbons has nails very similar to this guy's, but there's something that's not the same. I mean, maybe it's the angle, and it really is him, but I recall his fingers being longer and bonier."

Jason pressed "play" again and they watched the action. The man in the suit reached into a pocket and pulled something small from it, which he stuck in the side of the nearest computer. He took off his other glove and typed on the screen.

"Jason could you enlarge—" Peri began.

"Forget it, Peri." Jason paused the video and pointed. "I can't get the resolution, and the screen is angled, which would distort the letters even more."

"You're right." She tapped her fingers on the table. "I'm grasping at anything."

CHAPTER FIFTY-ONE

"I'M NOT EVEN sure what this shows us, or what we're looking for," Fletcher said. "What does this have to do with the two murder cases?"

"I don't know, but there's got to be a connection. Tressa wanted the UTran, and was buttering up Dev to get it. Dev wanted her tricks of the trade, so he was doing an equal amount of buttering. Alicia told me today that the UTran doesn't work—the only part that is working is the software Tim wrote. And now he's dead."

"The gizmo doesn't even work?" Fletcher stepped back, mouth open. "What about all the hoopla? The news articles? Interviews?"

"All fabulous hype, and the company owners are seemingly frantic to make the dream come true." Peri told him what Alicia had said. "Is Art still at the station?"

Fletcher shook his head. "He was on his way to a hotel with one of our officers, and slipped away. Got a BOLO on him. We're trying to get a warrant to track his phone."

Peri rubbed her neck. "Phone...you still have Tressa's phone, don't you? Maybe she has that app that lets you share your location with family and friends."

"Great idea, Peri." Jason jumped from his chair and rushed to the table holding Tressa's belongings.

"Wait." Fletcher held his hand up. "I'm not certain of the legality. If we need a warrant to access his phone's GPS, we could need one to access it through a third party app."

"Damn," Jason said, and sat down.

"Unless…" Peri strolled to the table. "Unless you got the information somehow, without accessing it yourselves."

The Chief's eyes narrowed. "What's that supposed to mean?"

She'd found the phone and picked it up. Three taps later, she was in the app.

"Oops, I accidentally found Art Gibbons. Want to know where he is?" She held her finger in the air, poised for one more tap.

"No." Fletcher glared at her. "Yes. But no. This is why I hate working with PIs. They encourage boundary-crossing."

"Not crossing. Maybe stretching." She looked at the phone. "I want his location—and you're not the boss of me."

"Peri, don't be a child—"

She pressed the button. A map appeared, with a stationary blue dot. *Temecula, how interesting.* A few more taps, and the screen cleared.

"Well," Jason said. "Aren't you going to tell us?"

"In the spirit of keeping the PPD a law-abiding force, no." She turned to Benny, who was standing by the door. "Let me call Skip and see if he can come get us."

"I called Sam. She will pick me up. I do not want to be here."

She noted his cross expression. "I'm sorry, I've been ignoring you. I was so involved in these clues—clues that you noticed first. Thank you, Ben."

His frown relaxed a little, to more of a sulk. It did not appear to be working toward a smile, so Peri knew better than to ask him if Sam could drop her off at Brian's, even though Benny was getting a ride. She pulled her phone out and called Skip. It rang a couple of times before she heard the lab door open and a low, dulcet voice.

"What's up?" Skip walked in the door, holding his phone. He glanced at Fletcher, who was talking quietly to Jason, then back at her. "I just wanted to review a few things with the Chief. And you?"

"Studying evidence, looking for clues, same old same old." She hugged him. "Could you give me a ride to Brian's to pick up my car?"

"Why is your car at Brian's?"

Uh-oh. Fessing up to Skip was never easy. "I was meeting Alicia there, Benny joined us, and someone following Benny tried to run us over and take a flash drive away."

"Peri—"

"First of all, it was not my fault, and second…it wasn't my fault. At least I knew to run to the police as soon as they started chasing us—I mean, Benny. They were chasing Benny."

She felt his body stiffen as they hugged, before his arms squeezed her closer. "I'll be so glad when this thing with your brother is over, and we can relax."

Something about his phrasing sounded unusual to her. "Oh? Are 'we' going to relax?"

Skip smiled. "We can talk about it while I take you back to your car."

His hand on her back guided her out of the lab and down the hall to the entrance. Benny scampered along behind them, the heels of his Italian loafers clicking frenetically. Peri barely had time to dig her sunglasses from her tote. A bright red Kia Soul sat in the front row of the civic center parking lot, Sam Hollis leaning against the passenger door.

The young woman acknowledged the trio with a wave.

Peri waved back, and turned to Benny. "Thank you again, for all your help. You're a good assistant. I'll call you as soon as I need—that is, as soon as I write up a schedule for you."

He smiled mechanically, but she saw the worry in him. Was he still wondering if he could be a good assistant and a good friend? *I can't worry about his issues right now.*

She paused at Skip's black SUV to watch Benny shuffle to Sam's car before hopping into the passenger seat.

"To Brian's," she said as Skip backed out of the parking space and headed north.

CHAPTER FIFTY-TWO

"SO, HOW ARE we relaxing?" she asked.

"I'm amazed." Skip shook his head but kept his eyes on the road. "You actually waited until we pulled out of the parking lot before the cross-examination began."

"I'm considerate that way."

He chuckled. "I've been thinking, Doll. Running numbers, talking to Katie."

"Katie?"

"The investment gal at my pension fund."

Peri sat up straight. *Was he going to say—that?* "And?"

"And." He took a large breath. "I've decided to retire after my disability time runs out."

She froze, staring at him, while a mad race of thoughts tore through her mind, trying to fit his retirement into some organized slot in her life.

"So? What do you think?"

"Umm…" She tried to find something benign to say, to buy her time, like when she told Benny his ugly Matt Helm turtleneck really looked like he was channeling his inner Dino. *Damn. I got nuthin'.* "You've been thinking about this for a while?"

"I have."

"It's just—you never mentioned it, so I'm a little surprised."

He was silent as they turned the corner onto Bradford Street. Peri thought about her earlier drive down this route, being followed by that sedan, barreling through the stoplight, trying not to get shot. The click of the turn signal brought her back, her body taut.

"I don't know why I didn't talk to you about it," he said at last. "Maybe because I didn't want to put one more thing on your heaping plate of Things That Might Happen. Maybe I wasn't ready to talk about it until I was ready to do it."

"Or maybe you were afraid I wouldn't get on board with it?"

"Maybe." His jaw clenched, in that way she knew. "But, I mean, you didn't ask my opinion when you left your job."

"You mean the PI business that you've been trying to get me to leave for five years now?"

"Peri, don't be like that."

"Like what? Like a woman who'd like to talk things over with her partner? I'm hurt, Skip. I know nothing about your plans, how Katie decided you could afford it, nothing." She paused, waiting for her inevitable angry-tears, but none came. "Is your house truly still on the market?"

"Stop it. I tell you everything."

"Really?"

"Almost everything. Look, I'm sorry if you feel left out, but it's really my business, whether I feel like I can still do the job."

"God, I hate that. 'Sorry if you feel,' that's no apology. Man up to it. You feel no remorse for not telling me. You're only sorry that I'm mad about it."

"Well, of course I am!"

"And that makes me mad on top of mad." Her eyes burned, yet no tears fell.

He pulled into the parking lot, sped to the back row, and braked hard, parking behind her rental car. "I'm sorry for that, too."

She opened the door, facing her car. "I didn't say I had to give my permission for you to retire—or that I even wanted to. But if I can't be your sounding board now, how are we even going to talk when we get married?"

As she stepped down to the pavement, she heard his guttural, "C'mon, Peri."

She stopped his words with a motion from her outstretched palm, and went to the driver's side of her car, digging into her tote for the keys. Her hand trembled as she unlocked the door. Sliding into the seat, she slammed her door shut, fed the key into the ignition, and revved the engine. A moment later, she glanced up at the rearview mirror.

He was gone.

She looked at the steering wheel, and her paste-white knuckles. Her eyes still stung, and now they were blurry. The tears ran at last. She allowed herself a few sobs, before taking a deep breath, wiping her face, and reining it all in with a shake of her head.

I hate crying.

She heard her phone jingling and retrieved it from her bag. Maybe it was Skip, calling to apologize, but it wasn't.

"I never do this, but I've got info on both murders." Blanche's voice was as soft as it could be and still be heard. "Bring the chocolate. I got the wine."

"You are a godsend," Peri said.

"You sound like you've been crying. What's up?"

"I'll tell you when I get there. I'll be bringing a lot of chocolate."

The throaty laughter of her BFF immediately lifted her spirits. Several bags of dark chocolate-covered nuts and berries later, she sprinted back to her car and pointed it toward the Debussy home in Yorba Linda. The wide green boulevards and gently rolling hills calmed her nerves, so that she pulled into their immense drive feeling comfortably numb.

The wine can take it from here.

CHAPTER FIFTY-THREE

PERI LET HERSELF into the Debussy house, kicked off her shoes and wandered toward the kitchen, calling as she went.

"Beebs? You in the wine cellar?"

Blanche was in the kitchen, peeling the foil from a bottle of Sangiovese. "Crazy woman, we don't have a cellar."

Peri held a bag high in her right hand, left hand extended for a wine glass. "I seek to barter these humble goods, for a glass of heaven's nectar."

Blanche poured two glasses, while Peri emptied her chocolate treats into a divided bowl.

"Chocolate covered almonds, chocolate covered shortbread, and chocolate covered ah-kie, a-say, whatever berries," Peri said as she worked. "How do you pronounce that?"

"Ah-sigh-ee." Blanche popped one in her mouth.

"Gesundheit." Peri picked up the bowl and nodded toward the patio. "You get the wine."

The two friends made their way to a pair of substantial cedar Adirondack chairs. Peri popped a chocolate-covered almond and felt the rich dark coating melt against her tongue, while the crunch of the nut between her teeth was satisfying. She followed it with a sip of wine, enjoying the tart cherry tones of the Italian grape.

"Wine any good?" Blanche asked.

"Works for me."

"So, girlfriend." Blanche held her glass almost to her lips. "What's got you all upset?"

Peri watched her friend drink, and took a long sip herself. "It shouldn't be anything, but it seems to be something. Skip just told me he's going to retire now."

"Great. He can hang around with the construction crew while you chill at my place."

"Yeah, but he discussed it with the Chief, with his financial advisor, and pulled papers before he even told me."

"Okay, that's not great. Any excuse?"

"Depending upon your viewpoint, either he figured if I didn't discuss quitting my business with him, he didn't have to return the favor, or he was afraid I'd try to talk him out of it." She picked at a cookie. "Does Paul discuss retirement with you?"

"Yes, but when he starts trying to tell me about some pension factor that is applied to his monthly income, and medical insurance, yadda yadda, my eyes glaze over." Blanche folded her legs into the spacious seat. "He should've told you first, and he didn't. You know he loves you, right? Throw a wine glass against the wall, and move on."

Peri chuckled. "You're right, I'll forgive him. I just need some time to be mad."

"Justifiably so. Now, want to hear the latest news from the slab?"

"Absolutely."

Blanche took another long sip of wine, and began her clinical recitation. "Female victim, one Tressa Velasco, 42, died of exsanguination, sometime between 1 and 2 am, on Monday. TOD was determined using internal temperature and assumes no external factors that would slow or quicken decomp.

"Twenty-five stab wounds, two of which are significant, one in the upper thigh which nicked the femoral artery, and the carotid above the clavicle. All wounds on the front of the body, all deep enough to suggest there was no hesitation, and several defensive wounds on the victim's hands.

"Good," Peri said. "I mean, it lets Dev off the hook. His RA is so bad, he couldn't wrap his fingers around a knife and plunge it into a body."

Blanche nodded. "Sounds right."

"How about Tim Neal?"

"Male, 27, he's more interesting." She leaned in. "Guess what killed him?"

"From what I saw, it looked like his head was bashed in."

"Nope." Blanche smiled. "Gunshot."

Peri sat forward. "Before or after the beating?"

"Before, mostly. A few bruises about the shoulders and forehead, indicating bleeding below the skin. But I found a small caliber bullet that had blown through the base of the brain and got stuck in the roof of his mouth. The rest of the pummeling appears to be an attempt to confuse COD." She chuckled. "As if."

"So, from the base of the brain…" Peri traced along her head, from the back toward the roof of her mouth. "The killer's gun was pointed up?"

"Yes, ma'am. Police are looking for a short guy with a gun. They already have the baseball bat."

"There's enough to point to the bat specifically?"

Blanche nodded. "Splinters in the wound, specific shape to each blow."

"Wow." Peri relaxed back into the chair. Her friend's backyard twinkled, lights strung across the fence, the patio, and the trees. "I should get some of these fairy lights for my new backyard."

"How's the reno coming?"

"Noisy. Everyone's trying to do a good job, then get outta my hair, and I'm trying not to be a bitch about things." She turned to her friend. "God, I want it to be over."

"Soon, my dear. Why isn't Skip doing some of the babysitting? He's still on disability."

"Yeah…I should ask him to do it."

"Ask? Is this your house alone, or do you both own it?"

"I guess I feel like I'm protecting him still. He was shot, in a coma, and I couldn't help him—at all."

Blanche patted her arm. "Maybe he doesn't want to be babied. Maybe he wants to be in the house, supervising stuff."

"God, I'm an idiot." Peri sat up and slapped her own forehead. "I'm all cranky about Skip's retirement, but I haven't kept him in the loop about the house. I'm not treating him like a partner, why should he return the favor?"

"I wouldn't call you an idiot." Blanche laughed. "Maybe a gal with good intentions."

"On a highway to hell."

A male voice interrupted them. "Why is there only a stairway to heaven?"

"A matter of meeting demand." Peri looked over her shoulder. "Hey, Paul."

Blanche's husband leaned in and kissed his wife. Peri got a small hug before he gathered a handful of cookies. "What's new?"

"Just talking about my brother's case and the latest victim," Peri said.

"What was that product you were talking about last time I saw you?" he asked.

"Universal translator, from Ro-Bet Engineering, LLC." She reached over and poured herself another splash of wine, before filling Blanche's glass. "Seems to be universally desired, but I found out it doesn't even work."

"Really? I didn't hear that." Paul stepped inside and came out with his own glass. "I heard there's a bidding war for exclusive rights to it."

"Like, for delivery now?" Peri asked.

"I believe so." He sampled the berries, then opted for the nuts. "What's for dinner?"

"Whatever Tlaquepaque is serving," Blanche told him. "We're going out tonight, remember?"

He appeared confused. "Oh, yeah."

Blanche watched him disappear into the house. "We don't really have plans. I just tell him that sometimes. Every once in a while I get lucky and he thinks he's forgotten."

"You're bad." Peri laughed. "I better go, if you're gonna change in time to make your reservations."

"True, I'd better hurry, or they'll give our table away." She stretched, a deadpan expression on her face, and picked up the bowl of chocolates. "Want to take these home? I don't want to eat all of them, and the kids are gone."

"Give them to Paul, with my compliments. Poor guy."

CHAPTER FIFTY-FOUR

"YOU NEED TO slow down." It was Skip's thirtieth warning within the last thirty minutes. "The Embassy Suites is not going to disappear."

"But Art might." Peri adjusted her body against the driver's seat, while pressing down on the accelerator. "We're still 45 minutes from Temecula."

"What exactly do you think Art might tell us?" Skip asked.

She could feel his eyes on her. "I want to know why Tim was at Art's house. I want to know how well Art and Dev know each other, and what Art's relationship with Tressa was really like. I want to stop feeling like I'm clueless."

"You want a lot, don't you?"

It was almost 7 a.m. when she pulled into the parking lot. She cruised the grounds, studying the cars.

"Are we sure that Gibbons drove his own car down here?" Skip asked.

She smiled. "No idea, but he drives a Mercedes Series E coupe."

"Metallic red, no less."

"Yeah, why does he care what we—oh, look, there it is—back corner."

"Hmpf," Skip snorted. "Parked across two spots."

"Jerk," she said as she drove past, stopped, and turned her car to back into the half-spot next to his.

"Peri—" Skip's voice sounded cautionary.

"I'm being careful." She slowly maneuvered into the space, focused on keeping her fender away from his car. Smiling, she quoted one of Skip's favorite movies. "I'm an *excellent* driver."

"Just concentrate on not scraping that work of art next to us."

Within a few minutes, they were parked, a slim inch or two of space between them and Art's vehicle.

"Now what, Filly Marlowe?" Skip asked.

"Very funny. Either we sit here and wait for Art to come out, or one of us sits here and the other goes into the hotel to flush out the quarry." She turned to face him. "What would you recommend?"

He looked out over the lot, up at the hotel, from corner to corner. "What I recommend is that we pull up into that space ahead." He nodded toward an empty space across from Art's car. "We lay low, wait for Art to come out. When he tries to leave, we block his exit."

"Isn't that illegal?"

"No, we do it all the time."

She stared at him. "Police do it all the time. Are we the police?"

"I am."

"You're on disability. Won't we get into trouble, what is it called, unlawful restraint or something?"

"I still have my gold shield. And we won't hold him permanently, just until he answers our questions."

"Maybe it's false imprisonment."

"Not if you're. In. Law. Enforcement." Each word barked at her.

She shrugged. "Which, his lawyers could argue, is questionable, as you're not on active duty."

"Well, your plan isn't that brilliant, either." He motioned to the sliver of space between his door and Art's car. "How am I supposed to get out? And what keeps him from seeing your car and running?"

She considered his words. "You're right. You can't run yet, so I'd have to chase him."

Once she had backed into the new space across from the Mercedes, she heard Skip sigh. "Don't be a ninny," she said. "I wasn't going to hit him."

"Mm-hm." He unhooked his seatbelt and adjusted the seat back. "You get first watch."

"First watch? Are we going to just stay here until he comes out? What if he doesn't come out today? Or tomorrow?"

"How long has it been since you've done surveillance? This is the job."

"Don't get snooty. I know how to sit and watch. I just want answers. Don't you?"

He nodded, and looked at his watch. "Tell you what. It's 7:30 now. Checkout's at noon. If he's not out here by 12:30, one of us will go in and get him."

"Okay. That's a good idea. I'll take the first shift."

She took a sip of her coffee, and settled back. Skip's eyes were already closed. He was able to take quick naps, wherever and whenever.

The sun was still behind the hotel, which was good. Temecula in June could be a dress rehearsal for Hell. Peri knew people who lived here and loved it. They also had solar panels to offset the air-conditioning costs. The saving grace of visiting her friends here was that she usually stopped at one of the many wineries.

Sacrifices must be made.

She was trying to remember which one served the fine sherry—it was Monty-something, or Mount Something—when a familiar face approached from the hotel's exit.

"Skip." She nudged him.

He was wide awake in a split-second. "We got him?"

"Nine o'clock." She didn't turn her head, but slunk down behind the steering wheel.

Skip also stayed down in the passenger seat. They watched Art walk toward his car, glancing behind and around him, still cautious.

"Okay, timing is everything here," Skip said in a soft yet commanding voice. "When he gets into his car, you start the engine and pull across to block him. I'll get out and keep him from running."

Peri nodded, her heart pounding with adrenalin. Art was at the end of the aisle, approaching his car. He reached in his pocket, withdrew his phone, and pushed a few buttons. The Mercedes let out a soft rumble as its engine started.

"Oh, crap," she said. "He's got remote start."

Skip was calm. "Just wait. When he gets in his car, we'll cut him off."

Art walked around to his driver's side door and opened it. A police siren screamed down Rancho California Road, causing him to jerk his head up and look around. He made eye contact with Peri.

"Oh, crap," she said.

Art turned and sprinted toward the hotel, leaving the Mercedes' door ajar. Skip and Peri leapt out to give chase. Skip ran, limping, towards the hotel, attempting to cut off Art's path, but Peri had another idea.

She ran back to the Mercedes and hopped in, driving it around the aisles to catch up to Art. As she drove past him, she slowed enough for him to see his car being taken for a joy ride.

"Hey." He raised his hands and ran toward her.

She pulled over to the curb and lowered the passenger side window. "Want to go for a little jaunt, Art?"

Skip caught up to them, rubbing his leg. He went to the driver's side and knocked on the window. "Really? Grand theft auto was a better plan?"

She glanced at him, and returned to Art. "Skip's not here to take you in, and I'm just a PI. All we want to do is talk. Have you had breakfast? There's a great place close by."

Art scowled at her, but there was a trace of fear when he saw Skip staring at him from over the roof. "Can I at least drive my own car?"

"Get in," Peri told him, patting the passenger seat. "I'm an *excellent* driver."

CHAPTER FIFTY-FIVE

SKIP FOLLOWED IN Peri's car, and five minutes later, they were pulling into the lot at Annie's Café. Peri unfolded herself from the seat of the coupe, as Art stood and glanced from the restaurant to his car, and back.

"Come on, Art." Peri walked around and patted him firmly on the shoulder. As she spoke, she encouraged him forward, toward the front door. "It's a cup of coffee. Maybe some pancakes. Do you like English breakfast? They've got a killer English breakfast, real proper with the beans and tomatoes."

Before he could argue, they were inside and seated. Once they'd ordered food and three steaming mugs of coffee were delivered, Peri leaned forward.

"How'd it all happen? At your house, I mean."

Art sat ramrod straight, bringing his mug of coffee up to his lips, tasting, and setting it on the table for more cream and sugar. Peri sized him up as she inhaled the aroma of her own cup. Still with the over-corrected posture, the properness of drinking, the blank expression on his face. He looked paler, if that was possible, and even leaner. Skeletal.

Nodding at Skip, she turned to Art and softened her voice. "Tressa's death is hard, huh?"

235

His posture collapsed as he bent over his coffee, one trembling hand covering his forehead.

"Care to talk about it?" Skip asked, scooting his chair a little closer.

"No one understood why we were together." He threw the words out, as if he didn't care. "They thought she was in it for the money. I have money, old money. Inheritance."

"I had no idea," Peri said.

He shrugged, pausing as the waitress delivered their breakfasts, before continuing. "Something people don't understand about north Orange County. There's quiet money, extraordinary wealth, in the commonest of homes. Something else people didn't understand—Tressa loved me, before the inheritance."

He looked up at Skip and Peri, as if daring them to argue.

"I believe she did, Art." Peri kept her voice soft.

"When she was found in that room...the way she was found...I didn't know what to think. I always trusted her, then suddenly I'm in an interrogation room and they're making it sound like Tressa was this horrible person. She wasn't horrible."

"Maybe they didn't understand why she learned other companies' secrets and brought them to Howard Aerospace," Peri said.

"Exactly." Art nodded. "She was loyal to the company, always. Wanted them to succeed."

"And she deserved to be compensated for that."

"Yeah, the money..." He brushed back a tear. "The money wasn't about greed. It was for me. She constantly told me she wanted to be an equal partner, a real contributor, to our marriage. I told her it wasn't necessary, that my wealth was inherited, so it didn't really count. But she was driven to give me as much as I'd given her."

He bowed his head, weeping softly. Peri gathered a forkful of biscuits and gravy, and looked at Skip, unsure of where to go next. Skip gave her a small nod, taking the next turn, and gently patted Art on the shoulder.

"Sounds like it's been difficult for you," he said.

Art sighed. "You have no idea."

"We found some things at your house. Alicia Duarte's phone number, and a Ro-Bet company ID for Tim Neal with your picture on it. Were you trying to help Tressa get the UTran?"

He looked down at his meal, pushing his eggs around the plate. "Tressa wanted the UTran, badly. I guess you could say it was her dying wish. I thought maybe I could get the device for HAC's use, in honor of her memory. We went to school with Dev, but he wasn't budging. I knew Tim from UCI, so I thought perhaps he could help me get a copy of it. He was…not anxious…to help. My next plan was to call Alicia and offer her a better job with a raise to join my team."

"In exchange for the device," Skip said.

"How did Tim happen to be at your house?" Peri asked.

"I invited Tim over," Art said. "I was going to try to talk him into selling me an exclusive to the UTran."

"What did he say?" Skip asked.

"Said it didn't work. Said his portion of the code was the only thing functioning, but he hoped Alicia and James would get their stuff running soon."

"Did he happen to say how the work was going? Like, was success likely?" Peri asked. "And whose hard work would make it possible?"

"He said Alicia's code was tricky stuff. Determining the length of the data streams, parsing their contents. But he thought she'd make the breakthrough before James ever got his part written and tested."

"Because...?" Peri asked.

"Because, in Tim's opinion, James is a slacker. Very secretive about his work, argues when you tell him his stuff has errors, disappears for hours at a time, and is completely defensive at any hint of criticism."

"So what happened when he got there?" Skip asked.

Art looked at his breakfast, and put his fork down. "I invited Tim inside. I tried to talk him into selling, but he wouldn't budge. We were arguing in the kitchen, and I heard noise out by the pool, like someone screaming. I ran out to see what's going on, when my phone buzzed me. An unknown ID sent me a text, saying to get out of the house."

She nodded. "Okay, then what?"

He paused, lowering his increasingly shaky voice. "I started hearing loud voices coming from inside, Tim and someone else. Then...scuffling and something breaking, like china. I was on my way in, to break it up, when I heard a gunshot. I ran to the garage, jumped in the coupe, and drove away."

CHAPTER FIFTY-SIX

SKIP HELD HIS hand out. "Can I see the text?"

Art took out his phone, touched the screen a few times, and gave it to the detective. Skip studied it, while Peri tried to lean over far enough to join him.

"Here." He shoved it at her.

Smiling, she took it. "Thanks."

The text was more or less as Art remembered it. She touched the name Unknown Caller, and the phone gave her more details, including the calling number. It looked familiar, so she took out her own phone and plugged the number into the keypad. A name came up.

"Well, whaddya know, my favorite person."

Looking at Skip, she showed him the screen. The number belonged to Officer Peter Darden. Skip glanced at it, looked at Peri and raised an eyebrow. "Fullerton?"

"What a jackass." She scowled. "I'm glad, at least, it wasn't someone I like."

Skip turned to Art. "Thanks for talking with us. It's not easy to know who to trust. Think you can go to the Placentia Police Department, make a report?"

The pale man nodded.

Skip took out a business card and a pen. "This is Detective Logan's number. Tell them you'll only talk to him. He'll take care of you. And don't tell anyone else where you are or where you're going."

Art gave him a wan smile. "Who would I tell? I've got nobody left."

"I'm so sorry, Art," Peri said.

He sat upright, placing his palm on the table. "I'll do what I can to help catch the bastard."

Peri smiled. "So will we."

Art pulled his wallet from his back pocket, but Skip held up his hand. "Don't worry about this. We'll get the bill."

"Consider it payment for the information," Peri said. "And for letting me drive your car. It's a beauty."

"I didn't have much of a choice. But thank you for the breakfast." He rose, adjusted his collar, and walked out.

Skip turned to Peri. "What have we got so far? We should start putting these pieces together."

"On the big picture, we've got two murders." She took a small notebook and pen from her tote. Tapping the pen against her chin, she stared across the room, at a painting of an idyllic country picnic. "Two very gruesome murders. I mean, they both look like rage killings, and yet there was a specific setup, and misleading evidence. Who does that?"

"A guy who's had a long time to hone his anger."

"A guy? Are we sure?"

Skip shrugged. "Statistically, yes."

"Okay…they seem to be related to a magical device that may or may not work."

"I think a trip back to the engineering firm is needed." Skip pointed to the notebook, so she wrote it down.

"Probably, but who is telling the truth and who isn't? Alicia and Tim say it doesn't work. Rodolfo gets up in front of cameras and says it does." She tapped the pen again, this time against the table. "Tressa gave those photos to Dev, which led us to the video, but no one can figure out what the video is showing us—and why is someone trying to nail Dev for these crimes?"

"Maybe if Dev saw the film, he could decipher it."

She rolled her eyes. "So simple, I should've thought of it."

"Well, Doll, you're not used to getting answers from your brother."

Smiling, she reached over to squeeze his hand. "We've got three things to do—visit Ro-Bet, show Dev the film, and question Officer Darden. What's first?"

"How about if we divide and conquer?"

"Okay, you visit Ro-Bet and I show Dev the film, then we interview Darden together?"

"Actually, I was thinking, you visit Ro-Bet, I show Dev the film, and we let Logan interview Darden."

"Logan? And why are *you* talking to Dev?"

"First of all, I know Darden's general type—young, insecure about his job but too proud to say so. Logan outranks him. Even if he hates it, he's going to talk to him."

"You're right, but I still wish I could be there to see him squirm."

"Of course you do, but karma is just as tasty when it's delivered by someone else. Trust me."

"I guess so." She rubbed his arm. "But Dev?"

"Because you're his little sister." Skip leaned over and kissed her forehead.

Her smile vanished. "I wish I could argue with that."

CHAPTER FIFTY-SEVEN

SKIP AGREED TO meet Peri's brother at Brian's. Dev had refused several locations, from his house, to various coffee shops, and especially the police department. As long as he showed up, Skip didn't care. The detective sat at the tall bartop in the corner, his back to the wall, watching everyone come in and go out.

His appointment strolled in, looking around the room. Skip put his hand up, index finger in the air. The small motion got Dev's attention, and he wandered to the table, yawning as if this meeting was already boring.

Shauna appeared beside them to take their order.

"Shauna, this is Peri's brother, Dev."

Dev flinched at the introduction, but grinned and shook her hand. "Shauna, Peri's mentioned you. She says this is one of her favorite hangouts, because you give her such great service."

The pretty blonde smiled. Skip watched, stone-faced. After they ordered and she walked away, he stared at Dev.

"Smooth, Chief. I can see why you're in marketing."

Dev's smile slipped back into his normal, sour expression.

"I do what I have to, when I have to do it."

"Why can't you ever do that for your sister? What does it cost you?"

"She knows the real me. If I tried anything, she'd call b.s."

Skip shook his head. "What was it about your family that stuck in your craw so hard, it turned you into a jackass?"

Dev glared at him. "My family is none of your business. Now, what did you want to show me?"

Skip slid his tablet toward Dev. "Those photos Tressa gave you—turns out, they're still shots from this video."

"So?"

"So the police have watched this, I've watched it, and no one can figure out why it's important." He pressed Play. "It seems to hinge on that person in the white suit."

Dev watched the video, while Skip watched him. Just as with Skip's introduction of him, there was a small flinch.

"Want to talk about what's going on?" he asked.

"I wasn't at work that day. Rodolfo had scheduled a couple of calls for me to take, in person."

Skip nodded. "Can you tell who's in the white suit, or what they might be doing?"

"I told you, I wasn't there."

He pressed Play again. "Look at the person in white. Is there anything about them—their posture, their height, their hands—that looks familiar?"

Dev watched it again, and shook his head. "I don't know what you want me to say. I wasn't there. I couldn't be sure."

"Goddammit, Dev, I'm not asking you to pick a guy out of a lineup. I want the name of someone it *might* be, someone to focus on."

Shauna arrived to deliver two pints. "Can I get you some waters?"

Skip shook his head no, but Dev's smile lit the dark corner.

"Thank you, Shauna, that would be delightful."

Skip sat back on his bar stool. "I should've let them put your ass in jail and toss the key."

"What is your problem, *Skip*?" He spat the name, mocking him. "I wasn't there. I've got nothing to tell."

The detective stared, silent. Dev drank and looked at the baseball game on the large TV above them.

"I've been a detective for fifteen years," Skip said at last. "In law enforcement almost thirty. I got good at reading people, finding their tell, that thing they do or say when they're lying. You've got a little twitch to your shoulder. You didn't twitch when you said you weren't there. When you said you got nothing to tell, yep, twitch.

"Here's the thing, Dev buddy—we are going to catch this guy, because the clues are all there, and we're getting closer. He doesn't like you, for some reason. Keeps trying to pin the murders on you. What do you think he'll do when we get him? I think he'll drag you in as a co-conspirator. He'll have just enough proof, and the D.A. is going to look at whether you cooperated with law enforcement, and think, well, he didn't exactly help us catch the guy, so, yeah, maybe he was in on the whole thing."

Dev put his beer down and stared at Skip, eyes widening.

Skip leaned in and growled, "And if you call Peri and beg for her help, I swear I will take my badge off long enough to punch you repeatedly in the face."

Dev sat back, his hand slipping away from his glass, his breath quickening. He nodded to the tablet. "One more time."

The video replayed, until he said, "Stop it there."

Skip paused the replay, and let Dev pick up the tablet and study the frame closer. "If we need to, our lab tech can enhance the still."

"No." He shook his head and handed the tablet back, pointing to the image. "That's James' hand."

"Peoples?"

He nodded. "His nails are always manicured, but a little long. They look like claws. I asked him about them once. He told me, 'that's the way all the rich guys do their nails.'"

"Thanks for helping." The words burned Skip's throat as he said them. "And by the way, you're wrong about your relationship with Peri being none of my business. I'm marrying her. Seeing the woman I love in pain because her jackass brother doesn't even like her enough to send her a Christmas card, that's very much my business."

"Look, you want me to say that I'll try to be a better brother, and I'd like to say it, just to get you off my back. But it's something she's going to have to accept. We weren't close as kids, we didn't bond over our parents' deaths, we're not close now."

"But why not?"

"I didn't like being raised by hippies."

"Peri calls them beatniks," Skip said.

"Whatever, I wanted to call them Mom and Dad and have a curfew and rules and boundaries—and normal clothes. Proper button-down shirts, pressed slacks. No Birkenstocks."

"Okay, fair enough. But at some point, don't you look at your family and think, that's the way they wanted to do it, and now I do it differently, and it's all right?"

Dev turned away from him, scowling.

"Really? You're how old, and can't accept your parents for who they were?"

"Leave it alone, Skip."

"More important, you're going to hold some kind of lifelong grudge against Peri, all because she didn't hate your folks?"

"I'm warning you." A flush of crimson rose, from his neck, around his ears, to his cheeks.

"Warning me? Against what?"

Dev opened his mouth, took a breath, and slid off the barstool. "Look, I don't expect you to understand. Or Peri. Things are the way they are. Am I free to go, Detective?"

Skip nodded, so he turned and headed out the door.

"I'm guessing you're ready for the bill." Shauna was at his side.

"Thanks." He reached for his wallet.

She looked toward the exit. "Peri's brother is an…unusual guy."

Skip smiled. "Yes, he is."

"He's a salesman, isn't he?"

"Is it obvious?"

"Oh please," she laughed. "All the compliments, calling me by name all the time. I see through that act."

Skip filled in the credit slip and gave it to her. "Yeah, it is an act."

He got up and walked out the door, into the still-bright late afternoon sun. Dev was right. Peri would see through him if he tried his salesman act on her. Her brother didn't want to be her brother—it was that simple.

I'll just have to be there whenever she feels the emptiness of that.

CHAPTER FIFTY-EIGHT

BY THE TIME Peri walked into Ro-Bet, the police had released the news that it was Tim Neal, not Art Gibbons, who was murdered.

"Dammit," she mumbled as she took the elevator. "Couldn't they have waited until I'd interviewed the employees one more time?"

Emily was not at her desk, so she knocked on Rodolfo's door.

"Come in."

Peri was surprised by his appearance. He was still dressed to the nines, but his face was haggard, his eyes sunken.

"I apologize," he said. "I've just had to deliver devastating news."

"Tim, I know," she replied. "I'd reschedule this if I could, but—"

"No, no." He offered her a seat. "Whatever we can do to help catch Tim's killer."

"I'm sure you understand, the police think the murders of Tressa Velasco and Tim are connected." Peri sat, smoothing her chinos. "I think they somehow revolve around the UTran."

He straightened a stack of papers. "We may have designed a groundbreaking device, but I hardly think it's worth killing over."

"To you and me, probably not. Could I ask you a sensitive question?"

"Certainly." He smiled.

"Does the UTran work or not?"

Still smiling, he cocked his head. "Whatever do you mean?"

"I've seen the video proclaiming its wonders, I've heard rumors that there's a bidding war for it, once it's certified. I've also heard, from other sources, that it's not working yet." She leaned forward. "Frankly, I don't care, except in the context of who might have murdered for it— either to get their hands on it, or prevent it from being sold, or..."

Rodolfo threw his hands up. "I hope you don't suspect me. My engineers tell me it's complete and working, except for the certification testing."

"Which engineers?"

He walked over to a file cabinet, pulled out a large folder, and placed it on the desk, in front of Peri.

"Here. According to the status reports, all teams. reported being on schedule for completion two weeks ago." He opened the folder and pointed to the papers on top. "This is their final report. Everything is done."

Peri paged through the report, which was filled with spreadsheets. Funny words ran down the side of each page, with dates across the top. Numbers filled in the boxes. She pointed to one. "Could you decipher this?"

"Oh, so sorry." He leaned over her shoulder, making her aware of his woodsy cologne and his minty breath.

"Down the side are the names of the software modules. Across the top are the week dates. The numbers inside the boxes represent the percentage of completion for each module by date."

She nodded, and leafed through each report. "So every week, the engineer figures out how close to finished they are, then fills out the box, yes?"

"Yes, and they turn in a hardcopy of their signed report."

"Mm-hmm." Peri held up one signed page. "And they wouldn't lie, right?"

"Absolutely not." He scowled. "They sign the report, for heaven's sake."

"Mm-hmm."

"Stop saying that." He opened the door. "Come with me. We'll have a talk with the team."

Happy that he wasn't clamming up or throwing her out, Peri got up and followed him. Emily was still MIA. Rodolfo marched down the hall, reports in hand. Her long stride made it easy to keep up with him.

Alicia was in her cubicle, looking at her monitor, scribbling numbers on a legal pad next to her keyboard, and sobbing. Their shadows across her desk caused her to look up.

"Oh, Peri, we just found out." She stood and launched herself at Peri for a hug.

"I'm very sorry," Peri told her.

"Can I speak with you for a moment?" Rodolfo held the paper out. "Do you recognize this report?"

Alicia took the paper and glanced at it. "Yes, it's my status for…" She studied the left corner. Her eyes drifted to the chart, brows furrowing. "Last week, but…"

Her boss stood, eyebrow cocked. "But, what?"

She looked at Peri, who held her palms up and shook her head. "But this—this isn't the report I turned in. I mean, it says I signed it, but all my modules should be set to 80%. They won't be finished until testing is finished—oh, and that should be set to, like, 50%. Who changed it to say 100%?"

Rodolfo's eyes widened. "Are you saying you haven't completed your modules?"

"Technically, the code is all written, but in testing, I found a lot of problems, which I'm still fixing." She pushed the report back at him, her mottled face turning pink. "But I'm getting closer. I should have them done any day now. And James should be getting close."

Rodolfo's face lost its burnished tan, as his voice rose. "Does any of it work?"

"Tim's stuff. His code worked great. We had plans next Friday to integrate our pieces. Except for James." She sat down and wept again.

Rodolfo balled his hand into a fist, and pounded his forehead. "We're supposed to be in certification. All that humble-bragging I did on camera about our success—what am I supposed to do, call it all back?"

CHAPTER FIFTY-NINE

ALICIA MET HIM, decibel for decibel. "When did I ever tell you my stuff worked? I'd be doing a happy dance through the offices if I got it working."

"Do you hand your reports to Rodolfo directly?" Peri asked.

"No, Tim collected them every week—mine and James'."

"Emily sets them on my desk on Friday afternoon," Rodolfo said. "So either Tim modified them before giving them to Emily…"

"Or Emily forged them," Peri said, and looked at Rodolfo, who looked at Alicia.

Rodolfo shook his head. "Even if she was smart enough, it's too much like work."

"Too bad we can't ask Tim," Alicia mumbled through her tears.

Peri glanced at Tim's cubicle, cluttered with stacks of papers. "Maybe we can."

She walked into his office space and leafed through the first pile she saw. Rodolfo and Alicia followed her.

"Super smart and super messy." Alicia gazed around.

"And from the looks of it, super into hoarding every scrap of paper he ever touched," Peri said. "Which means, if he replaced the status reports you gave him with updated numbers…"

"Those originals are still in here." Alicia took a stack and rifled through it.

"While you do that, let me call Emily and see if she has any information." Rodolfo took his phone from his pocket and pressed the screen. "Emily, come down to the lab…Yes, now…No—For fu—for Pete's sake, it's not rocket science. Get your ass down here."

Peri tried to ignore the conversation, but couldn't stop smiling as he ended the call. "People think it's easy to be the boss."

He put his hand up. "You have no idea."

Peri and Alicia were halfway through the piles on the desk when Emily strolled into the room, coffee mug in hand and an insolent roll to her red, swollen eyes.

"What?"

"Emily, who turns in status reports to you on Friday?" Rodolfo asked.

"The engineers, of course."

"Yes, the engineers." Now it was Rodolfo's turn to eye-roll. "Names, please."

She shrugged and picked at a spot on the lip of her mug. "Sometimes Tim, sometimes James, Peter, or Katy."

"Who are Peter and Katy?" Peri asked.

"The hardware team," Alicia said. "They're the next row of cubbies over."

"Emily," Peri said. "Maybe you could help us sift through these papers and pull out any status reports. You know what they look like."

Emily stood still, blinking at Peri, and sipping whatever was in her mug.

"Emily." Rodolfo barked her name. "Get in there and help."

She scowled, and drifted into Tim's cubicle. Peri picked up a stack from the corner and set it in front of her, motioning to the only chair. "Here. Sit. I wouldn't want you to overwork yourself."

Emily pouted, although Peri could see new tears running down her cheeks.

"We're all upset about Tim," Peri told her, putting a hand on her shoulder. "We need to find his killer."

The young girl turned away, yanking her shoulder from under Peri's hand. She plopped into the chair and picked up one piece of paper, barely glancing at it before throwing it to the floor.

"Here's one of Tim's." Alicia held up a paper, then studied it. "See? Nothing has been completed through initial unit test."

"Can I see that?" Peri held her hand out. "Rodolfo, do you have a status for May 20th?"

He leafed through the stack and pulled out a report. "This report says he completed 100 percent of his modules."

Alicia studied the report from Tim's office. "This says May 20th, he was only 80 percent complete. Seriously, would we have been working so hard if we were finished?"

"I assumed you were trying to get us certified. That's what these statuses said."

"May I see the bad report?" Peri asked. Taking it, she carefully aligned both reports together and held them up to the light. "This report has been forged. Tim's signature on these two papers is precisely the same, down to the pen-stroke."

"No one signs their name exactly the same," Rodolfo said.

Peri felt her phone vibrate in her pocket. Chief Fletcher was calling, so she stepped out of the cubicle.

"Officer Darden is coming in at 4. Want to be here?" he asked.

She looked at her watch. Thirty minutes. "I'm on my way."

Rodolfo had joined Alicia and Emily in the quest for the missing status reports. Papers were piled everywhere as they sifted through the scribbled notes and computer printouts.

"Rodolfo, could you let me know what you find?" Peri asked. "And, by the way, where's James today?"

Alicia peered over the cubicle wall. "No idea. He should be around."

"Is it odd for him to be absent?"

"Not exactly," Alicia told her. "He kind of ghosts you. He's here, then not here, then back again."

Rodolfo frowned. "Why wasn't I told this?"

"Because I'm not his boss, and I'm no snitch."

"Emily," Peri said. "You said either Tim or James turns in the status reports, right?"

The girl, still slumped in the chair, nodded. "Uh-huh."

Peri tapped her chin, looking at the reports. "If you don't find anything in Tim's office, maybe look in James' files."

Rodolfo's voice deepened, stern and decisive. "You can bet I'll be looking through James' office."

"Call me if you find anything interesting." Peri strode out the door.

CHAPTER SIXTY

CHIEF FLETCHER STOOD at the front desk, waiting for her. Evelyn buzzed her into the station, a pasted-on smile replacing her usually dour face.

"Evelyn." Peri greeted her with enthusiasm. "Thank you for opening the door. How have you been? How's the family?"

The clerk's face froze. "Good. Fine."

Fletcher motioned for Peri to follow him. Before she did, she turned back to Evelyn. "We really must do lunch someday."

Out of the corner of her eye, she saw the smile disappear from Evelyn's face. It didn't even fade, it just halted, as if suddenly overcome by a bad smell. Peri grinned, and continued down the hall.

"Stop teasing that woman," the Chief said as they walked toward the interview room. "She bites."

"You, too? I thought it was just me."

They rounded a corner to the left and entered the door to the observation side of the interview. Detective Logan sat, stretched out in the chair, using all the space on his side of the table. Officer Darden, hands clasped, sitting upright, did not look so relaxed.

Logan placed a folder between them, opened it, and pointed. "This is a text sent from your phone, Pete. Care to explain it?"

"No sir." The ruddy-faced young man glanced at the paper, and at Logan. "But I will."

Logan stayed in the same spread-out position, but Peri saw the slight forward adjustment in his shoulders.

"Okay, so, before I decided to become a police officer, I was a little reckless." Darden paused here, allowing a large gap of silence.

"Most of us here were," Logan said. "It's probably what got us interested in police work."

Darden looked up at him. "Yeah, but you didn't have to worry about social media, and camera phones, and the internet and stuff."

Logan nodded. "True enough. How bad was it?"

"Bad. I mean, getting wasted at a party is one thing, but…photos of me on a sofa, lines of coke on the table in front of me, big, goofy grin on my face…" Here, his voice became a painful whine. "My hand wrapped around some girl's breast…I still don't know who she was. And I realize how it looked, but I swear I didn't do any of those lines…at least, not that night."

"So? If those photos are out there, they're out there."

"But they weren't. I found the friend who posted them, explained I was cleaning up my act, and asked him to remove them. He deleted the photos, and I did a search on the 'net, looking for more. Each time I found one, I contacted the person, had it deleted, and searched again, until nothing showed up."

"Thought you were in the clear?"

Darden nodded. "I had to have been—the academy wouldn't have accepted me otherwise, right? Then one day, I get a text from an unknown number. It's that photo, with the words, 'I need a favor' underneath."

"For the record, why don't you tell me, what was the favor?"

"Incriminate Dev Chaplain in the murder of Tressa Velasco. Do what it takes to keep the spotlight on him."

"Did they tell you how, or leave it up to you?"

"Oh, no, they had specific instructions, told me where to hide the knife, to make up an excuse to find the photos in Chaplain's office, so forth."

"And the text to Art Gibbons?"

"They wanted Dev alone in the house, to take the blame."

"Did they also want us to think it was Art that was dead?"

"At least for a while." Darden shrugged. "No idea why."

"And you never investigated this blackmailer?"

He shook his head. "I was afraid. If he caught me snooping on him, he might turn me in."

Logan rubbed his forehead. "I guess. Still, doesn't say much for your cop skills, Pete."

"I'm no Superman. This cop gig isn't what I thought it would be, but it's good pay and bennies."

The detective stood so violently, his chair toppled behind him. He pounded his fist on the table. "Goddammit. You're exactly the kind of officer we don't need in the department, almost as bad as the ones who have a score to settle with the world. You took an oath, to protect and serve. Who are you protecting here? Or serving? Your own ass, that's all."

Darden's expression remained neutral, but his body shrank back.

Walking away, Logan picked up his overturned chair and set it at the table. He remained standing. "So, what can you give us to find this person?"

"But the photo—"

"I don't give a rat's ass about your precious photo. And even if we never see it, our department knows about it, so there's nothing else to blackmail you with—or is there?"

"No, but," Darden's eyes pleaded, puppy-dog style. "Can't we just keep this between you and me?"

CHAPTER SIXTY-ONE

LOGAN LAUGHED AND pointed to the two-way mirror. "Hate to tell you, Sport, but my Chief's been watching and listening the whole time."

Now it was the young officer's turn to stand quickly. He backed toward the door. "You set me up! I want my union rep."

"Sit down." Logan pointed to the chair. Darden didn't move, so he raised his voice "Sit. Down."

Darden sat.

"You set yourself up, when you tried to hide your past. You should have come clean at the academy. Past drug use doesn't mean you can never become a police officer, although it sounds like you're not that invested in being one."

Darden opened his mouth, but the detective held up his hand in silence before continuing. "And you can have your union rep just as soon as we're through and we hand you off to the Fullerton PD. They'll be having the discussions on whether to discipline or terminate you. But right now, you're going to give me anything you have that might help us catch a killer."

Logan handed him a pad of yellow legal paper and a pen.

"What do you want me to write?" Darden looked up at him, pouting.

"Let's start with the phone number you received the texts from. And of course, we'll need all those texts."

"I deleted them."

Logan smiled. "I'm sure the phone company will help us retrieve them."

Peri touched the Chief's arm to get his attention. "Ask him how he got the knife that he hid behind the toilet."

Fletcher gave a small nod and took out his phone, texting the question to Logan. The detective checked his messages and gave a thumb's up to the mirror. It was quite a change, she thought, from the days when the detective would be called from the room for a quick discussion. Cell phones were like notes being passed in class.

Peri watched Darden write, noting the quick, jerky movements of his hand. The awkwardness wasn't unusual for someone his age, who spent most of his time typing papers instead of writing them. Halfway down the page, he stopped and shook his wrist a few times.

"Aw, wee lamb," she said. "His wrist is too weak to hold a pen for long."

"The young ones are all like that," Fletcher told her. "They're better at technology."

She sighed. "I suppose so. But no more letters? I've always gotten a thrill out of going to a museum and seeing letters from famous people. Now, museums are going to display the famous author's tweets. Depresses me."

Fletcher patted her shoulder. "It does me, too. I think it's harder to let go of things as we get older, which is too bad. Things change, and when we can't accept it, we're the ones who suffer by being cranky all the time."

"You're a smart man. I knew there was a reason they made you Police Chief." As she laughed, she felt a buzz in her pocket. A text from Alicia.

JAMES NOT AT WORK. NOT ANSWERING PHONE. FOUND MY STATUS REPORTS IN HIS DESK.

"We may have another suspect," she told the Chief, and gave him the short version of her morning at Rodolfo's company. "I'm going to call Skip, but is it possible you could tell me if you find anything about the blackmailer?"

"Peri, you know—"

"I know plenty, including that you don't have the time or resources to keep me in the loop. But this is my brother. Please, Chief, just this once?"

He scowled, and nodded. "Because it's your brother."

Peri strode down the hall to the exit. "Gotta run, Evelyn, catch up later, I promise," she said as she left, her phone against her ear, waiting for Skip to pick up.

"You've reached Detective Skip Carlton of the Placentia Police Department," the voicemail began.

As lovely as his voice was, Peri pressed a button to interrupt it and leave her message. "Skip, I think we should go to James Peoples' place and scope it out. I've got a feeling about him."

She had just ended the call when her phone vibrated. Thinking it was Skip, she answered without looking at the ID.

"Miss Peri, don't you want my help?" Benny asked.

She wracked her brain for the last time they spoke and what she might have promised him. "I'm sorry, did I miss a meeting?"

"You said you'd call when it was time for me to work. And that you'd give me a schedule."

"Yes, I did." She gazed at the Placentia Civic Plaza, bright in the warm June sun. "Hey, you can help me. Can you be at my house in two hours?"

"Maybe. What should I wear?"

"Uh, I'd say, something you can move around in."

"Where are we moving?"

She wanted to snap, *just put on some sweats*, but knew he didn't own any. "I need to go to a suspect's home and interview him, if he's there. If he's not there, I may want to take a look around, scope things out. Does that give you an idea of how to dress?"

"Oh, yes. Bowling shirt and wide-legged slacks. Soft-soled shoes so we don't get caught."

"I'm not saying we'll do anything illegal."

"We never do anything illegal, Miss Peri." He sounded offended. "We are fighting crime. There's nothing illegal about that."

"Of course," she said. "See you in two hours."

CHAPTER SIXTY-TWO

AT HOME, PERI reviewed her notes on James Peoples, got on her laptop, and dug deeper. She knew that he'd gotten his master's at UC Riverside, and that in the eight years since graduation, he worked at six companies. Alicia described him as a prickly person to work with, so perhaps the frequent job changes were a reflection of his social skills.

She searched on his name again, but found nothing else about him. *He should have existed before UCR, right?*

She tried a genealogy database—nope, nothing there. Peri sat back and drummed her fingers on her leg. How does someone suddenly spring to life on the internet? *Unless*, she thought, *they changed their name.*

"Who are you, really, James?" she asked as she searched through the Office of Vital Statistics and Records in California.

Bingo. James Morton Peoples had been born on August 19, 2008, when he legally changed his name from Jaime O'Brian Pueblos, in San Diego County. A search on Jaime O'Brian Pueblos was much more interesting than James Peoples. Jaime had gotten his undergraduate degree at the University of Arizona.

"Wait, that's where Art and Dev and Tressa went." She got out her phone and scrolled through the photos, until she found the one with Dev and three others. It was clear to her now, that the young woman was Tressa, and the tall nerd was Art, which left the short punk-rocker. He didn't look like James. She studied the spiked white hair, the piercings. "But do you look like Jaime?"

Jaime Pueblos also owned property—in Placentia. According to the records, he had owned it since May 2008. It was, perhaps, the last thing he did as Jaime. She was surprised to see the house was located within walking distance of Placita Santa Fe, the city's historical downtown district. Packed with interesting shops and restaurants featuring five-star authentic Mexican food, the neighborhood was decidedly Hispanic.

Peri checked her notes. James listed his address as an apartment in Brea.

There were logical reasons for him to own property he didn't occupy. Income from a rental, or living arrangements for a relative. Still, it was worth looking at.

Hopefully, I can get enough information without breaking and entering. Skip hates it when I do that.

Now she had to convince Benny that if he wanted to help her, she was driving.

Benny was not thrilled by this news. "You drive too fast."

"I promise not to drive over the speed limit. We have to go downtown, so parking is limited. Plus, as much as I love your car, the Caddy is distinctive. When we need to fly under the radar, my little rental is the better choice."

"I understand, but I don't like your driving."

Peri shook her head, pursing her lips. "I don't mind if you don't like my driving, I don't like it myself. I grieve over it long winter evenings."

"What are you talking about?"

She laughed. "Sorry, it's a line from a movie. Dino wasn't in it, so you wouldn't have seen it. Shall we go?"

Benny frowned but nodded, so she grabbed her tote and keys. "Trust me, I'll be careful."

Peri made sure she traveled at exactly the speed limit as they turned onto Chapman, and then down Bradford Avenue. The neighborhoods changed considerably in those few miles. Wide boulevards with umbrellas of camphor trees above and crowds of yellow day lilies below, soon changed into less manicured areas of old trees and broken sidewalks.

Palm trees lined Bradford, and the tidy, grassy lawns fronted houses that were now businesses. The street ended at Placita Santa Fe, also known as Bradford Square to the people trying to revitalize the area, bring in a train station, and apartments.

"A good idea, mass transit-wise," she mused as she drove. "But maybe not so good for the people who've lived here for so long."

"Stop talking. You have to drive." Even as a passenger, Benny had his rules.

She pulled into a space a block away from her destination, on Santa Fe past the 301 Café, a local favorite for tacos, burritos, and beers.

"Where's the house?" Benny asked.

"Up around the corner, on Walnut." She pointed as she unbuckled her seatbelt.

He looked up the street, where block walls were mixed with chain link fencing, most windows had security bars, and the trees were so large, grass no longer grew in the front yards.

"Why aren't we driving up there?"

"For a couple of reasons. One is, I'm already pretty conspicuous in this neighborhood—and before you say anything, you stand out, too." She reached into her back seat and grabbed a clipboard with papers hanging from it. "Two, if he's at home, I don't want to frighten him by seeing a strange car drive up. So, we're going to pretend to be from a local church, inviting people to attend our services."

He rolled his eyes. "Miss Peri, who is going to believe that?"

"I'm hoping no one here recognizes me." She held up one of the papers. "Besides, it's not exactly a lie. I got these flyers from a friend of mine who goes to Placentia Presbyterian, down the street. I figure, if I actually pass these out, I'm getting karma points."

"You're weird."

"Are you in or are you going to wait in the car?" She opened her door.

He remained in the passenger seat until she was on the curb. Sighing dramatically, he got out and slammed the car door. "I'm in."

CHAPTER SIXTY-THREE

THEY STROLLED DOWN Walnut, stopping at houses to plant a flyer here and there. Peri recognized James' house from the image she'd found on the internet, but she remained unhurried, taking in all the scenery on the street.

"Why are we taking so long?" Benny asked.

"Because I want to see if there are any busybodies around. So far, I haven't seen anyone peek out of their curtains."

They passed by a long, rectangular beige stucco with Big Wheel tricycles on the dusty front yard. A round face appeared at the open door, so Peri walked up the driveway. Benny followed her, with a reluctant shuffle.

"*Hola*," Peri said. "*Estamos invitando a la gente a nuestra iglesia.*"

"I didn't know you spoke Spanish," Benny said.

"*Un poco.*" She held a flyer out to the woman, who took it and smiled.

Smiling back, Peri said, "*Que tengas un buen dia,*" before returning to the sidewalk, Benny in her footsteps.

"Wow, that was amazing, Miss Peri."

"Not really. I'd love to really learn to speak it, but in conversation, the words go by so fast, I don't understand.

And I feel stupid asking someone to slow down and speak like a gringa."

No one was home at the next house, so they walked on to their destination. The other homes in the neighborhood looked well-used and well-loved, but James' house was neglected. There were no trees, no plants of any kind in the yard to explain the lack of grass. Gray patches dotted the house where the stucco needed replacement. The windows looked original, and Peri knew this place had to be fifty years old. His detached single-car garage sat at the back of the small yard.

She strolled up the cracked drive, studying the house.

"He's not home."

A tall Latino man waved at her from the chain link fence and green hedge next door. She waved back and strode over to him. He appeared to be about her age, gray-haired and pleasant looking, with a smile on his face. His property was the antithesis of James' dump, a small hacienda-style house of arches and bright tiles, sitting on a well-maintained lawn.

"Hi, I'm Jill Clinton." She extended her hand and prepared to kick Benny if he disagreed with her.

"Really?" The man was still smiling. "Because I could've sworn you were Peri Minneopa."

A surprised laugh escaped her. "I am sorry, have we met?"

"Not exactly, but my family helped you out with a case once. Young girl found dead in Kraemer Park. You interviewed my sister. I was in the next room, just in case."

"Wow, that was a while ago." The memory of a frozen hand and beautiful ring flashed across her mind. "Your name is?"

"Jose Lopez. You can call me Joe, good to meet you."

"Well, now that my cover is blown, maybe you wouldn't mind telling me about your neighbor here?" She pointed to James' house.

"He's not much of a neighbor." Joe shook his head. "I mean, I'm kind of a hermit, because I work from home and can't have people interrupting my day. But in the evenings, I'm on my porch, or walking the neighborhood. I know everyone. But this guy? I admit, we were a little worried about a white guy moving in, ten years ago. Gentrification, and all that."

"Yeah, doesn't look like that's going to happen," she said.

"I only met him because I heard the U-Haul in the drive and went over to introduce myself. It was only him. Told me his name was Jaime Pueblos, but he looked white and didn't speak Spanish, so I was a little suspicious. I offered to help him unload the boxes, but he almost bit my head off. Said no one touches his stuff. Moved everything by himself."

"That's interesting." Peri began writing on one of the flyers. "Wonder what's so untouchable about his boxes?"

"He's in and out at all hours," Joe said. "I know because his car makes such a racket, and it's outside my bedroom window."

She stared at the house. "Sure would like to see inside."

"Well." Joe dropped his voice to a whisper. "I'd be glad to look the other way if you want to help yourself into the place. I'll even be your lookout."

"Sounds good. Have you got your phone? I'll give you my number—text me if you see him coming."

"You got it."

She turned to Benny with her keys. "Go get the car and park it over here, in front of Joe's place, okay? In case we need a quick getaway."

"I don't like driving strange cars."

She sighed. "Are you working for me today?"

"Yes."

"Then work. Go get my car. Stay in it, leave the motor running." She handed him the clipboard. "It'll be nice. You can enjoy the air conditioning. I have a place to plug in your iPod, so you can listen to Dino."

That put a smile on his face, and off he scurried, to complete his task.

"Who is that guy?" Joe asked.

"Believe it or not, my assistant." She shrugged. "Do you have a baseball cap I could borrow? In case there are cameras?"

Joe went into his house, returning with an Oakland Raiders cap.

"Just tell me if it's like, filled with explosives." He smiled. "Of course, if he's shooting pornos, maybe I'll try to be a better neighbor."

She smirked. "I'll keep you informed."

CHAPTER SIXTY-FOUR

STOPPING AT THE garage, she looked up at all the eaves. She was reasonably good at finding cameras, even the smallest dots of lenses. There didn't seem to be any, but she pulled the cap down so the brim shadowed her face, and tucked her blond hair underneath.

The back entrance to the house was a simple affair, two cement steps and a door with three small windows at the top. The door used to be blue, but half of the paint had chipped off. Peri stepped up, tools at the ready. The lock was an easy pin, so she zipped it open with no problem. There was no deadbolt.

James' skills in engineering could have him booby-trapping this house in a million different ways, and Peri did not want to set off any alarms, or worse. She turned the doorknob in small increments, listening for any extra clicks that should not be there.

Of course, if I do hear a click, I'll be dead within seconds.

Her forehead beaded with sweat, as did her palms, and she grasped the doorknob tighter. She felt the latch release and the door pushed out slightly. As she pulled, she examined the doorway for any trip-wires. A small thread lit in the sun, and she stopped. Creeping up the top step, her vision followed the end of the strand. It went to the doorjamb, where she couldn't see any further.

A small gust of wind took the door and shook it. She gasped as the thread stretched, and broke. The strand of a cobweb drifted down to her nose.

"Son of a—" she whispered.

Convinced the door was not armed, Peri opened it and slipped inside, leaving the door ajar. She was in a small, dark kitchen. The trash, piled in the corner, gave off a pungent scent, no doubt enjoyed by the many flies in the room. The counter was filled with paper plates on one side, and empty pizza boxes and soda bottles on the other. She pulled the door shut behind her.

Peri used the flashlight on her phone, and moved on, through the darkness. The windows had been covered with cardboard and sealed with duct-tape. She walked slowly, shining her light all around, looking for any sign of cameras or trip-wires. Her heart was in her eardrums, beating a staccato.

It was a small home, as small as it looked from the outside. Two bedrooms, one bath, living room and kitchen. The living room was empty, except for boxes. The labels on them said they had held TVs, computers, gaming consoles, etc. They were all empty.

She kept moving until she found a closed door to what she believed was a bedroom. It was locked, further piquing her interest. Angling her light down, her paranoia was validated—a narrow wire was strung across the doorway, at ankle level.

If there was a wire down below, what kind of security was in the lock?

"This might be a job for the police," she muttered.

Sweeping the light behind her, there was another door. That knob turned. Again, she opened it as if the room might explode. Creeping in with soft footsteps, she stood in the middle at last, throwing her flashlight's beam around. Her mouth dropped open.

"Oh. My. God."

A king-sized mattress sat on the bare floor, covered only in a rumpled blanket. The one pillow, sans pillowcase, slumped in the corner. As in the living room, the windows were completely covered.

Photos of Tressa Velasco decorated three of the four walls, plus the ceiling. There were large photos, small photos, professional headshots, and candids. Many looked as if she didn't realize she was being photographed. Peri recognized a few as the ones Alicia was supposed to plant. There was not one vacant spot.

Peri turned to the fourth wall and shone her light at it. If seeing Tressa had made her gasp, this wall nearly stopped her heart.

There were more photos of Tressa on this wall, but they were not the photos of a loved one. A red marker had been used to draw gashes on her body, a target on her face, and blood spatter everywhere. A black marker was used to draw a noose, a knife, a gun.

Several other people's photos were there, too. Dev, Tim, and Alicia were there, as well as Art, and Rodolfo. All had a word written over their heads: DIE. Except for Tim. Across his face, in red, was DEAD.

CHAPTER SIXTY-FIVE

PERI NEEDED A photo of this room, but the light was dim, and she didn't dare turn on a lamp. She did her best, hoping her cell phone's technology saved her. As she snapped the last photo, she got a text from an unknown number.

IT'S JOE. HE'S BACK. I DISTRACT HIM.

She tiptoed out of the room, and back to the kitchen. Locking the door behind her, she jumped down the steps and ran behind his garage. She could hear voices coming from the front yard, and silently thanked her new friend for the distraction.

The only place to go was over the chain link fence and hedge, into Joe's yard. Climbing up, she threw herself onto the bushes.

Being botanically challenged, she had no idea what kind of plant she was clambering over, but she knew from each poking rip, they had thorns.

"Ow-ow-ow," she muttered, trying not to scream out loud.

She hit the brick patio with a thud and a moan. Lying still for a moment, she tried to decide whether anything was broken enough to require medical attention.

Everything that was supposed to wiggle did, and nothing flapped about unless she flapped it.

A little ibuprofen and I'll be fine.

Until she heard the barking. Dogs. Big dogs, from the sound of them, who'd encountered a stranger in their territory.

"Oh, no," she groaned, and looked to her right. Two enormous pit bulls raced toward her, jaws drooling. She hid her face with her hands, and cooed at them. "Please, puppies. Good dogs. Be good."

The first muzzle hit her in the back like a truck. She gasped for air, still trying to talk to the dogs and keep her face from being chewed off. Dog spittle sprayed her arms and neck, and she curled into more of a fetal position.

The next muzzle pushed itself down the neck of her shirt. She could hear the snuffling, and an almost-mumbling sound from both dogs. They weren't growling or barking, it sounded like two old men trying to decide which way to go on a map.

That's when she felt two tongues, licking her arms and neck. She peered through her fingers and saw two tails wagging, one white, and one steel gray. In slow motion, she let go of her head, propped herself up, and held a hand out to one of the dogs. At that, they both laid down and gave her their pink bellies to rub, tails still wagging violently.

"Aren't you good dogs," she told them, and used each hand to scratch a tummy.

She'd been scratching them for a while when Joe came into the backyard. "Oogie, Boogie, leave her alone. They're friendly, as long as you're friendly."

Peri lifted herself to a standing position, and looked down. She didn't look as injured as she felt. Dusting her pants while she petted the dogs, she said, "I guess they look fierce enough if anyone tries to sneak into your place."

"Oh, they're good guard dogs, all right. They saw me talking to you, heard our voices, knew you weren't a burglar. They're smart like that."

She limped toward the gate. "Doesn't it confuse them, calling them Oogie and Boogie?"

"Not really. They never come when they're called anyway."

She laughed. "Thank you so much for your help, although I'm not sure if I got any intel for you. One of his bedrooms is locked and I didn't get time to unlock it."

"I'm gonna keep an eye on him." Joe nodded toward the house. "Creeps me out, man."

"If you see anything, call the PPD and ask for Detective Logan. I'm sorry I don't have his card on me."

"Or I can call you, right? I've got your number."

"Oh. Yes, call me." She looked back at the house and shivered. "I'll send the cavalry."

Benny was rocking out to "Mambo Italiano" when she got into the passenger seat. "Miss Peri, why are you sitting there? Why aren't you driving?"

"I got a little scraped up." She slumped down in the seat and looked at James' house. His car was in the drive, a silver Nissan coupe, with tinted windows. "Could you please drive me home?"

"Only if you don't nag at me for driving too slow or too wrong."

"Promise." She saw the front door open and sank even further down. "He's coming out."

James/Jaime walked onto his tiny front stoop and looked up and down the street, holding something in his hand. Peri couldn't tell what it was. At one point, he looked at their car and stared. She felt his gaze permeating the space, but she remained quiet. He moved toward them and she held her breath.

"Benny," she whispered. "Go—Now."

"Why?"

"Just do it!"

"Are you scared? Why are you scared?" He rolled away from the curb and inched the car down Walnut Street.

"Because James is a scary man. And I didn't even see his whole house."

"Well that's too bad but now you have to stop talking because I'm driving. And no rolling your eyes and sighing at me, either."

Peri slumped against the passenger seat and closed her eyes. Her phone vibrated, so she took it out. Skip. Finally.

"Hey, Doll, what did you need?"

CHAPTER SIXTY-SIX

A HOT SHOWER and cold compresses made Peri feel a lot better. She sprawled in one of the lounge chairs, soaking in the quiet of her backyard, and trying to ignore the muffled sounds of the paint sprayer in the house. It was cabinet painting day, but the good news was, they were almost done—with the kitchen.

The French doors opened, and Skip came through, carrying a tray of pizza and beer.

"Veggie pesto pizza?" she asked.

"I know what you like." Skip set the tray on the table and prepared a plate for her.

"Yes, you do." She smiled as he handed it to her.

He sat and took a swig of beer, pointing to her ice pack. "Want to share what happened?"

"We've been overlooking James Peoples. He's flown under everyone's radar, but that guy's got a serious creep factor." She told him about going to check out his house and what she saw inside the room. "And there's another bedroom that's locked and has a tripwire."

"Are you telling me you broke into a house?"

"Joe said I could." She took a bite of pizza.

"Who's Joe?"

"James' neighbor. Oh, but get this—Joe knows him as Jaime Pueblos. He changed his name. Tell me that's not suspicious."

"That's not suspicious."

She glared at him. "Okay, you don't like the whole breaking-and-entering thing. At least I'm willing to let the police take it from here. Actually, I'd rather the police take it from here. I don't want to try to open that locked door."

Skip shook his head, and smiled. "When you were trying to deal with the shooting, you were so glum and moody, I wished you could get more of your sass back. Now I'm wondering why I wished that."

"I am feeling better, it's true, although I'm a little sore at the moment. I didn't think I wanted this case, didn't think I wanted to do any investigating of anything, anymore. Now I'm glad I did. It feels like waking up from a long sleep."

"Speaking of sleep, mind if I stay over tonight?"

"Of course. Isn't this house ours?" She ate another bite of pizza.

"Yes, I just…" He shrugged. "I'm feeling bad, like I've let you deal with all this renovation mess, just because you're the first occupant. Trying to get my place sold isn't taking up that much of my time."

"It's okay. I've actually been feeling bad myself. I've been making all the decisions and not letting you be a part of it. It's how I've always done things. On my own." She smiled at him. "Guess that's gotta change."

"We're both independent."

"And hard-headed."

He grinned. "Only when it counts."

"Speaking of independent, can we discuss your retirement?"

"What about it?"

His reply had a testiness to it that made her want to back away. *Nope, diving in anyway.*

"I'm just curious, since I've closed my shop and you're retiring—what do we do with ourselves now?"

"I'm not sure—golf more? Travel? Not work?"

She took another drink, gathered a little more courage. "Aren't you worried that you'll be bored?"

"Maybe." He stretched out in his lounge chair, and reached for his beer. "All I know is, it's been nice to not set the alarm, not put on the suit, the holster, the whole outfit."

"Even the badge?"

He grinned. "I admit, the badge is a tough one. It's been my ID for years."

"You'll have to find out who else you are, once your detective days are over."

Skip got up and walked over to her, leaning down to kiss her forehead. "I'm sure I'll be fine. How about you? Will you be too bored?"

"No," she blurted. "That is, I don't think so. I wanted to close up shop, right?"

He smiled and stroked the top of her head. "Right. Well, the game is on, and I'm gonna go watch it. Want to come?"

"In a bit." She dragged her laptop from the side table and put it on her lap, wincing as it hit her hip. "I want to do a little more digging before I call it a night."

He took the rest of the pizza and disappeared. The construction workers had quit for the day, bringing blissful silence to her house. No—to their house.

Peri had pages of notes on James Peoples, but was still curious about Jaime Pueblos. A photo would be good. She entered his name in the search box, and found a smattering of entries, including a seldom-used page for finding people from high school and college. She clicked on it.

According to the website, Jaime Pueblos was a student at Ramona High School in Riverside, followed by four years at University of Arizona. The only comment was from one classmate, voting Jaime "the most likely to build a rocket, or a bomb, or a bomb that goes on a rocket."

Not a stellar endorsement, she thought.

Peri sat back in the chaise, rubbing her temples. A guy who went into life as Jaime Pueblos and came out James Peoples. Why? Could it have been racism? It was possible, but she couldn't believe it. Most companies would have swept up a programmer with a Hispanic name in a heartbeat, happy to check their affirmative action box.

She looked at the photo again, of Dev and his friends. Dev wasn't talking to her, but maybe Art had some useful information. She dug out her cell phone.

"Art, this is Peri. Do you remember a student at Arizona named Jaime Pueblos?"

The silence on the other end was thick, and cold as a stone wall.

"Yes," Art said at last. "He made Tressa's life hell while she was there, and the school wouldn't do anything about it."

"What exactly did he do?"

"That typical, 'won't take no for an answer' crap. She joined him for coffee once, *once*, and he decided she was his. I finally got involved—as a friend. She and I weren't even dating at the time."

"What happened?"

"Tressa told him to meet her one morning in Dr. Halliday's classroom. Dev and I met him instead. Believe me, I tried to reason with him, but he was unreasonable. Kept smirking at me, saying I was just jealous, she would always be his, he knew she loved him. Dev was always more physical than me—he finally slammed him against the wall by his throat and told him she sent us to make him go away."

"And did he?"

"Yes, that was the end of him bugging her. We all graduated, went our separate ways."

Peri displayed Dev's photos on her laptop. "Could you describe Jaime?"

"Short, dark hair with dyed white tips, all spiked. Piercings, I think, in his lip and maybe his nose."

"Any idea why he'd change his name?"

"What do you mean?"

"I mean, he's James Peoples now. He works at Ro-Bet."

"No wonder she was so antsy lately," Art said. "Why didn't she tell me?"

"I need to warn you about something, Art." Peri told him about the photos in James' bedroom. "The last time I talked to Alicia, they hadn't seen him at work. I recommend staying anywhere other than home."

"I'll pack a bag right now. Thank y—" An explosion cut off the last word.

CHAPTER SIXTY-SEVEN

"ART!" PERI REDIALED. The phone went to voicemail.

She leapt from the chaise and ran through the house, to the bedroom. "Skip, I was on the phone with Art and I heard a gunshot, or a bomb."

Skip sat up, away from the pillows on the bed. "What did it sound like?"

"An explosion. And I can't get Art on the phone."

"Let me call Logan." He reached for his phone, buried in the blankets. "Logan, I need someone to check Art Gibbons' home. Possible ten-eighty, Peri was on the phone and heard an explosion, she can't reach him now…Good…Thanks."

Peri came out of the closet holding a pair of shoes.

"What are you doing?" Skip asked, setting down his phone.

"Going to Art's house."

Skip shook his head. "No, Peri."

"But—"

"No. Peri." He was insistent. "You are not needed there."

"But I have information."

"Will that information help Art if he's dead?"

"No."

"If he's alive?"

"No—well, maybe?" Peri shrugged. "I feel like I need to be there. I want to see that he's still alive. I have to give Logan the information Art gave me."

Skip got up and held her. "You can talk to Logan later. Right now, he needs to take care of what might have happened. Afterward, he'll want your statement."

She flung her arms up, and stomped her foot. "Are you going to stop me from investigating every murder?"

Skip pulled away. "Am I what? I thought you were closing up shop."

"I am, but—admit it, I'm pretty deep in this one. I've got to see it through." She looked up at him. "Tell me you understand."

He stared at her for a few moments, brushing the stray hairs from her cheek. "Yeah, I do. Why don't we go together?"

She grinned and pushed away to get ready. "Perfect."

The drive to Art's house was quick in the light traffic. Even so, Peri had to work at keeping her impatience at bay.

"Isn't your therapist giving you any tools to cope?" Skip asked.

"Yes, why do you ask?"

"Because your fingers are drumming a hole in my upholstery."

"It's called tapping. Emotional Freedom Technique."

"I don't think you're doing it right."

"That reminds me, I have an appointment this Friday." She put her hand in her lap. "Sorry, I just want to get there."

"We're getting closer."

She shrugged. "I feel bad. I should have called Art as soon as I saw that wall. Or Dev. Or the police. They needed to be warned."

"And you can tell all this to Logan, and the police will take care of it." Skip's voice stayed calm, in the midst of Peri's storm.

When they arrived at Art's house, five patrol cars, a black SUV, and an EMS truck sat in the circular driveway. Peri wanted to run ahead, but she stayed with Skip, who strolled forward, using his cane to support his leg. Detective Logan's partner, Detective Powell, was at the door, looking at the couple with a blank face.

"Detective Powell, how nice to see you," Peri said, hoping to start with a pleasant exchange.

"This is for police and emergency personnel only, ma'am." He glanced at Skip. "Carlton, I didn't know you were back from disability."

"I'm not, exactly. Peri, here, has information for the police, pertinent to the shooting."

"Shooting? What shooting?" Powell looked puzzled.

"When I was on the phone with Art, I heard a horrible explosion. Sounded like a gunshot."

Powell smiled. "No guns, ma'am. It was truly an explosion."

"And Art?" she asked.

"Survived, ma'am."

Peri grabbed Skip's arm, and exhaled. "I'm so glad. You have no idea. I thought he was—"

"Good news," Logan walked through the foyer to interrupt them. "He wasn't."

She smiled. "How is he?"

"Little rattled, probably some concussion, but he'll live. And he was able to tell us about your phone call." Logan frowned as he looked at her. "I want to be pretty angry with you, breaking into a house like that. But it does give us a more solid suspect."

"Are you going to pick him up?"

Logan shook his head. "We don't have anything to hold him on, yet. Jason's working as fast as he can on Darden's phone, but I don't have anything definite enough to get a warrant for."

"I'm just glad he's okay." Peri opened the gallery on her phone and swiped through her photos. "I'm afraid it was dark in the room, so it was hard to get good pictures. Oh, here's one."

She showed it to the detectives.

"Looks like we got a real sicko," Powell said.

Logan pointed at her phone. "Send that to me. Maybe I can get a warrant somehow."

Peri texted the photo as requested. "Now what?"

Skip and Logan exchanged glances.

"Now we go back home," Skip told her. "And let these folks do their jobs."

"If you can contact your brother, tell him what's going on," Logan said. "I'm guessing that Peoples still thinks Dev is being properly railroaded, but it wouldn't hurt to keep him safe."

"I'll try." Peri turned toward the car, frowning. Skip followed.

"You look sad." He reached out for her and rubbed her neck as they walked.

"No, I'm happy that Art didn't die. I'm still kicking myself for not warning everyone in time." She slowed her pace to fall in with Skip's, laying her head on his shoulder. "I suppose I'm still wishing Dev would at least keep in touch with me during all this. Am I such a horrible sister?"

"No, I think he's an ass." Skip kissed the top of her head as he wrapped his arm around her waist. "But I'm in love with you."

CHAPTER SIXTY-EIGHT

PERI ROLLED OVER and looked at the clock. Six-thirty. Sun bounced off the window shades, diffusing the light in the bedroom. Too early to rise, normally, but today her mind was already in the starting gate.

Skip slept beside her, an occasional snore to say he was still there, still breathing. She studied his face, from the tips of his short, gray hair, down through the sunburst creases at the corner of his eyes, past the high, defined cheekbones, to his full lips and stubbled chin. He was so handsome, it sometimes clouded her brain.

There was a moment's sadness where she envied his ability to age well, while she went fifteen rounds with gravity every day.

But mostly, there was love and gratitude, and a healthy dose of lust.

Last night, they'd made love like they used to, before all the injuries and the trauma. They'd returned to physical intimacy earlier, but the act was careful, precious. There were minefields to avoid, and each caress had a question mark attached, asking if this was okay. And each time she'd kissed him, she was so damned grateful he was still there, and that made her feel like she was on hallowed ground, ground that was too sacred for animal pleasure.

But last night she was Peri, the woman who loved pleasing Skip, and having him return the favor. Her skin was more her own again, and she wore it better.

Skip opened his eyes, and gave her a sleepy smile. "Is it time to get up?"

"Not really, but I'm awake."

He pulled her to him. "Then let's do something else."

She officially got up at eight, throwing on her sweatshirt and shorts to go make coffee. The kitchen cabinets had been given their last coat, and she squinted at them in the morning light. They were supposed to be gray, but the sunlight gave them streaks of gold, like a vein of precious metal running through marble. She picked up her coffee mug and walked as she sipped, back and forth in the kitchen, staring at the paint from all angles.

Skip joined her with his coffee. "Whatcha looking at?"

She pointed. "Does the paint look funny to you?"

"Hmm, maybe. Funny, how?"

"It looks like marbling. See all the random stripes of gold?" She gestured as she spoke.

"Yeah, I guess I do. It's probably just the sunlight." He kissed the top of her head. "Does it bother you?"

"Nah, I guess not. I wasn't expecting it." She chuckled. "Life is full of stuff I don't expect."

"If it really bugs you, we'll have them redo it, or do some kind of window treatment."

"No, I'll give it a couple of days. I may get used to it." She turned her face up to his for a kiss. "In the meantime, I'm going for a run."

He smiled. "Sounds great."

Peri plugged in her tunes and trotted to the end of her street, where she turned left. Her plan was to jog across Central to the country club, then past the civic center. She wasn't sure of the mileage, but for the first day back in months, it would have to do.

The area was just hilly enough to make her work, but not enough to keep her mind from working. She was surprised by how hard she had to push herself up the grades, how much she was sweating and labored.

I didn't expect these inclines to be so steep. Life is full of stuff I don't expect.

At the top of Alta Vista Street, she stopped. Life was always full of the unexpected—she used to roll with it, embrace it, leap on its back and ride it like she stole it. The shootout had taken that from her.

"No, it wasn't the shootout," she said to no one. "I've been shot at before."

But I've never shot anyone.

She had picked up that gun in the warehouse to get it out of enemy hands, or so she thought. It wasn't meant to be used, unless it was to defend her client. That word "unless" now seemed large. There was no unless. When she picked up that gun, in the middle of a gunfight, the expectation was that she'd have to use it. She just didn't want to admit it.

I picked up the gun in self-defense, and I used it for that reason.

Her cell phone vibrated in its holder, interrupting her thoughts. She pressed a button on her earbuds to answer the phone call.

"Peri, Steve Logan. Jason was able to trace the phone calls to Darden. Burner phone."

"Tell me there's a way to trace that."

"Yes, but it's not easy. What we have in our favor is that whoever is using it, has been using it for a long time. We've called in a cyber-expert to help us out."

"In the meantime, any luck with that photo and getting a warrant?"

"Peri, it's not even 9 am." Logan chuckled. "Let the judges get to their chambers first."

"Sorry. I'm getting a bad feeling about all of this."

"I hear ya. I'll call you as soon as I find anything."

"Thanks, Steve." Peri ended the call and turned, loping down the hill to resume her run. Usually, she stayed on wide, well-maintained sidewalks, but today, she opted for the bicycle lane in the street. The asphalt felt more forgiving on her knees. She focused on her steps, her breath, her body, but her mind kept drifting away.

Jaime Pueblos stalked and bullied Tressa Velasco in college. Then he changed his name to James Peoples— why? He went through a string of jobs—why? It was as if Jaime Pueblos and James Peoples were two different men, one still living in his college obsession, and the other functioning in society.

She kicked hard going down the last hill to her house, feeling her heartbeat pound in her head, before pulling up to a walk in her drive. A couple of slow, strolling laps in front of her garage, breathing evenly, brought her pulse down to a manageable level. Skip would scold her if he saw her pushing herself this hard.

"God, Peri, you're gonna have an aneurysm," he'd say.

I may well have a heart attack, but I'm going to solve this case first.

CHAPTER SIXTY-NINE

ON HER WAY into the house, she called Rodolfo. "I realize it's early, sorry. Have you seen or heard from James yet?"

"Not yet, and I confess, I'm worried. I've been trying to call him since yesterday. Even Alicia's tried. There's been no response."

"Would you mind if I came over and looked through his desk for clues?"

"You can," he said. "But we've already picked over his desk, ourselves, just looking for any idea of where he might be."

She didn't want to offend him. "I'm sure you have. I'm hoping to find anything I can pair with new information I learned yesterday."

"Oh, of course. Come over."

She had thrown on her clothes and was trying to fluff her hair out with some gel when the doorbell rang. Benny stood on the front porch, looking dapper as always in a pair of chocolate trousers and a coral short-sleeved shirt of some silky material.

"What do you need?" she asked.

"I thought I could help you today. Sam is at work, catering an event."

Peri opened her mouth to explain that she didn't really need his help today, but this was the most confident she'd ever seen him. He didn't whine about wanting to help, he didn't make it about his comfort. He expressed a generous thought, of helping her.

"Sure, come on in, and let me finish getting ready." She held the door for him.

"Where are we going?" he asked as she headed toward the bedroom.

"Ro-Bet Engineering," she called out over her shoulder.

Ten minutes later, they were comfortably ensconced in his Caddy, cruising down Chapman Avenue, with Dean Martin serenading them in the background. The light was red at the corner of Bradford, so the big sedan slowed gradually to a stop, like an ocean liner coming in to port.

"Miss Peri," Benny said. "Do you love Detective Skip?"

"Yes."

"How does it feel, when you love someone?"

Peri looked over at him. He sat upright, hands precisely at 10 and 2, staring at the road before him. "For me, when I'm with Skip, I don't want to be anywhere else. I want to share my day with him, then spend time doing stuff with him."

"Stuff like what?"

"Like, anything. Have dinner, go to a movie, or a party, or whatever."

"So, do things you both like?"

She smiled. "Not necessarily. Skip loves baseball. I'm not that big a fan. But I'll go with him to see the

Angels play because I love being with him, and I love watching him enjoy himself."

As she ended her sentence, he stuck his right hand toward her. "Okay, you have to stop talking. The light is green."

She was silent until the next red light. "Why are you asking about love?"

"Because." He shook his head. "I know I'm not like most people. I don't always understand…how other people work. I never had a girlfriend, ever."

"Did you ever meet girls that you liked?"

"A few. But I knew they would never like me back, so…I tried not to think about them."

She watched him struggle for his words, and her heart broke a bit. Benny was alone. Until now, she didn't realize that he knew it, and that it mattered. "I'm sorry."

He shrugged. "It's okay. Now I have Sam as a friend."

"And you're not really sure how much of a friend she is?"

He shook his head again. "Huh-uh. I like spending time with her. I even like to do things for her. Last night, we went to an event with all kinds of fancy food that I didn't like at first. She kept describing stuff to me, though, and I ended up liking a lot of it."

She opened her mouth, but his chubby hand went up as the light turned green. Relaxing back in her seat, she waited for the next stoplight. She hoped there would be enough lights for them to finish their conversation.

At the next stop, his voice took a somber tone. "I like spending time with Sam, Miss Peri. Maybe I like it too much. It will hurt when she goes away."

"Is she going somewhere?"

"No, but she will. Everyone does."

Poor Benny. Left behind by so many he loved. Socially awkward, hating to be touched, yet wanting some kind of human experience. She wanted to tell him that Sam would never leave, but she sensed that would be the wrong thing to do.

"That would hurt, if it happens, but maybe it won't. Sam seems to like you a lot, since she's hanging out with you so much. But if it doesn't work, it will hurt, and you will have me as a friend, and Skip, and the Nichols."

His expression lightened. "I still go to their house to play with Matt Helm."

"Yes, and think of what's happening right now. You're learning how to hang out with someone—a girl you like. Maybe Sam won't end up as your girlfriend, but you'll learn how to act when the next girl comes along."

"You're right." He smiled. "I am learning to be with someone."

She opened her mouth to add one more thing, and saw the warning hand come up. Turning back in her seat, she watched the road as they coasted down the street. *Sam must really like him, to put up with all his rules.*

As they turned into the parking lot, Benny said, "We're not going to walk around the cars and get chased by the police again, are we?"

"No, but thank you for asking. We're going to the office. I've got some investigating to do, and I think I have a job for you as well."

Benny squeezed his eyes closed during the elevator trip, gripping a handrail. "It smells in here."

"Of teriyaki." She sighed. "It could be so much worse."

Rodolfo met them at the elevator. "Come with me. Alicia has discovered something."

CHAPTER SEVENTY

ALICIA WAS IN her office when they arrived.

"Oh, good, you're here," she said. "I hacked into James' computer and found something interesting."

"One minute." Peri stood at the cubicle doorway and turned to Benny. "You remember me telling you about the man who died?"

"The man who was...like me?"

"Only a little bit—in his organizational style. His office reminds me of the way you keep things in your home."

He stretched taller. "I know where everything is."

"Exactly. I want you to go to Tim's office and see if you can find any kind of correspondence with a man named Art Gibbons. Can you do that?"

"You want me to investigate something?" His voice rose, giddy.

She smiled. "Yes. I think it's a perfect job for you."

While Rodolfo led Benny to Tim's cubicle, Peri stepped inside Alicia's space to see what she'd found.

"Okay, we keep all our software files in an area where they have to be checked in and out. That way, only one person can modify them at a time." Alicia pulled up a listing. "But James set up a mirror-image of what we have, and added some modules of his own."

"I hear you speaking English, but I'm only getting a little."

Alicia grinned. "James had his own version of the system."

"A working version?"

"Sort of, but not. It's kind of a 'display purposes only' version. It has canned messages and canned responses, to make the average observer believe it works. But you couldn't plug it into anything and make it translate."

"Art Gibbons swears he saw the UTran work," Peri said. "Think this is what he saw?"

"If James showed it to him, yes."

"Computers can get pretty fancy with timestamps, and user IDs. Can you verify that James is the only one who ever touched this thing?"

Alicia nodded. "Pretty sure. Our files are all subject to the same security ware. It's possible that James could disable it, but it's not easy to do and he might not have thought he needed to."

As Alicia worked, Peri pulled another chair into the space. "How well do you know James?"

"Hmm, not extremely well. He was hired after I was, went to University of Arizona, then UCR, majored in computer science, minored in both Applied Mathematics and Applied Physics, which is nuts. I don't know anything about his personal life. I have no idea if he's even married."

"Yeah, about that…did he ever talk about Tressa Velasco?"

Alicia turned to answer, but a familiar male voice responded.

"Talked to me about her a few times," Dev said.

"Dev!" Alicia leaped from her chair and hugged him.

"What are you doing here?" Peri asked.

"I work here." He scowled at her. "I'm no longer under suspicion. Darden's discussion with the PPD cleared me."

"Good," she said. "I'm glad. Did you meet James before he worked at Ro-Bet?"

Dev looked puzzled. "No."

Peri leaned forward. "How about Jaime Pueblos?"

"Who's Jaime Pueblos?" Alicia asked.

Dev's expression changed, slowly, from confused to surprised. His eyes widened. "He's Jaime. The one who kept harassing Tressa."

"I confirmed it with Art last night."

"School wouldn't help her, so Art and I threatened him." He stared at his sister. "Now it makes sense. He had a weird conversation with me a day before she was murdered. I didn't get it at the time."

"What was it about?"

Alicia slipped from the cubicle. "Be right back."

Peri pointed to the empty chair beside her. "Sit. Spill."

"I was coming back to work after meeting Tressa for lunch. She was chatting me up about the UTran, and I was chatting her up about software safety certification. It was the little game we played, to see who would give the other more information.

"So I'm on my way to my cubicle, and James pops up, like he usually does. Asks if I had a nice lunch, makes stupid small talk. I give him some quick answers—he's creepy and I don't trust him. Then he says, 'Tressa helping you out?' I nodded, then asked how he knew I was with Tressa. James just gets that weird-assed, crooked smile on his face. Then he asks, 'Does she ever mention me?' I get real short with him, tell him, 'No.'

"He scrunches up his face, gets all pissy, and says, 'Well, she better start.'"

"Of course he did." Peri stopped writing, and stared at her notes. Should she tell Dev what she found? What would he be able to add to the discussion? She felt a vibration in her pocket, and pulled out her phone.

"Peri, where are you?" Skip asked. "Tell me you're not at Ro-Bet right now."

"As much as I aim to please, I can't. I'm in Alicia's cubicle. We found—"

"I don't care what you found. Logan just broke into that locked room in Peoples' house. Guy's got an arsenal, enough to blow up the entire block."

"Oh, wow. But how does that—"

"Listen carefully, Doll. There are things noticeably missing from the room. Turns out, he is very organized, and keeps a careful inventory. We think he's got a Glock and an AK-47, along with a few boxes of ammo. And we believe he's heading toward Ro-Bet."

CHAPTER SEVENTY-ONE

PERI FELT HER stomach drop toward the floor. "We'll evacuate at once."

"Be careful. I don't want him to attack you as you're coming out. We've got a BOLO out on him across the tri-city area. Fullerton PD is on their way to the site, along with SWAT. Find a place to hunker down and wait for them. I'll give Berkwits a call, tell him you're in there."

"Thanks. Love you."

"Love you right back. And keep your head down."

"Hey, Miss Peri, I think I found something." Benny appeared at the cubicle, excited.

She turned to look at the faces around her. Rodolfo, Alicia, Benny, and Dev—all potential casualties. Beyond them, she could see workers in clean suits, working in the lab. To her right, an emergency exit door. To her left, the door into the reception area.

"Is Emily still out there?" she asked.

"I think she went to lunch." Rodolfo looked at his watch. "Do we need her?"

"No, no, it's good that she's gone." Peri held her hand up, gesturing for their attention. "That was Skip on the phone. The police believe that James Peoples is on his way here, heavily armed. Fullerton PD and SWAT are on their way."

She watched the faces near her pale.

"What do they want us to do?" Rodolfo asked.

Peri looked around the area. The space wasn't ideal. "They want us to hide, but I don't see a lot of opportunities. I'd like to evacuate, if possible."

"What if he's waiting for us?" Alicia's voice was barely a whisper.

Peri turned to Rodolfo. "Can we get to the floor above us? Or the floor above that? My thought is to evacuate this space, but go up instead of down, stay in the building, as far away and as separated as possible. We need to give the police time to get here."

Rodolfo nodded. "We could get to the 9th floor easily through the emergency exit, up the stairs."

"Perfect." She pointed to the lab. "Someone get those workers out."

Alicia scrambled out of the cubicle and ran to the other room. Peri watched the pantomime as she got the workers to step into the side area, and begin disrobing.

"Let me check out the stairwell first," Peri said, stepping to the aisle. Her heart raced, thinking about the last gun battle she was in. This wouldn't be a battle, if only one person had the guns. She wiped her moist palms against her khakis, and looked around. "Where did Dev go?"

Heads were shaking, but no one answered.

"What should I do?" Benny asked.

"Umm," she muttered. *What should he do? What should anyone do? Why am I in charge?* "Stay with Alicia. Help her stay hidden."

Her answer seemed to appease him, and he joined the young woman, explaining that he was there to protect her. Peri smiled, to keep herself from screaming.

"I'm here," Dev said, as he reappeared at her side. He held his hand out to her. There was a gun in it. "I went to my office to get this. I'm sure you can use it better than me."

Peri stared at the pistol. "The police, and I, looked through every inch of your cubicle. Where was this?"

"Oh, no, this is a recent addition. Like, today. After Tim died, I decided I needed to protect myself."

"I thought you couldn't pull a trigger with your RA."

"I mostly can't." He shrugged. "Not quickly, anyway. But something's better than nothing." He offered it to her again.

"No. It's not." She continued to stare at the gun. "Every time you pick up a gun, you make a decision that you will use it."

She pictured Tim, being ambushed in another man's house. And Tressa, suffering through years of stalking, to be brutally murdered. There was only one thing to do.

Peri took the gun. Everything about it, from its heft to its texture, returned her to that night. The flash of seeing Donny Jackson point his gun at her, the slow motion of her finger pulling the trigger on the Glock in her own hand, and Logan's voice, telling her, "You got him in the gut."

The words ran on an extended loop through her brain, and made her want to toss the gun on the floor. Right now, she couldn't afford trauma. Taking a big breath, she looked the gun over to see if it was loaded and ready, and nodded at Dev. "Let's get everyone out of here."

The lab workers were still painstakingly removing their clean suits, hanging them nicely. Peri burst into the space and yelled, "No time for that, just go, now!"

Startled, they dropped their suits and ran for the door. She met them at the emergency exit, held her arm out to wait. There was no window, so she opened the door enough to see the landing and a staircase to her right. It was empty. Storing Dev's gun in the back of her waistband, she pushed the door open further, keeping both hands firmly on the handle in case she had to pull it closed, or smash it into anyone on the other side.

The seconds were ticking by, but she dared not rush. Opening and peering, further and further, until at last the door was open and the way was clear. Holding it open, she gestured. "Up, everyone. At least one floor. Two if you can do it quickly. Find a place to blend in with people, or hide in one of the restrooms. Go!"

The first person ran through the door and bounded up the stairs, followed by the second. Peri turned to the third, and heard a pop. The third engineer, a middle-aged, plump man, fell to the floor.

"You're not leaving." James Peoples stood in the aisle, his Glock pointed toward the emergency exit, and Peri.

CHAPTER SEVENTY-TWO

PERI DROPPED DOWN to see about the fallen man, who was moaning, and a second pop brought an explosion in the wall above her.

"Leave him."

James was not alone. He held Emily in one arm, clamped around her waist. Her normally pale skin was ashen, but she showed no emotion. When Peri stood, he pointed his gun at the young girl's head, shoving it so hard against her ear she yelped in pain.

"You think you're so smart." He smirked as he walked closer. "You're all morons."

Peri held her arms up, hands away from her body. "I'm sure no one thinks they're smarter than you, James. Or should I call you Jaime?"

He turned his head away from Emily and spat. "I hate that name. I'm no immigrant."

"I never said you were. You can't tell from a name. Lots of people in this country who've been here a long time have names that sound foreign." She tried to keep her eyes on him while her peripheral vision swept the room, looking for the others. It looked like they'd hidden or run. Now it was just the four of them—her, Emily,

James, and the engineer on the floor. "How can I help you, James?"

"You can't." He growled this, and pulled Emily tighter, swinging his aim between her and Peri. "You've messed it all up, you and your investigations."

"I can't help it, James. I was hired to do a job."

"It's Dev's fault. He needs to take the blame for this. It's all his fault." James was howling now, half-whining and half-roaring. "Where is he?"

"I don't know." The gun was pointed toward her, and any moment, she expected to hear the report, feel the sting.

"Don't lie to me." He stuck his gun into Emily's cheek, rubbing it into her bones. "Dev? Dev Chaplain? Come out or I kill her."

There was no noise, and Peri thought perhaps they'd made their escape—but how? They would have had to cross paths with the gunman if they went out the front door.

"James?" Rodolfo eased his way out of Dev's cubicle. "James, you're a wonderful employee. We can fix all this."

James pivoted toward his boss, pointing the Glock at the tall man's chest. He stared for what seemed like an eternity. His face remained expressionless, although his reddened eyes darted from one person to the next.

While the gunman stood still, Peri crept forward, in a slow, silent shuffle, keeping her eyes on Emily. Emily looked at her, eyes frantic, mouth pursed as if holding in the screams. Peri gave her a small, reassuring nod. It was time to make a choice, to reach in her waistband for the gun, or try to grab the girl first.

"James." Rodolfo tried again. "I care about you. Let me help."

"You think I care how you feel about me?" James lowered the gun to his side, his voice flat. "She was the only thing I ever wanted. The. Only. Thing. If she'd just gone along, agreed to be mine, none of this would've happened. She knew what she was doing—moving away, going out with all those men. Cheating on Art with Dev— oh, she denied it, but I saw the way she looked at him."

Rodolfo kept working. "It sounds hard, James. You need to heal from it."

James lowered his head, relaxed his grip on Emily. "Heal from it? As if I can. Why do I bother? Why am I even talking to you? You, with your big ideas about a translator. It was never going to work. Never. But Tressa wanted it, and Tressa should have everything she wants."

Rodolfo made brief eye contact with Peri, before focusing on James. He stepped forward. "James, we can make it work. For Tressa."

"Shut up shut up shut up!" James' face was purple, veins in his neck bulging. "You don't get to say her name!"

Uh-oh. Peri bent down and ran toward him as he pushed Emily aside and raised the Glock. She managed to catch his midsection with her shoulder as she grabbed Emily, and still running, pulled her toward a file cabinet they could get behind.

Knocked off-balance, his first shot went high, into Rodolfo's shoulder. His boss immediately fell to the ground and crawled back into the cubicle, hiding behind Dev's mini-fridge. James kept shooting, at the cubicle walls, at the windows of the lab, until the Glock was emptied.

"I hate you," he screeched, throwing the gun at the lab. "You all need to die."

Swinging the AK-47 around from his back, he aimed at the top of the tall filing cabinet Peri and Emily hid behind, and fired. The noise was deafening, as the bullet passed through the cabinet, into the wall beyond. They would not be safe here.

Peri had pulled the gun from her back, but he still had the advantage. She looked around—the lab, half windows, half solid wall, was behind her. James was now firing into all the walls, trying to hit whatever was on the other side. It wouldn't be long before he started going into each space to see what he'd shot.

She timed her shot to go with his, one round, at the lab windows, hoping he didn't notice the extra pop. The closest window shattered, scattering glass shards everywhere. She shoved Emily over the half-wall, pointing for her to get behind the equipment in the back of the room.

Peri waited by the cabinet, her gun ready. Her plan was to wait until he came closer, and pray her reflexes were faster. Her entire body vibrated with fear.

Stop shaking. Stop. I need a clean shot.

CHAPTER SEVENTY-THREE

THE ROOM WENT quiet, and she heard his footsteps going away from her. She tried to look around the cabinet, to see where he was. The creak of a door snapped her into a realization. The restrooms—everyone must have rushed in there to hide.

While James stood at the door to the restroom, she hurried to Dev's cubicle. Rodolfo was still there, holding his bleeding shoulder. Peri stripped off his tie and stuffed it into the wound. He winced, but took the tie and held it tight.

"Come out, you cowards," James yelled. "Or I'll shoot you through the stall doors."

Peri flattened herself against the wall as the restroom door opened. Dev came first, followed by Alicia, and finally Benny. As he passed, Benny glanced at her. She shook her head and brought her finger to her lips. This was not a good time for him to notice her.

James walked out, gun up, but his finger was not trigger-ready. Dev and Alicia were across the aisle already. Benny strolled, wandering a bit from side to side.

"Can you walk any slower, you idiot?" James poked at him with the gun barrel, trying to prod him along.

Instead, Benny stopped and half-turned. "Stop pushing me."

Unprepared, James slammed into the little man, tripping over his own feet. Peri leapt forward, tearing the assault rifle out of his hands and shoving Dev's gun into his back. He stiffened, as she pulled the rifle, with its strap, over his head.

It was almost off, when he whipped around and grabbed her hand, trying to wrench her pistol away. A shot went wild as they wrestled. She was still holding the AK-47 above her head, trying to get it off him. Having a free arm, he slapped her face, then punched at her ribs, trying to loosen her grip on the Glock. Each blow folded her in half, and knocked air from her lungs. Still, she clung to the rifle.

She managed to toss her gun away from them, to free her hand for fighting back, punching him repeatedly in the face, until the blood ran from his nose. Her ribs complained as she brought her fist up, but she kept hitting.

The strap of the AK was still around his neck, stuck around his ears. With a desperate effort, she brought her knee up, hard, to his crotch. He doubled over, retching, allowing her to shove him away with one hand, and rip the assault weapon away with the other.

The gun felt heavy, so she threw it behind her. Dev ran after it, picked it up. The air was thick with smoke, and her ears still rang from the shots fired. She was aware of her breath, coming hard and rapid. Out of the corner of her eye, she saw Rodolfo walk out of the cubicle, holding his arm.

"You bitch," James whispered, staggering to his feet.

"Right. You kill two people, but I'm the bitch." She shook her head. "Men."

"Doesn't matter, they won't touch me." He smirked through the blood on his face. "Haven't you heard? I'm crazy."

A random pop startled her. James gave a gasp of surprise, before looking down. Blood flowered on his shirt, and he dropped to the floor. Peri turned to see Emily holding Dev's gun, staring at the body in front of them. The young girl's shoulders drooped, the gun hanging from her fingers.

"He killed my Tim," she said. "We were going to get married. He was my heart and he's dead. He's dead."

Peri's phone vibrated. She saw Skip's number, and answered.

"Come on in," she said into the phone. "Shooter is down, two employees injured. Send up the paramedics."

The door slammed open within moments, letting in the horde of policemen and emergency personnel. Rodolfo sat, clearly dazed, while they worked on his arm. Emily, Alicia, and Dev were all treated for scrapes and cuts from the flying glass. Benny was, as usual, in pristine condition.

"Thank you, Ben," Peri said as the paramedic took her blood pressure and tested her bruised ribs. "Your tripping James was just what I needed."

"You're welcome." He looked down at the floor, his right leg jiggling, and his hands rubbing his ears. "But I didn't mean to."

She smiled. "Then it was a happy accident, which still makes you a good assistant."

"Thanks, Sis." Dev stood by her, a bandage on his hand. "I'm sorry."

"For what?"

He shrugged. "Mostly for getting you into this mess. But for today—I could have never taken that guy out the way you did. I-I froze."

"It's okay. That's my job, to help take the bad guys out."

"That was your job, right?" Skip asked.

She turned, wincing, and tried to put her arms up for a hug, but pain stopped her. "This was not my fault."

He kissed the top of her head, smoothing her hair with an affectionate caress, and kneeled down in front of her. "How are you?"

"Okay." She sighed. "Really, okay."

The EMT removed the blood pressure cuff from her arm. "You should get x-rays of those ribs, not that you can do anything about it if they're cracked. But otherwise, I think you're fine."

"They'll need a statement from you, eventually." Skip told her, nodding at the detectives. "And you can always talk to me."

She leaned toward him, kissed him. "Funny how different it is this time. I mean, I didn't shoot him, so maybe it's that. But I picked up that gun intending to use it. I took responsibility for it, which is what I've been avoiding acknowledging with my warehouse memories."

"It's kind of a cop's burden. You strap on the gun, knowing that when you have to, you will use it."

She smiled. "The best part is, I'll actually have something to talk about with the therapist on Friday."

Skip chuckled. "Only you."

CHAPTER SEVENTY-FOUR

SIX MONTHS LATER.

"Peri, will you have this man to be your husband, to live together in holy marriage? Will you love him, comfort him, honor and keep him, in sickness and in health, and forsaking all others, be faithful to him as long as you both shall live?"

She gazed into Skip's dark eyes and smiled. The living room of the historic Bradford House, decorated in all its Christmas glory, twinkled in the background, and the smiling faces of their close friends and family glowed in the diffused light.

All we need is a soft dusting of snow, and we could be in a Hallmark Christmas Movie. She grinned. "I do."

Skip did not take nearly as much time to affirm his commitment. Rings were exchanged, vows recited, and the deed was done. The officiant told them they could kiss, so Skip pulled her close. She took his face in her hands and held it for a moment, before wrapping her arms around him and pressing her lips to his.

Despite the refined venue, the small crowd cheered as if they'd seen a home run. In the small room, there was no need for a wedding march, in or out. Everyone got up and mingled, hugging and congratulating.

"This is the nicest no-frills wedding I've ever attended," Blanche said.

"Of course it is," Peri told her, and pointed at the two handsome men talking to the reverend. "Willem and Jared helped us design and plan it."

Willem grinned at his name, and looked up. "We just went through a wedding—we learned all the pitfalls, right?"

Jared nodded. "Maybe we'll go into the design-construction-wedding-planning business."

"What's happening next?" Benny asked from Peri's elbow.

"Next, we go for pizza and beer, like any good wedding," Skip told him. "Meet us across the way, at Craftsman."

A party of sixteen fit easily in the restaurant, and the management let everyone order off the menu as long as the newlyweds picked up the tab.

"It's not as much a wedding reception as it is a party," Peri told Skip's daughters, who had flown out for the occasion. "Hope you don't mind."

"Mind?" Daria said. "I'm taking notes. This is the way I want to get married. No muss, no fuss, no trip to Crazy Town."

Amanda nodded. "I always thought I wanted the big traditional blowout, but this looks like so much less work."

"Not only less work, but less money," Peri said. "Money we spent on a real vacation."

The girl's eyes widened. "Oh, yes."

Someone touched Peri's arm, and she turned to see the owner of the restaurant, holding a magnum of champagne. "Your friends thought you should at least be traditional enough to have a proper toast."

"Veuve Clicquot?" Peri looked around the room, holding up the bottle. "Who did this?"

Blanche held up a slice of pizza. "I did. Whatcha gonna do about it?" Her husky vocals gave the dare a dangerous yet laughable quality.

"I'm going to drink it—along with my friends, if they wish to raise a glass."

This got a positive response, and soon sixteen glasses were filled—even Benny's.

"Is this okay?" Sam asked him. "You don't drink."

"I can drink, I just don't like it." He raised his glass, along with everyone else. "But for Miss Peri, I will take one sip. It's tradition."

Blanche stood on a chair, giving her glass a light tap with the blade of her dinner knife. "Attention! We are here to celebrate the marriage of Peri Minneopa and Skip Carlton. And no, they're not hyphenating their names."

"I may take hers," Skip said. "How's Skip Minneopa sound?"

They roared, as expected from a group drunk on beer and confessions of love.

"I've known these two for a long time," Blanche continued. "And I've known Peri even longer. Who knew, when we were in high school in Salinas, that we'd both end up in southern California? As Dickens might say, I've seen them through the best of times and worst of times, and this is the pinnacle of best. May you have a long and happy marriage, of safe travels, and great adventures, together. Cin cin!"

Peri tasted the fruit and almonds of the rosé, closing her eyes to savor the wine and the moment. She leaned her head against Skip's shoulder and held up her glass. He touched hers with his own.

"To happy," she said.

"To happy," he agreed with a smile.

She glanced around the room, enjoying the company. Willem and Jared were deep in discussion with Chief Fletcher and his wife. Steve Logan was chatting with Amanda, Skip's oldest, while Daria talked to Paul and Blanche's son, Nick. Paul and Blanche were sitting with Dev, who had decided he could show up and be his sister's brother for at least one day.

She found Benny just in time to see him take a second sip of champagne, make a face, and hand the glass to Sam, who laughed and drank it. What she saw next made her sit up and poke Skip in the ribs.

"Ow, what?"

"Look at Benny and Sam," she whispered, nodding in their direction. "They're holding hands."

Skip looked at them, and smiled. "Wonder what kind of wedding they'll have?"

"Sam's a caterer, so the food will be fabulous."

"You're like the Army, Doll." He kissed her nose. "You travel on your stomach."

"As long as I can still run it off, I don't see the problem."

Benny walked over to their table. "Miss Peri, I have something to tell you."

"Okay."

He took several big breaths, sighing every time, and looking at Sam, who kept smiling at him in encouragement. "I-need-to-resign-my-position-as-your-assistant."

The words were so fast and run together, Peri had to ask him to repeat it three times before she understood. She wasn't sure whether to laugh or be snippy. "I'll be sorry to lose such an important employee, but I understand."

"You see, Sam's boss offered me a job at Alta Vista. I'm in charge of restocking and organizing our linens, glassware, and table settings."

"Congratulations. It's the perfect job for you." Too much champagne made her want to hug him, but she stopped herself and patted his shoulder. "Good luck with your new assignment."

He looked over at Sam, who nodded and smiled.

Logan strolled over to the happy couple, and winked at Skip. "So, going to the Grand Canyon?"

"A little further than that," Skip said with a grin. "Peri?"

She climbed atop her chair. "Hey, everyone, a couple of things. First, for anyone wondering, we are going to New Zealand for the honeymoon. I'm not much on postcards, but I'll try to send you all an email. It will say, 'Wish you were here.'"

The crowd laughed.

"Second, for those of you who are thinking that Skip and I will die of boredom in our retirement, I have good news for you. When we get back, there will be a new business in town. Rumor has it, it's a private investigations team, run by a former detective and his lovely wife. If you need background checks, surveillance, whatever, just call on C.M. Investigations."

Logan's mouth dropped open for a second, until he laughed and led the applause.

"And last, the most important thing. As you can imagine, not even the wedding cake is traditional for us. We don't need to shove it at each other's faces, and there's always too much left. So enjoy your mini-molten lava cakes with ice cream."

Skip helped her climb down and ease back into her chair, just as dessert was served.

"Oh, look, they're in the shape of hearts," she cooed at the plate of chocolate sin in front of her. She studied the heart, and felt a surge of gratitude. *Here I am, surrounded by family and friends that I adore, and I'll be going home to a beautiful new house with my loving husband. If it gets any better than this, I might die.*

Skip lifted a forkful of cake and ice cream toward her. "How about a little tradition?"

Peri opened her mouth and let him feed her a bite. It tasted like contentment.

THE END

ACKNOWLEDGMENTS

Where to start...I must first acknowledge that this book was an ugly baby, one that didn't tell me its story right away, one that made me slap my characters around until they gave up their secrets. And now, after a difficult labor, I love it.

I must always thank my editor, Jennifer Silva Redmond. Without her, I would time travel, eat food before it is served, and continuously scamper. She saves me from my vices.

A big thank you goes to Carol Betancourt. She won a silent auction item to have a character named after her in this book. Her name is already great, but she preferred to have her husband's name in the book, Rodolfo. It's a fabulous name, and I hope I've given him the fabulous role he deserves. Thank you for not being "John Smith."

Joe Felipe always gives me exactly the cover I'm looking for.

Finally, a big thank you to my husband, Dale, for constantly checking his watch and asking when I'm going to become famous. I'm working on it, honey.

ABOUT THE AUTHOR

Gayle Carline is a typical Californian, meaning that she was born somewhere else. She moved to Orange County from Illinois in 1978, and landed in Placentia a few years later.

Her husband, Dale, bought her a laptop for Christmas in 1999 because she wanted to write. A year after that, he gave her horseback riding lessons. When she bought her first horse, she finally started writing.

These days, she divides her days between writing humor columns for her local newspaper and writing mysteries for a larger audience.

In her spare time, Gayle likes to sit down with friends and laugh over a glass of wine. And maybe plan a little murder and mayhem.

For more merriment, visit her at:
http://gaylecarline.com.

Also by this author:

Freezer Burn (A Peri Minneopa Mystery)
Hit or Missus (A Peri Minneopa Mystery)
The Hot Mess (A Peri Minneopa Mystery)
A More Deadly Union (A Peri Minneopa Mystery)
Clean Sweep (A Peri Minneopa Short Story)

Murder on the Hoof
From the Horse's Mouth: One Lucky Memoir

What Would Erma Do? Confessions of a First Time
Humor Columnist
Are You There, Erma? It's Me Gayle
You're from Where?
Raising the Perfect Family and Other Tall Tales
Holly Jolly Holidays

CPSIA information can be obtained
at www.ICGtesting.com
Printed in the USA
FSHW021205310120

9 781943 654147